WAR CREEK

A Novel

Susan Marsh

D1052370

MP PUBLISHING

WAR CREEK

First edition published in 2014 by

MP Publishing
12 Strathallan Crescent, Douglas, Isle of Man IM2 4NR British Isles
mppublishingusa.com

Front cover design by Claire Bateman.
Jacket photography by Mirjan van der Meer, Rooze Photography.
Book design by Alison Graihagh Crellin.

Publisher's Cataloging-in-Publication Data
Marsh, Susan Lee.
     War Creek/ Susan Marsh
     p. cm.
     ISBN 978-1-84982-241-1
1. Washington (State) --Fiction. 2. Teenage pregnancy --Fiction. 3. Fathers and daughters --Fiction.
I. Title
PS3613.A76995 W37 2013
813.6 --dc23

ISBN 978-1-84982-241-1
10 9 8 7 6 5 4 3 2 1

Also available in eBook

*To the North Cascades, which drew me from an early age,
and whose beauty I will always cherish.*

CHAPTER ONE

Sunlight touched the cottonwoods, their leaves dark and glossy as if it were the middle of summer. Agnes slowed at the War Creek bridge, wishing she were among the tourists heading farther up the canyon to camp and fish in the shade of those fragrant trees. She paused to take in the warm June air and the cheerful declarations of a Ruby-crowned Kinglet. A lone wisp of cloud blotted the sky like a dab of tissue.

Her eye followed the Twisp River upstream, still dark and indistinct in morning's shadows. Then she looked downstream—the direction of retreat. She considered turning around and speeding away. Her father's words came back to her like a fresh slap: *Don't show your face around here again.*

In the twenty years that had passed since she turned up pregnant and her eldest brother was killed in Vietnam, Agnes had not shown her face. But now her father needed help, and her older brothers were unavailable. She resolved to simply have it over with: help him pack his belongings and vacate the ranger station where he had presided for over forty years. Then get out as soon as possible. It wouldn't take a week.

She turned from the river road and crossed the bridge to where War Creek Ranger Station waited. A compound of wooden buildings surrounded by tall ponderosa pines, the sight of it brought a sense of returning to another lifetime. Fifteen miles upstream from the town of Twisp, a farming and ranching community on the banks of the Methow River, War Creek had once been a half-hour bus ride to school. The town had grown but the farms along the lower Twisp River remained as Agnes remembered them—pastures dotted with grazing horses and Shasta daisies gone wild; patches of thick forest, the cottonwoods that shaded the water. The station was remote when she was growing up, but now, as she crossed the bridge, the distance from town felt trivial. Perhaps because those final fifteen miles had come at the end of a five-hundred-mile drive from Helena, Montana. Perhaps because she wasn't stopping to let children out at every cluster of mailboxes. And, she noticed, the section of road upstream of the forest boundary, where county maintenance ended, had been paved.

Her sense of the familiar wrestled with the knowledge that she was no longer part of this place. She had grown up at War Creek, the hub of activity for a ranger district that had since been incorporated into the adjacent one. Officially closed, it now served as a place to park her father, the retired War Creek District Ranger. He stayed on as a volunteer to look after the station and feed the horses, advise tourists on hiking routes, and generally maintain a Forest Service presence in the river corridor. Perennial tourists who came to summer cabins and campgrounds stopped to visit with him, and all the ladies brought him cookies.

Agnes surveyed the ranger station before her. The corral rails, cribbed to scallops by generations of pack stock, had been replaced. The barn, toolshed, and house—a four-square structure where the district ranger had kept his office and raised seven children—bore a new coat of Forest Service brown, with crisp white trim. The rough grass was closely clipped, the apple trees pruned. A U.S. flag hung from the top of a warped pine pole. From all appearances, Ranger Bradford Clayton was still very much in charge.

Agnes turned into the compound and cut the engine. Her insides felt like a dropping elevator and she took a few deep breaths to calm herself. Then she closed her eyes and remembered: last night she had dreamt about the bear.

Her eyes flew open at the sound of boots scraping floor planks.

He stood on the screened-in porch in faded flannel sleeves with blown-out elbows, weathered khakis, wide suspenders. A full hand shorter than Agnes, even in his prime he had been dwarfed by the other Forest Service men, but his broad shoulders and long torso made up for his lack of stature. *Built to work*, he used to boast. His chest had barreled and his crew cut of sandy red hair had gone silver and shaggy. He rocked from one foot to the other, arms crossed and hands tucked under as if he were chilled. Agnes smoothed the front of her blazer and checked her skirt for bagel crumbs before pushing the car door open.

A deep-throated growl issued from under the porch.

"Knock it off." Clayt stamped his foot.

Agnes moved toward the house and Clayt stepped to the top of the wide porch stairs. They stood for a moment facing one another, he guardian of his fiefdom, she the supplicant at the gate. Agnes broke the silence.

"I made it."

"So I see."

"When was the last time you saw a barber?"

He ran a hand through his hair and shrugged. "You look like you're headed for a job interview."

She had hoped her schoolteacher clothes would place her on equal ground—the professional adult, poised and responsible. But Clayt saw through this disguise to the true nature of the equal ground on which they stood: unemployed.

As if by signal they moved to the porch steps and took seats on opposite ends of the same wide plank. Together they stared off into a row of ponderosas, the ones he had planted before Agnes was born, now thirty feet tall with trunks thick enough for house logs. Mismatched bookends, Clayt and Agnes: he was broad and florid-faced while she was slender and bony. His hair was wild and nearly white, hers glossy black and tied at the nape. They resembled one another only in the details—eyes a blend of green and blue and gray, his in a permanent squint from years outdoors, hers cautiously appraising. They shared a high forehead and lips that pressed together in a reticent line. Each of them waited for the other to speak.

"Find a place yet?" Agnes asked.

"Got a situation. Young feller got hisself lost, head a Eagle Creek."

Agnes made a small noise in her throat. Avoiding the issue already—not an encouraging sign. She hadn't driven five hundred miles to help him recover a lost hiker.

"He'll turn up, don't you think?"

"Been missin' since Sunday." Clayt chipped a flake of loose paint off the railing with his thumbnail.

"I'm not sure what you can do about it."

He pinned her with his glacial stare as if only an imbecile would say such a thing. "There's plenty I could damn well do, if anyone cared t' ask."

The growl from under the porch again.

"Tuck," Clayt ordered. "Come say howdy. Far as I know she don't bite."

"The place looks good," said Agnes.

Clayt glanced over his shoulder, shrugged, turned back.

"The paint job, Clayt. The new corral rails. I noticed. I'm just letting you know."

He pressed his palms into his knees and stood.

They walked across the patch of mown grass to the corral and tack shed. Agnes absorbed all she saw, trying to sort what was new from what she remembered. Behind the barn the footpath had grown over and would have been hard to find if she didn't know where to look. Two horses murmured as they came around from the back of the barn.

"Howdy, boys," Clayt said. "This here's Jasper," he told Agnes as he scratched the tall bay's forehead. "That's Agate."

"He's a good-looking boy," Agnes said. Agate, a paint seventeen hands tall, greeted Agnes with a gentle snort.

"Shipshape," Clayt said. "Never know when they'll pay another surprise visit. I tell you the supervisor's a woman?"

A mule joined the horses and leaned against the corral rails. "And I'll bet this one's name is Socks," Agnes said.

Every mule she could remember was a rich chestnut brown with white socks on all four legs. The mule's chest was matted with pine pitch. Agnes picked at the pitch and inquired about the female forest supervisor.

Clayt shook his head. "Sorry sight—don't know one end of a horse from th' other. She's never even been a ranger—not that there's any real rangers anymore. Where'n the hell do they find these people?"

"I know a woman ranger in Montana," Agnes said. "She's good."

Agnes had worked for the Forest Service in Montana during the summer in the years she taught school. She had loved the assignments, from cleaning campgrounds to patrolling the backcountry on horseback. She had grown up in the agency's arcane culture and had always admired the dedication of people who worked long hours in the hot sun, rain, and insects just because they loved the place. If it hadn't been so hard to get on permanent, she might have been a ranger herself, rather than a grade-school science teacher.

Clayt went on. "This one's a piece a work. Come waltzing out here all gussied up in lipstick and high heels like a God-damn floozy."

Agnes laughed. "To what did you owe such a momentous visit?"

"Kicking my ass the hell outta here, what else?"

"That couldn't have been a surprise."

"C'mon around."

He led her past the shed that served as partial shelter for his beat-up pickup and two winters' worth of cordwood. Fire shovels and Pulaskis and McLeods hung neatly in their proper places. Agnes noted that a double-bit ax was missing, the faded orange spray paint leaving its silhouette on the pegboard. She glanced at the pile of crumbling clay pots in a back corner and pulled her eyes away from all that remained of her mother's garden. Lovingly tended, then abandoned when her mother left, it had reluctantly surrendered to the lawn. Agnes read its protest in the defiant clump of rhubarb, its flower stalk standing like a ragged flag.

Clayt relaxed a degree as they completed the tour around the compound. He settled onto the bottom porch step and busied himself with another flake of paint.

Agnes sat. She could hear the Forest Service radio traffic coming from inside the house. "At the rate you're going you'll have that railing down to bare wood by nightfall."

Tuck's nose began to inch from under the steps. Agnes cooed. A low-slung Border Colliemix slunk out and crouched on the grass in a ready-to-herd stance, eyes alert for any move, the tip of his white tail flicking with a hint of a wag.

"Visit was only a formality," Clayt said. "She and I knew where things stood. But by God and all the angels in Heaven, I ain't done fighting." He shot her a tight smile. "Nothing the matter with this place—it was built to last."

Agnes smiled back. "Like you," she said.

"There goes another load a them flippin' clowns," he said, nodding toward a six-pack pickup speeding west along the Twisp River Road. "Before long we'll have ten more a the sonsabitches lost in the woods."

Clayt's face reddened with anger but his voice betrayed defeat. Fresh paint on the barn, fresh trim on the windows, but his expression was a haggard record of deferred maintenance. He rolled the paint he'd worried free between his thumb and forefinger. Thick and flexible, more plastic than paint, a tiny brown cigar.

"Ain't done fighting," he repeated, his gaze lost in the cottonwoods on the far side of the Twisp. "Never will be."

Clayt grunted and pushed himself off the step.

"You plannin' to unload your car or what?"

The smell of the house caught Agnes by the throat. Cold, musty corners and varnished pine wainscoting, a hint of mothballs and mildew, of moisture collected for decades under the roof shakes. Smoke from the wood cook stove and polish from her mother's piano—both of them long gone. She paused in the doorway of her former bedroom, darkly paneled with a low ceiling and wide fir planks on the floor. The bare walls held yellowed squares, the ghosts of her mother's simple but enthusiastically rendered paintings.

On the far side of the room a lace curtain gently undulated, its hem purling like the Twisp at low water. A plain chest of drawers, twin beds covered with white chenille spreads, immaculate as summer clouds. Agnes had been thrilled to inherit the bedroom after her twin brothers, John and Patrick, grew up and left. Until then, as the youngest child and the only girl, she had slept in a narrow closet of a room meant for storing Forest Service manuals and records. Clayt had more children than paperwork, so Agnes had shared the space with his locked file cabinet and a stack of unopened mail from the supervisor's office.

Agnes arranged her socks and underwear in an empty drawer of the pine dresser and draped the rest of her clothes across the bed that had been John's. The dresser's mirror reflected a stranger to the room. Agnes shed her blazer. Better, the mirror said. She kicked off her shoes and laid her skirt on the bed, wondering who she'd meant to impress by wearing such an inappropriate outfit. She quickly changed into jeans and a short-sleeved shirt, glanced in the mirror with relief, and closed the door behind her when she left.

She opened a bottle of Sauvignon Blanc she'd picked up in Coeur d'Alene and began to rummage through the kitchen cabinets. Cans of Dinty Moore beef stew, Spam, Boston baked beans. A bag of broken spaghetti, the corner gnawed open by a mouse. Salt and pepper packets, spilling their contents over the liner paper. His kitchen looked like a backcountry patrol cabin.

"What do you have to eat?" she called.

"Somethin' wrong with stew? I got some leftover biscuits."

She closed the cabinet door and stood with her hands on the edge of the sink. "I guess I'll eat a biscuit," she said. "As long as they aren't full of lard."

"On some vegetarian kick, are you."

"Where do I find a corkscrew?"

"You were raised on trout and venison and it didn't hurt y'none."

Clayt retrieved a coffee can from under the sink and peeled off the lid.

"A little worse for wear," he said, handing her a bent, misshapen corkscrew.

"What have you been using this for?"

"Haven't."

She offered him some wine, but he made a face.

"Ain't served in a chalice, it ain't wine."

"Suit yourself." She turned to a dark oak display cabinet holding a set of official Forest Service china—heavy platters, stacks of plates and cups and saucers. "I love this old stuff," she said. "Mind if I use one of the cups?" She opened the glass door. "You even have the sugar bowl."

"That lady Forest Sup was sure as hell interested in getting her hands on it."

"I'll bet. Don't let her near it."

Agnes poured wine into the cup, decorated with a bold green line near the lip and the Forest Service shield. Its tall symmetrical conifer in the center was one of the pines growing on the mountain behind the station. She smiled, thinking of the mug her roommate Joan had given her. In place of the multi-branched tree on the Forest Service emblem was a stump. The lettering around it said *Forest Circus—Department of Aggravation*.

She pulled a chair from its place at the table, a heavy varnished thing made of pine logs and thick plywood panels. It scraped noisily over the plank floor.

"Cheers," she said, raising the cup. "More in the fridge if you change your mind."

"I won't."

"So, did you talk to anyone at the Historical Society?"

"They ain't got a pot to piss in."

"Did the supervisor—what's her name, anyhow?"

"Something fluffy—Sara Lee? I forget."

"Did she recognize all the work you've done here?"

"Had her mind set before she got outta the rig."

The phone rang and Clayt grabbed it. Rather than saying hello, he barked his name into the phone the way he had when he was ranger. *Clayton.*

"News?" Agnes asked when he hung up.

"Just Collins, passin' on the gossip."Agnes looked away and Clayt gave her a chastising look. "Him and me go way back, y'know that. We still watch each other's hind ends."

In the old days, people talked about how Peter Collins and Brad Clayton brought out the worst in each other. "He's a mean old drunk," Agnes said.

Clayt scrutinized her face for a long minute. "You could stand to learn a bit of charity, missy. Hate the sin and love the sinner."

She kept a neutral expression as she tasted her wine. Clayt might have done the same once.

"Okay now," he said. "You make yourself scarce while I rustle up some grub—and don't make a face, it'll be something you'll eat. Skedaddle."

Agnes took her wine and started for the porch. She ought to tell him it was good to see him, good to be home at War Creek, but decided to wait and see whether either statement was true. He stood with crossed arms against the sink, waiting for her to depart.

Beyond the barn and corrals ran the indigo waters of the Twisp River. The footpath, once beaten in by Agnes and her brothers, led upstream to a gallery stand of cottonwoods at the river's confluence with War Creek. Agnes followed to see if she could still find the way. Her feet dented the same soft soil they had packed long ago, her brothers running home with a string of trout, Brownie wagging his bushy tail behind them. She knew each boulder and exposed tree root as if the years had evaporated. A chance to see the place where War Creek met the Twisp was the reason she'd been willing to come at all.

Willing, she thought. *Not exactly.* Her brother Patrick had badgered her, saying the rest of them—scattered from Seattle to the Bay Area to cities in the East—were too busy with jobs and kids and other obligations. Even Matt, who, like her, had no children to chauffeur to various sports and lessons, who lived only a few hours away in the Seattle area, showed no enthusiasm for taking time off work to help his father. Agnes had swallowed tears most of the way from Helena, angry with herself for buckling under, knowing that the emotional equilibrium she had worked hard to establish and maintain would be disrupted if she ventured back to Clayt's domain.

But, she thought with a flash of defiance, it was her domain as well. Born here, she had more claim to it than he did. Growing up a Forest Service brat at a remote ranger station, she had loved the forest, the mountains, and the rural way of life. As she prepared for this trip she had packed clothing for more than a few days. Perhaps she would linger in the neighborhood. Why not check out the national park to the west, or take a ride on the *Lady of the Lake*, the tourist boat that took people to the far end of Lake Chelan? Some of her Montana friends knew more about these places than she did. She was settled and content in Helena, a close enough approximation of home with its wide blue skies and ponderosa pines. She found a house she could afford, an affable roommate to help cover costs, and summer work between school years with the Forest Service. In spite of these advantages, she understood that the place she had chosen to settle was a stand-in for the one she yearned for. War Creek.

She had known about the Saint Vincent's School closing months before it happened, and had tried halfheartedly to find another teaching job. Nothing was available aside from opportunities to substitute. The previous summer had been her last with the Forest Service as well. Budget cuts, she'd been told. She knew when funding was tight within the agency the first thing to go was the seasonal workforce.

With nothing waiting for her now, she stood beside the river where her trajectory had begun, as if she could start again. In the gabbling music of the Twisp she imagined a quiet conversation. She couldn't quite make out the words; it seemed as though the waters whispered to each other from behind a closed door. In low, sympathetic tones, they were talking about her.

She shook the image from her mind. *Get him moved and get out.* This would be her mantra for the coming week. She would write it on a piece of paper and tape it to the wall above her dresser.

The Twisp was lower than she remembered it being in June, the time when runoff should be peaking. A hopscotch of boulders emerged at the river's edge, whitened by caliche and furry with dried moss. Insects moved everywhere, from the chalky river rocks to the highest branches—an iridescent beetle stumbling between smooth stones, a cluster of tiny midges vibrating in midair. Fishing weather. There was a time when Clayt would wolf dinner, grab a box of the tiniest black flies he could manage with his skillet-sized hands, and scurry toward the river, not to be seen again until well after dark. Sometimes his employees, Roger the recreation and trails guy, and the goofy range tech everyone called Fred Flintstone, went with him. Agnes would listen from her bed as darkness deepened, the double-hung window cracked a good five inches to let in the warm night breeze. She would guess how many nips from the bottle they had shared by the volume of their distant bursts of laughter. She resolved to get Clayt down here later for a farewell cast.

A log lay ahead, thirty feet long from the base to where the crown had broken off, and four feet thick. The cottonwood had come down in an autumn storm in the mid-1960s when Agnes was a girl. She had used one of Roger's double-bits to hack a section of the trunk into a rough approximation of an armchair.

Thereafter, when mild weather allowed, she took her library books and homework to the cottonwood armchair, or simply sat with her dog Brownie and listened to the merging of the waters. The log, with its rough-hewn chair, still remained, and Agnes hurried toward it.

The late sun shone through the trees and the emphatic song of a Yellow Warbler haunted the canopy, trumpeting its claim to this place, its voice blending with the music of the river. A honeybee hovered, drawn by the residual wine in her cup. She waved it away and bent to scoop layers of fallen, rotted leaves out of the chair. The wood was punky and starting to disintegrate, but as she settled into the seat she had made so many years before, she was delighted to find that her frame still fit its contours.

The wine warmed her from the inside while the evening breeze slid through the treetops. Silk from an early hatch of ballooning spiders drifted in long silver threads above the river, some tangled into knots like fishing line. Her eye followed one filament as it rose higher and higher, nearly disappearing into the clear air. She set the cup on the sand beside her and closed her eyes, breathing deep to fill her chest with summer.

An image of her childhood dog came to her: Brownie running along the sandy path delirious with joy, his bushy tail with its white tip swinging in all directions. Even in his old age, he never missed a chance to totter along this trail beside her.

"Aye, Brownie," she said aloud, imitating the deliberate brogue Clayt used once in a while to impress strangers and honor his immigrant parents. "We're home." The sound of her words brought sudden tears. *Home, indeed*, she thought. *Where did we all disappear to?*

Her mother had left when Agnes was seventeen, not even waiting until her daughter returned from giving birth at a home for unwed mothers in Spokane. "Couldn't bear t'see you after the shame you brought down on us," Clayt had said by way of explanation. Agnes had run to the river in an effort to exhaust her fierce grief and disbelief. The cottonwood log had accepted her, as it accepted her now, as if welcoming home a long-lost sister after twenty years away. Sitting here had taught her how to pause, consider, and listen—to herself most of all.

She let her gaze drift downstream to where the gravel lane came off the county road, crossed the river, and entered the ranger station compound. Beneath the bridge were the remnants of an older one, the one she had crossed to fetch the mail and meet the school bus. All that remained was a crumbling concrete abutment, nearly invisible beneath a tangle of brush.

Clayt had fought to save the old bridge when an inspector out of the regional office in Portland declared it inadequate; her father had argued that the bridge, built in the 1930s with the rest of the ranger station, was part of the compound, and whatever they replaced it with would lack its dated elegance. He had been right: the old bridge, with its graceful arch and detailed panel work, had been replaced with a standard design— overbuilt and obtrusive, and entirely without character.

From her cottonwood armchair, Agnes used to monitor the comings and goings of the valley, watching its commerce of campers and hikers and pack trains through the frame of the old bridge. She would pause midway on the bridge between the school bus and the ranger station to watch the water flowing under her feet toward the Methow, the Columbia, through the mountains and to the ocean she had never seen. The river led to the unknown, and it drew her imagination the way its current drew her brothers' cottonwood-bark boats.

Now she knew where the river led. She had seen the ocean, the lush forests on the west side of the mountains, the prairies and scablands on the east. She had made a life for herself in the Montana Rockies. Now the river had led her back to where she began.

CHAPTER TWO

Agnes took the porch steps two at a time. The screen door slapped behind her as she went inside.

"Got t' fix that damn thing," Clayt mumbled from his seat at the table. "Not used t' having kids runnin' in and out."

Her mother's wince at the sound of that constantly slamming screen door returned. "Sorry."

"Thought I might have t' come fetch you," Clayt said. Napkin crumpled, forearms crossed on the table, a hint of amusement in his eye. "It was ready so I ate."

Agnes rinsed the plate he'd left in the sink and eyed the contents of the cookpot. "Want any more?"

"Eat."

She divided the remaining spaghetti and tomato sauce between them. "Smells pretty good," she said, setting the plates on opposite sides of the table.

"Won't poison you."

"I can still squeeze into the log seat."

"Haven't gained a pound, from the looks of it—y' gave me way too much for seconds."

Agnes poured herself another cup of wine. Between bursts of static, the Forest Service radio brought snippets of news Agnes strained to hear. The lost hiker.

"Turn it up," he said.

The telephone on the wall rang and he scraped his chair back to reach it.

"Clayton."

Silence while he listened to his caller. Agnes turned the radio down.

"Pissin' in the wind," he said. "Should of taken the West Fork, there's an old trail—I coulda shown the…"

He shook his head like an exasperated teacher with a room full of D students.

"I know exactly where a feller'd get hisself lost up there," he continued. "And what he'd do about it." Another pause as he listened. "I don't give geography lessons over the phone," he snapped. "Stop by the station."

He gave directions and laid down the phone, grumbling.

"You know, I think I could stand some a' that wine after all."

"Who was it?" Agnes asked.

"Name a Hunter Swann. One a them bear guys."

Agnes searched his face. "Bear guys…"

"Parta that bunch bringin' back the griz. They got this collared sow, released in the park but she must not of liked the accommodations—too damn many rules, I s'pose. Anyhow she made her way t' Eagle Creek. I hope to hell…" His eyes shone as he looked in the direction of a window. "Don't matter now. Let's tidy up. Swann said he'd be by within the hour."

Clayt left the table to open the screen door, responding to a sound that Agnes failed to hear. Tuck slunk in, and after making a wide arc around the table settled onto a braided rug.

"Dog'll get used to you," Clayt said.

After dinner Agnes took a shower. She stood at the mirror to run a comb down the part in her hair and for a moment she paused, caught by what she saw. Usually in a hurry, checking that her hair was okay while brushing her teeth, she hadn't studied her face in years. The mirror held a faint image of a girl. It was into its heavy beveled glass that she'd once stared, her face flushed and mottled and shining with tears, her right cheek still bearing the impression of his hand.

She abandoned the comb and yanked at the doorknob, desperate to escape the mirror. But where would she go if she fled? There was little privacy beyond the bathroom, which had the only door in the house that locked. She took a few deep breaths until she could look into the mirror again, her long damp hair a tangled mess.

"What are you doing here?" she said to her reflection. "What possessed you?"

She dwelt for a moment on the unfairness of the situation—how was it that none of her brothers could make time to help the old man move? She saw them lined up behind her in the mirror, each a head taller than the boy in front of him, Agnes the youngest, the dark and quiet one standing before five wild redheads and blond Will. Will, thirteen years older, was the most remote to Agnes, gone before she was old enough to count her six brothers. The idea of Will was more real than the boy had been. He was followed each year by five more brothers in turn, and after a few years' pause, Agnes. Clayt called them the Maccabees, an unruly brood sniping at one another and finding excuses for delay before being marched to the station wagon for Mass on Sunday mornings. Agnes broke into a smile at the image, and seeing her smile in the mirror helped her breath come easier. She was almost glad to be here, glad to have the free time to stay for a week if necessary, whatever it took to get him moved and settled.

A commotion in the other room brought her around. Tuck barked and scratched at the door and she hurried to finish with her hair, twisting it into a damp and slovenly knot and clipping it to the back of her head. She wasn't sure if she was expected to make herself scarce while the men talked or if she would be allowed to join them. As a girl she had never been encouraged to show an interest in men's activities, but she had been intrigued by her father's outdoor life, had loved the company of horses and mules. She'd shadowed Roger as he cleaned and put up the tack, helping when he let her, even if it meant shoveling manure. She was similarly intrigued with what the visitor that evening might have to say, for the last grizzly bears known to inhabit the mountains above War Creek had disappeared before Agnes was born. It intrigued her to know that such a bear now walked the silent forests and dew-draped meadows of Eagle Creek, a few miles from where she stood.

"Company's here," Clayt shouted.

She was to be included. She hurried to the kitchen.

"We could probably stand a pot a Joe," he said over his shoulder before he opened the front door.

The visitor filled the doorway. Agnes thought if it were possible to cross a human and a bear, he would be the result: dark hair that could use a haircut, full beard, stocky like Clayt, but with long legs and the muscled tautness of a younger man. Hunter Swann removed a dark green baseball cap with an embroidered bear paw on the front and introduced himself.

Agnes waited for Clayt to introduce her as his daughter, but he turned away and gestured for Hunter to sit at the table. She avoided Hunter's questioning eye as the heat rose to her face. Her name and status didn't matter; she had been summoned to make coffee.

"I've heard that you enjoy a spot of the Irish once in a while," Hunter said as he sat down. Clayt straightened as if to ask *whose business is that*, but Hunter grinned and pulled a bottle of Bushmill's from his jacket pocket. "Care for a drop while we talk?"

Clayt laughed heartily. "Y' have good taste," he said. "Agnes, how 'bout a couple a shot glasses?"

She rolled her eyes and turned toward the stove to heat the coffee water. "Coming up."

Just what he needed—a jug of hooch in front of him. She was mad at Hunter before she had even been properly introduced. She brought two Forest Service coffee cups and two shot glasses and set them down between Hunter and her father with a bit more force than was necessary.

"My daughter," Clayt said to Hunter. "Fresh from Montana, come t' light a fire under her old man's rear end."

"Good to meet you," Hunter said. He stood.

"Likewise." She held out her hand and he shook it with genuine warmth, looking her in the eye.

Hunter filled the shot glasses and looked around for a third. "Agnes, don't you indulge?"

"Not unless invited."

"Well, criminy, miss. I'm inviting."

He pulled a chair out for her. She met his gaze and looked away, embarrassed to be treated like a lady in front of her father. She knew she would hear about it later.

The three of them sat around the table with the whiskey bottle, coffee pot, and a tin of gingersnaps Agnes had found unopened in the cabinet. Tuck nuzzled Hunter's sleeve and he reached down to scratch the dog's heavy ruff. Agnes watched as he leaned into the stranger, this dog that had so far not allowed her to approach.

She fought an old familiar sense of being a small boat come loose from its moorings. She did not belong at this table among men and dogs and talk of bears. As a child she had strained to overhear such conversations, knowing that for a ranger's little girl it was not possible to be included. Now that she was, at least partially, she still felt like an eavesdropper. Her roommate, Joan, whom she'd met when they both had summer jobs at a Forest Service district just outside of Yellowstone National Park, used to talk about how she wished she had been born a boy. She wore her hair short and favored overalls, and had been pleased when an adult asked her mother how old "he" was.

Agnes had never felt that way. She only wished that girls could do what they wanted without constant correction. The disparity between what she wanted and what she was allowed, what interested her and what was supposed to interest her, set her adrift from whatever was going on around her.

She stared into her coffee and let the whiskey sit untouched, feigning invisibility as her father launched into his standard interrogation, his questions sounding more like commands.

Before Hunter arrived he had gathered topographic maps of the search area and now unfolded them onto the table.

Hunter answered with patience and good humor, sending an occasional glance toward Agnes to include her in the conversation. His face was craggy, his hands were rough and scarred. The remnants of stitches traced the base of his thumb, and the tip of his ring finger was missing altogether. She wondered about the mishaps that had left their history on his hands, accidents involving hunting knives, barbed wire, grizzly bears.

Clayt leaned over a map. "Now," he said. "Where's this sow hangin' around?"

Hunter penciled a circle on the map and Clayt frowned.

"It's hard t' see how your bear and this lost fellow could of missed each other. What's it been doing up there?"

"She seems to have settled in around Eagle Pass. Eating marmots and avalanche lilies."

"How can you tell what she's eating?" Agnes asked.

Clayt shot her a look that said *don't interrupt*, but she could see Hunter appreciated her interest.

"I've been following her around since the release, tracking by radio signals and investigating the places she's been. Whenever I come across a scat I bring it back for analysis." He looked at their expressions and laughed. "Field biology isn't as exciting as it sounds. We spend a lot of time dissecting poop."

Agnes couldn't stifle another question. "How?"

"I put the scat in a vial of alcohol or water and agitate it until it's a slurry, like thin soup. Then I spread it out to dry so I can examine—"

"That's enough detail," Clayt interjected.

Hunter exchanged a glance with Agnes and they both smiled.

Clayt grunted disapprovingly. "I don't know why that bear isn't down in some a the timber sales we put up when I was in charge. There's huckleberries, mountain ash…"

"She might be in the fall," Hunter offered.

"Better not be. I plan to visit myself." Clayt shifted his weight and regarded Hunter. "What's the chance this bear'll be around by fall?"

Hunter paused, considering the implied challenge.

"He's thinking about his berry patch," Agnes said.

"Bears tend to avoid cutover areas and open roads, unless they have no choice."

"I put up that sale for wildlife. The elk and deer seem to like it just fine," Clayt said.

"Bears are not so tolerant. That's why the Service picked North Cascades for this project—one of the only places left with enough wild country."

Clayt sipped his whiskey and winced with satisfaction. "Bears used t'hang around the valley all the time, especially in the fall. One year we had one raidin' orchards and compost piles."

Hunter became interested in details but Clayt put him off. Suddenly vague about the bear he had announced a moment earlier, he said it was a long time ago.

"We get reports of sightings once in a while," said Hunter. "Most of the time they turn out to be black bears."

"I know a grizzly bear when I see it," Clayt said.

"I don't doubt you. All I'm saying is there's no established population."

"Most folks around here consider that to be just fine. And they don't see any reason t' spend their tax dollars bringin' trouble into the valley."

"I don't make the decisions," Hunter said. "It's my job to help keep the bears out of trouble."

"More coffee?" Agnes asked.

Hunter pushed his chair back. "I've taken enough of your evening. I greatly appreciate the information." He faced Clayt and put his hand out. "It's been a pleasure, sir," he said. Then he paused. "Do you mind if I ask you a question?"

Clayt stood to shake his hand. "I'm all ears."

"Seems like you ought to be up there."

"Come again?"

"Leading the search. Guiding."

"Like I told you, nobody asked."

"He's retired," Agnes put in. "So maybe it didn't occur—"

"The hell it didn't," Clayt snapped. "Everyone knows I'm the one t' ask about this country."

Hunter adjusted his cap and moved toward the door with an idea playing across his face.

"I'm concerned about the War Creek sow," he said. "Not only on account of that lost hiker, but all the people up there running around. Her signal shows she's been staying put, not her usual pattern. She may be injured."

"Most a them boys carry firearms," Clayt said.

"I need to have a look at her. And I'm going to need a packer."

Clayt's expression slowly changed as he realized what was being offered.

"Think it over. I'll be in touch." Hunter turned to Agnes. "Obliged for the coffee."

She sprang out of her chair to see him to the door.

"Thank you," she said as he started down the porch steps.

He looked up at her inquiringly. "For what—rankling your father?"

"For asking him to help."

"He'd be doing me the favor. Goodnight," he said, and walked down the steps to his truck.

Agnes dried the last of the dishes and rinsed the coffeepot, stealing glances at her father where he sat at the table scowling at the map. Hunter had left the bottle and she watched for an opportunity to snatch it away before Clayt drained it.

"That was interesting," she said.

Clayt didn't look up. "Don't you get yourself in a sweat over that character."

"He seemed to know what he was talking about."

"And what about your old man?"

"Did I imply…" She caught herself, turned back to the sink.

He shook his shaggy head. "Never able to keep your hands off the laddies," he said.

Tears stung her eyes and Agnes looked away. He might as well have kicked her. Supporting herself with the heels of her hands, she leaned over the kitchen sink and waited for a wave of nausea to pass. She was silent for so long Clayt poured himself a victory drink.

"Truth ain't pretty sometimes," he said.

Agnes spun around. "Truth, my ass. I didn't find your bear guy attractive in the least. From the look and smell of him he's more bear than man."

Clayt chuckled at this. "Don't think I didn't see you blushing away like a schoolgirl."

"I wasn't blushing," she said. "I was mad."

He held his shot glass up and squinted at her through the amber liquid. "And what, may I ask, did you have t' be pissed about?"

She took a deep breath and let it slowly trickle out before answering. "If you could only see yourself," she said. "The way you were ordering me around—make coffee, bring shot glasses, how about some more coffee, miss? You wouldn't even introduce me until you had to. I felt like a nameless servant, not your daughter."

"I don' know whatcher talkin' about."

"You know what, Clayt? It's past my bedtime." She heard him helping himself to another wee dram as she closed the bedroom door behind her.

"Tuck likes t' sleep in there," he called. "If you close th' door he'll scratch the hell outta it."

Silently she unlatched the door and left it ajar. Her eyes stung and her breath caught in her throat. Alone at last, out of his sight and his unfailingly critical scrutiny, her bottled-up emotions spilled over. She had worried this would happen. Clayt hadn't changed a bit, and as he took on his practiced role of the critical, unforgiving father, she had unconsciously slipped into her old skin: rebellious and defiant, a simmering anger underneath the appearance of normalcy. The anger of a child who had never been heard or understood.

It had taken all the effort she could muster, but she was proud of herself for making a graceful exit. Would she be able to repeat the performance the next evening, or the next? The coming days would be consumed with trying to persuade him to acknowledge his situation rather than efficiently packing and moving his household. It was obvious he had done nothing to prepare and was capable of dragging the torture out for weeks. Her brothers, though pleading their inability to help, would nonetheless be checking in, expecting progress. The weight of responsibility for things she could not control dragged Agnes to the bed. She lay on her back and pressed the heels of her hands into her eyes.

He'd always been a mean drunk, though he had never been rough with her the way he had the boys. But long before he slapped her that one time, she had feared his anger like a dog that had been whipped. A raised voice, a reddening face—she'd gotten her so-called blush from him—still made her shrink inside. All those trips to the tack shed with one of the boys, the yelps she heard as bridle leather met the bared flesh of a young behind. Once punishment was administered, the son would be given a chore for penance and Clayt would return to the house, his face stitched with anger for having his workday interrupted by bad behavior. By the time Agnes was the age of her mischievous brothers, it seemed they were allowed to run wild. She couldn't ride a horse or take a walk in the woods without supervision, though she longed to be a full-fledged member of the pack of Clayton Maccabees. By then, Clayt's drinking had increased to the point where he could no longer hide it. His temper had a hair trigger and Agnes never knew what would set it off. So she slunk around the house like Tuck in the presence of a volatile, unpredictable man whose affection she could not win.

Agnes turned off the light and pulled the thin wool blanket to her chin. The bed was child-sized, barely long enough to hold her without her feet sticking out. She got up and opened the window. Lulled by the scent of pines and the murmur of the river, her thoughts grew still at last.

CHAPTER THREE

Clayt flicked a number eighteen black gnat into an eddy with the grace of a long-seasoned fisherman, but the fly provoked no investigation from below. He cast in another direction while Agnes watched from the cottonwood armchair. She zipped her light fleece jacket to her chin against the morning chill.

"No use wastin' any more time on this malarkey," he said, reeling in. He rubbed his casting shoulder.

"We can head downstream if you want," she suggested.

He shook his head and eased onto the log beside her. "Skip it. Fish are havin' enough trouble in this drought without some old fool harassin' 'em." He propped his fly rod against the log and massaged his visibly swollen knees. Glancing at Agnes in the armchair he said, "I know one thing. You didn't get that skinny bum from me, now." He poked his belly under the waders and chuckled.

Agnes felt her stomach tighten. His remark would have struck her as no more than a joke but for the teasing she had taken from her brothers and their friends as a child. By six years the youngest, the only girl, and the only one with dark hair, she had provided them with ample ammunition to shame her when they were looking to pick on someone weaker than themselves. There had been talk since she was old enough to hear it about her differences, but Agnes saw both parents in herself. She had her mother's frame and coloring, her father's disposition. Still the question hovered in her mind—was Clayt making fun of himself or goading her the way John and Patrick once did? If she'd been born with a mane of wild red hair like the rest of them, they all would have found another attribute for which to berate her. But the question of patrimony stung her now, perhaps in a way he had not meant. She was aware of having primed herself to be overly sensitive around him, to add layers of meaning to anything he said.

Clayt and Agnes sat in silence, their eyes fixed on the river. Agnes imagined her mother, standing with her back to the mountains and facing the widening valley, her long hair coiled in a braid around her head, her slender waist accentuated by a flaring shirtdress and wide leather belt. The dress fell to her calves, leading men's eyes toward delicate ankles and feet made for dancing.

Mary had long been weary of the social isolation at War Creek, miles from town. The Collins clan, their closest neighbors, were a half mile away. The hard physical work and loneliness of being a ranger's wife and raising the children mostly by herself, the North Cascade winters bearing down from the west like a chill, damp cloth, wore on her. She had begged Clayt to move on, but his only offers for a transfer came from deeper in the backcountry—the Northern Rockies, central Idaho. A place called the River of No Return held little appeal for Mary. It seemed to Agnes that Will's death and her own unwelcome condition at sixteen had given Mary the excuse she needed to depart. How long had she been waiting for such excuses?

The gruffness returned to Clayt's voice. "Don't be mopin' about your mother, now."

"How did you know?"

"It happens."

"Ever hear from her? Or anything about her? It's like she fell off the planet."

Clayt's silence made it clear it was past time to change the subject, but Agnes persisted.

"Do you know if she's even alive?"

"I said don't mope."

"No moping," she said. "I was remembering a dream I had the other night, about a bear."

"You keen on bears, now, are you."

She looked at him. "I'd love to see that grizzly bear. Wouldn't you?"

He spat on the ground and pushed himself up off the log and stood facing the water.

Dreams had a way of vanishing like river mist on a summer morning—vivid for a moment and gone the next—and the act of trying to recall the dream was enough to make it flee. But this one had stayed with Agnes, for it was one of a series of recurring dreams that had started when she was in labor. As she recounted it to Clayt, she felt as if it were happening again.

The silver bear appeared, a fleck of luminosity moving in the forest. The bear's forelegs scissored under the massive hump of her shoulders and her polished claws tapped on stones like combs of tortoiseshell. The bear paused to raise her nose, then turned away, her muzzle following some unknown spoor along the forest floor. Perhaps she found a faint ancestral trail, a long-forgotten route into the past. She seemed to understand that her search would never end but the way would continue to reveal itself. Soon she receded into the shadows, a faint glimmer among the trees.

Clayt waited for more. "That's it?"

"Pretty much."

Clayt snipped the black gnat off the tippet and hooked it onto a patch of sheep fleece on his fishing vest. "All that crap about this so-called War Creek sow, it's gotten to ya."

"I've had the dream before."

"You're worried, I 'spect. A shame about Saint Vince, by the way. A damned shame."

It was the first time since Agnes arrived that Clayt had acknowledged what was going on in her life. She agreed it had been sad when the Catholic grade school in Helena lacked funds to continue operating, but she was not particularly sorry that her job had come to an end. If she were honest with herself, she would admit the timing could not have been better.

She had first gotten an offer from Saint Vincent's after a job fair when she was a senior in college. Not ready to leap into a permanent contract, she turned it down in favor of drifting for a while. After four years in Spokane, where Clayt had enrolled her in Gonzaga University, she moved to Moscow, Idaho, preferring a smaller town. With her teaching credentials in hand, it wasn't hard to find work as a substitute teacher, but Moscow, like Spokane, was too far from the mountains. She migrated eastward, deeper into the Northern Rockies, to Kellogg, Missoula, and Helena. Subbing suited her, giving her enough money to live on and the freedom to work when she wanted to. She found her first summer job with the Forest Service as part of a district work crew. She painted picnic tables, emptied trash cans, fought wildfires, and helped clear trails, surprising her crew boss with her adept use of a crosscut saw. The skills she had learned from Roger years before served her well, and she was nearly guaranteed a job the following summer.

Eventually she found herself wanting a home base, tired of apartments and Forest Service bunkhouses. A garden, like the one her mother kept at War Creek. Eventually, she called Saint Vincent's and asked if they had any positions. She'd worked there for ten years.

She stood. "Time to get the fisherman home for breakfast."

"Back's seizing up," he said. "Rain on the way."

"You haven't filled me in about your plans," she said as they walked back along the path above the river.

"What plans?"

"Don't play games."

"For the first and last time, I don't have no flippin' plans."

Agnes turned to face him and he nearly walked into her. "Look, Clayt. I came at your request—"

"As far as I'm concerned you can go home."

"What I was about to say—"

"Save us both a lot of trouble if you got the hell out of here."

"I can make my exit as soon as we get back if that's what you want. In the meanwhile, shall we try to get along?"

He was silent behind her as they walked. The barn and corral came into view, Agate and Jasper nickering softly with ears pricked forward.

"Grub time, boys," Clayt called.

Socks appeared from the other side of the barn and all three trotted to the gate. Each bore the same brand on his left rump: US. Agnes could see from the girth of the horses that Clayt had not been riding them.

"Hey, Socks, how's that noggin?" Clayt offered his shoulder and the mule vigorously rubbed his forehead on it. "Goddamned flies. They've been hell on this one."

Agnes brought sections of hay to the horses while Clayt smeared salve on Socks' fly bites.

When they reached the house, Agnes tried again to make friends with Tuck. A tentative approach, tail low; he allowed her to lower her hand to his nose, scratch his chin.

"See, told you he'd come around."

"Just as I'm about to leave," she said.

Clayt propped his fishing rod against the step railing. "Don't take everything I say as gospel."

"When did your word stop being gospel? I agreed to move you, but you haven't looked for a place to live, you haven't packed, and now you're telling me to get the hell out. Do you want my help or not?"

He stood for a moment as if trying to decide. "Dog could use another bag a grub."

A grocery run. Just what she needed to get away from War Creek for an hour or two and let the air clear. She ran into the house for her car keys, pausing for a moment to keep the screen door from slapping behind her.

"Back in a while," she said.

"Mind stoppin' at the liquor store?"

—

Agnes strolled each aisle at Helen's Market, taking her time, feeling the worn hardwood floor giving with a gentle creak underfoot. She thanked the checker, a young woman with a vaguely familiar look, and stopped to scan the community bulletin board outside. A Great Pyrenees at stud, a Quarter Horse filly for sale, a flea market next Saturday. An adolescent girl's careful lettering offered babysitting services with a fringe of phone numbers cut along the hem of the smudged sheet. Among the notices a flier caught her eye.

NORTH CASCADES GRIZZLY BEAR
REINTRODUCTION PROJECT
PUBLIC OPEN HOUSE
WEDNESDAY, JUNE 20
7:00 – 9:00 P.M.
TWISP VALLEY MIDDLE SCHOOL
ALL WELCOME

Below the flier a handwritten sheet encouraged the attendance of all who wanted to keep dangerous predators out of the valley. She tore off one of the cards stapled to the flier and shoved it between her yogurt and Tuck's kibble.

On the way back to War Creek she spotted a sandwich-board sign on the edge of town. RAVEN'S ROOST ROASTERS, OPEN 6 A.M. The board-and-batten cabin that housed the establishment reminded her of the cozy coffee place in Helena where she met friends and graded homework. She went in to investigate.

The aroma of baking chocolate filled the doorway. The walls were studded with handmade décor—stoneware sculptures, weavings, watercolors and photographs of local landmarks. Shelves of roasted beans, crocks of sourdough start, jars of local huckleberry jam and clover honey. Beyond the giant roasting machine that nearly blocked the doorway and the clutter of burlap sacks full of raw coffee beans, three small tables looked out onto forests, fields, and sky. True to Clayt's prediction, ranks of dark clouds had begun to slide eastward off the Cascade crest.

Agnes approached one of the photographs. A broad dome of exfoliating granite the color of tarnished silver stood over a lake so deep its water looked nearly black. She could pick out the trace of a trail winding through the fringe of larches surrounding the water. The picture had been taken in the fall, for the larches were bright butter yellow.

"Cutthroat Lake," she said to herself, and at the same moment a woman ducked through the kitchen door.

"Correct you are," she said with a hearty voice. "Welcome to the Raven's Roost. What can I bring you?"

The woman introduced herself as Orion, Rion for short. She bustled with practiced efficiency behind the front counter and asked Agnes about herself. She brought two cups of coffee to a table and offered Agnes a seat with a sweep of her arm. Older, fiftyish, wearing a crisp plaid jacket of the style Mary used to wear. Tall, like Agnes, but heavier, with cropped salt-and-pepper hair and eyes that had seen a lot of the world and hadn't been particularly pleased. Her gaze was sharp but kind as she sat at the table across from Agnes.

"Great little place," Agnes said. "Been here long?"

"About a year. And you?"

"About a day."

The string of brass bells hanging from the doorknob announced the arrival of a customer. A pale man with thinning hair in oil-smeared coveralls and a Caterpillar cap, he looked comically out of place as he squeezed between the shelves of coffee and a string of prayer flags.

"How's it goin', Rion?" he said.

"Honey Badger." Rion strode toward the counter. "Usual?"

"I'll take one of them sticky buns, too."

"Now there's a healthy lunch. I can make you a roast beef sandwich. Promise to leave off the sprouts."

"I need something to get me through fixing that God-damned tractor."

"Okay then," Rion said, and got to work, making small talk, addressing herself as much as anyone else.

The man looked around as he waited for his coffee. His eyes glanced past and returned to Agnes and settled there. She looked away under his unapologetic stare. Something about his stance, his voice, worked at her memory.

"You ain' Clayt's girl."

She stood and moved toward him. "I'm not exactly a girl these days," she said.

He nodded, half smiling.

"Her name is Agnes," said Rion. "Pretty name, don't you think? Old-fashioned."

"I knew it," he said. "I worked for your old man when you were just a little squirt."

"Roger?"

He took his cap off and bowed, and his smile broadened. "Been a while."

"Indeed it has. What are you up to these days?"

"Got myself a little farm downriver. Our oldest is off to college in the fall."

Roger, the bachelor trail crew foreman, not a lot to say, better with the stock than with people. Now he had a kid in college.

"Gotta run," he said. "Say hey to the old man—I owe him a visit."

"Will do. See you around."

Rion and Agnes returned to the table and their coffee.

"I can't believe I didn't recognize him," Agnes said.

"His apple-blossom honey is the best in the valley." She reached behind her for one of the jars on a shelf, pried it open, and passed it to Agnes.

Agnes spotted a notice on the wall beside the shelf of honey, the one she'd seen in the grocery about the bear meeting.

Rion noticed her gaze at it and laughed. "That's going to be a circus. Half the community is totally against it and the other half is scared to say a word. I hear they'll have bouncers in case it gets out of hand."

"I'd probably have to put my father in the first camp," Agnes said.

"Controversy is a good way to winnow out your clientele, I'll tell you what. The rumor mill has it I'm a bear lover just because I don't hate them. Business is down a third since all this came up." Rion paused. "Thinking about going to that meeting?"

"Probably."

"See you there."

CHAPTER FOUR

Rion set two cups of coffee on the table farthest from the front door and slid onto the bench opposite Agnes. "Some crowd last night," she said. "I made my escape as soon as I could."

"I tried to catch your eye," Agnes said. "You were right about the free-for-all." She stirred cream and some of Roger's honey into her coffee. "It's only one bear we're talking about here, with a radio collar and a full-time biologist to watch after her. People seem to think the woods are overrun with grizzlies."

Rion's smile was thoughtful. "Who was the old guy carrying on?"

Collins. "Friend of the family, you might say."

"I felt sorry for that poor sucker trying to answer questions."

"I was interested in what he had to say," Agnes said. "It was hard to hear with all the interruptions."

The door bells jingled and Rion rose to meet customers. The family entered gingerly, squeezing between coffee sacks. They studied the menu and Rion helped the kids decide what would be the most delicious combination.

"I want peanut butter and banana," said the little girl. She eyed the shelf of local preserves. "And honey," she added.

Her mother shushed her but Rion said she could easily fill that order. While she made sandwiches and gave advice on where to hike, Agnes thought about the previous evening's open house. Old Collins had been in fine form, firing off questions and answering them himself. The room was evenly divided from Agnes's perspective standing along the back wall—cowboy hats on one side, ponytails on the other. Hardly any women.

"I have a question," said one of the cowboy hats. "It's all well and good that this bear is minding her manners, but what's going to happen when she shows up here in the valley?"

Before Hunter could reply another comment came from the crowd. "Everybody knows what happened to that missing hiker. Only a matter of time before they find what's left."

This was followed by a wave of affirmative rumbles around the room. Then Old Collins stood up. "We don't want our tax dollars spent on bears. Hell, they can find their way out of Canada without you. I had a griz in my garden years ago. Dug every last carrot and ate my apples, the bastard."

Collins sat back and enjoyed the barrage of angry quest-ions he'd unleashed as the audience shifted from arguing with Hunter to shouting at each other. It was after ten o'clock before the place quieted down. The night janitor waited in the doorway.

"We need to let this man get his work done," Hunter said. "Thank you all for coming, and for your interest in this project."

"Interest, hell," said Collins. "This thing is getting shoved down our throats."

"Not everybody in this room hates bears," said one of the ponytails.

"Blow it out your ass." Collins turned to Hunter. "You can take your Goddamned bears and shove 'em."

Hunter turned off the slide projector, gave the group a slight nod and smile, and strode out a side door. The door closed behind him, leaving everyone to look at one another in astonishment.

"Chicken shit," Collins shouted.

But Hunter had another trick up his sleeve, the one that had softened Clayt. After leaving the group with turning heads and *what the hell* on their lips, he reappeared with a paper bag in his hand. With a significant look toward the audience, he set a bottle of choice Scotch on the front table with a loud rap. He poured a bit into a paper cup for himself and set the bottle back on the table.

"If you want to have a serious discussion, I'm all ears. But if I'm going to sit here for the rest of the evening taking abuse, I plan to get shit-faced drunk. Anyone care to join me?"

His eyes were steady and the hecklers glanced at each other. The janitor grinned and Hunter brought him a snort.

"I'll sure as hell join you," Collins said.

A few nervous snickers as Hunter produced more paper cups. Over the next hour a reasonably civil discussion ensued. While no one changed his mind, no one was punched, and the bottle became empty.

Agnes smiled at the memory. She looked up to see Rion watching her.

"You're a champion daydreamer," Rion said. "I've been standing here for a minute or more."

"Thinking about last night. I wonder if old Collins and the rest of them would have been so hard on Hunter if it weren't for that missing hiker."

"First-name basis already," Rion noted.

"You sound like my father."

"I sympathize with those geezers," Rion said. "I can see why they're not anxious to welcome bears into their backyards."

"Does that mean they shouldn't be allowed anywhere?"

"Not in town, thanks. Ever been around them? You must've in Montana."

"Not often."

Agnes had chaperoned school field trips to Glacier and Yellowstone, but she had never seen more than a speck through a spotting scope. Black bears, yes, sometimes right in town when the crabapples were ripe.

"We had bear-watching trips where I taught school," Agnes said. "A couple of spots on the highway not too far out of town."

"Had?"

"I'm not teaching anymore. The school closed."

"What'd I miss? Did you mention before that you were out of a job?"

"I'll find something. Can't say I'm all that worried about it at this point."

Rion nodded with sympathy. "I've shed my skin a few times, started over when I didn't think I was ready. But you change when you have to. I can hardly remember the things that mattered most to me ten years ago."

"What matters now is getting Clayt settled. I'll worry about myself later."

"What do you mean, settled? You are full of surprises today."

"Sorry—it's been a whirlwind since the moment I arrived and I don't remember what I've mentioned. He's getting the boot from Uncle Sam—apparently the old ranger station is a safety hazard and they want to tear it down. Know about any good rentals?"

Rion pressed her fingertips into her temples and closed her eyes, as if consulting some psychic force. Agnes had seen her do this before, her indication that she didn't have any answers.

"I wish you'd come sooner," Rion said. "Like maybe April. This place is dead most of the year, but when everybody's hiring for the summer, good luck finding a place to park. I promise to keep an eye out."

"I had a feeling from the start that this trip was going to be more complicated than I hoped. The only reason I'm in town is to help him move."

Rion was quiet for a long time before giving Agnes an appraising look. "You're here for a lot more than that."

Agnes flushed. This woman didn't know her from Eve. The Clayt in her rose up to tell Rion to mind her own damn business, but her flash of anger faded as she considered the truth in what Rion had said. Rion saw through her, it seemed, to a core she could hardly acknowledge herself. She resented it, and at the same time it gave her tremendous relief. With Joan and her other friends far away, she needed someone who understood her.

"So tell me," Agnes said, "what you think I'm here for."

"I see myself in you. What are you—thirty?"

"Thirty-six."

"When I was your age..." Rion stopped herself to laugh. "Don't I sound like an old bat!" With a mock-elderly voice she said, "When I was yer age, sonny..."

Agnes laughed with her.

"I have fifteen years on you, sweetie. I'm not being condescending, I call everybody sweetie. But I can remember the times in my life when everything was standing on end or upside-down and how I didn't know what to do next. It seems like you're in a similar place right now. I came here to put the past behind me and start over. Maybe you're doing the same."

Agnes nodded. "In some ways, yes."

"And in other ways, maybe you're here to find the past."

"If I can."

The odor of mothballs had Agnes sneezing before she reached the house. Leaving the front door open behind her, she hefted grocery bags onto the kitchen counter and slid the bundle of mail onto the table where Clayt sat with a stack of small, canvas-bound notebooks.

"What did you unearth?"

"Old logs." He patted a frayed cover. "1948. Book's in about the same shape I am."

"Mind if I look?"

The field logbook fell open at random, with many loose pages.

"Is this your handwriting?"

"Whose else would it be?"

"It's elegant, is all."

"Used t' teach penmanship in school. Along with comportment and citizenship. Who hears those words anymore? Found one for your buddy Swann. *June 20, 1948. Cleared trail to War Creek Pass and got Eagle Creek on the way out. Heavy deadfall, returned to station after dark. Aspen trunks clawed by a large bear."*

"1948? Wow."

"I remember that big ol' tree like yesterday—I could walk right up to it this minute with my eyes shut."

"So, what did you decide about Hunter's offer?"

He closed the logbook on his forefinger and looked at her.

"Sorry to interrupt." She turned to put the groceries away. "I was thinking I could help, is all. I know how to pack and wrangle."

The silence with which he returned this comment was infused with antagonism and she hurried to change the topic.

"I better hide this chocolate or I'll sit down and eat it all."

She took her stash of chocolate into the bedroom and tucked it deep into the back of her socks drawer.

"What in the world…"

A plastic bag, sticky and brittle with age, occupied the corner of the drawer. She nudged it into the light and picked it up. The dry, broken lumps within looked like remnants of an ancient brownie. But this was no forgotten pastry.

Agnes sat on the edge of the bed with the baggie in her hand as the memories filed into her mind, each holding its hand out to the next until they formed a line leading to the place she needed to see. She left Clayt to his journals and followed the familiar path through the cottonwoods, past her rough-hewn armchair. A roll of mist rose from the far side of the river and the lower slopes of the mountains slowly appeared, as if they were pulling lace nighties up and over their heads. Much to the disappointment of fire forecasters and farmers, no rain had fallen in the valley overnight.

The path ended and she could see across the mouth of War Creek to the clearing where an old logging road took visitors to the real trailhead, one she had never found reason to use since the station had its own trail leading into the backcountry. She continued into deeper forest, where the river had abandoned an old meander and only a soggy basin remained. Tall spruces locked crowns to form a dim, dense room in the depression, like a cellar. Agnes dropped into the depression where so little sunlight reached the forest floor the understory consisted only of fallen twigs and needles that crackled underfoot. She could no longer hear the creek. This was the forest, the specific place, where in her dream the silver bear appeared.

She wasn't surprised that nothing remained of the crude survey lath cross with Brownie's name painted in picnic-table brown. When she came here as a twelve-year-old, a week after Clayt had buried him, the cross had been pulled out and splinters of it were strewn over the forest floor. The grave had been empty as well, with no trace of her beloved Border Collie. She wondered then if Brownie had risen from the dead and was out spreading the gospel of canine resurrection.

She had searched for him, for any sign of what had happened to him, until she nearly stepped into a soft heap of fresh scat. She had picked it off her saddle shoe with a stick and it fell into moist sections like blocks off a punky log. It contained clusters of whitish, swollen things the shape of rice. *Dead maggots*, she thought with a shudder, but curiosity had bested her revulsion and she rolled some of the scat into a handkerchief and took it home. She had shown it to her brothers, John and Pat, who suggested she let it dry before saving it. Their idea on this was a smart one, it turned out. The scat had lain in a disintegrating plastic bag at the back of her bedroom drawer, intact, until now.

"You're white as a ghost," Clayt said when she returned.

She leaned against the door. "I went to visit Brownie."

"What th'hell for?"

"I never blamed you."

"Wish it could of been otherwise."

Brownie had been fond of herding—then chasing—cattle on the Forest Service allotment, a major fault in a dog that belonged to the ranger's daughter. After numerous complaints and attempts to break his habit, Agnes found one of the ranch hands trying to herd a group of cows and calves while Brownie happily scattered them. "That your dog, kid?" She ran to grab him. "His hide's going to be hanging on my shed." Clayt walked the dog to the mouth of War Creek with a rifle under his arm. Agnes didn't hear the shot.

Clayt had shown her where he'd buried Brownie, and together they erected a cross made from lath survey stakes. "Better t' have me put 'im down than let somebody else shoot the hell out of him," he told her. She couldn't argue, but she could not be consoled. It was the last time she remembered her father hugging her.

"Now y' got Tuck to play with," Clayt said. "If he'll have ya."

"Why wouldn't he? We're getting to be pals."

"Dogs can sense a person's soul."

She was not about to let Clayt get away with that remark. "He must have decided I have a clean one, then," she said.

Clayt made no comment as he placed his field journals back in the musty box from which they had come. "What'll I do with these, missy? Who in the hell would want 'em?"

"Don't you dare get rid of those. I'll take them."

"Nap time," Clayt announced, and disappeared into another bedroom. He called from behind his closed door, "Tuck'll be wantin' dinner if you don't mind."

She poured a cup of kibble out and filled the water bowl and placed them side by side next to the door. Tuck accepted her offering with a slight wag of his tail.

Agnes went back into her room and left the door ajar, in case Tuck decided to come in. She transferred the scat from the ancient Ziploc bag to a new one.

The scat still held the dried-up maggots, yellowed and shriveled as old toenail trimmings. Clayt had told Hunter there'd been a bear in the area many years ago and Agnes thought the crumbs in the bag could have come from the same bear, the source of rumors and unconfirmed sightings for months: beehives torn apart, the branch of a neighbor's apple tree broken off and stripped of fruit, horses galloping around pastures in the middle of the night. After Brownie's grave was excavated, Clayt had sent Roger out with his rifle, riding under moonlight along the trails and logging roads. Everyone in the valley believed it was a grizzly bear. Huge tracks, made larger in the telling. People got into the habit of watching the margins of the forest when their horses started herding nervously. With time, the rumors and sightings trickled away into legend.

Now Agnes knew the legend had been fact—she had this scat as proof. As she rolled the bag around the crumbling bear scat and tucked it back into the drawer, she thought it would be a good idea to show it to Hunter.

She returned to the front room and called her roommate Joan.

"Sorry to bug you at work," she said. "Have a second?"

"Thanks for calling," Joan said. "I've been wondering how it's going out there."

"I meant to call sooner, but it's been a little hectic. I think this visit might take more than a week."

"I thought you were planning on that."

"I was planning on having some fun, hiking in the area, not spending all my time…" She paused to make sure Clayt was still snoring, "Spending all my time arguing with my father."

Joan made a sympathetic noise in her throat. She had been Agnes's confidant for years, and often joked that she thought she knew Clayt as well as Agnes did from all the stories she'd heard.

"Anyway, if bills come—"

"I can cover them."

"You're not going to want to pay my Visa bill. Just send it along."

"Where to?"

"Isn't that a good question. Wait." She flipped through the slim regional telephone directory on a shelf below the phone, and read out the address for the Raven's Roost.

"I'll send the mail when it piles up, but take your time—all is well here. Hotter than a pistol, though. I think we're in for another big fire season."

CHAPTER FIVE

Agnes set Tuck's breakfast on the floor. The dog tolerated a quick pat on the back, his tail wagging now instead of tucked between his legs.

Clayt hung up the telephone and rubbed his eyes. "Roger's beggin' off," he said. "Too busy with his flippin' bees this time of year."

"Begging off of what?"

He looked around the room, eyes red and watery. "Ah well, wasn't sure I wanted t' go in the first place. T' hell with it."

"This bear trip with Hunter? Of course you want to go. I didn't know Roger was involved."

"Need somebody to help me with the stock. I'm too damned old t'lift a pannier fulla grain by myself."

"I have an idea."

"I don't mean to take you. A woman has no business in the backcountry, especially with a grizzly bear running around."

She stared at him. "Excuse me?"

He answered with a glare.

"You're the one who taught me."

"I let you ride. I took care a camp and all."

"It isn't as though I haven't sat on a horse since. I camped out by myself all the time in Montana. You can be the guide and I'll be the camp jack and wrangler."

"Like I said, t' hell with it."

"Fine. I'm going to find you an apartment, then I'll go without you—the trip would be more pleasant anyway. We'll report back."

"You'll think up any damn thing t' go."

"Don't you remember that I grew up loving this country, and tagged along with you and Roger every chance I got? Did you ever think I might want to see it again myself? And what's this bullshit about women not belonging in the woods?"

"Watch your mouth, missy. You go off talking like a gutter snipe and you'll not impress this Hunter."

"I couldn't care less about Hunter."

Agnes felt the blood coming to her face as Clayt reddened. The two of them and their tempers.

"Look," she said. "I know how to read a map and I remember those trails. If you won't help Hunter navigate, I will."

"Using what for stock?"

"I'll rent some."

"Why don't you take a little stroll and cool off, now. Get the blazes out of my hair."

Agnes grabbed her jacket and let the screen door slam behind her as she flew down the steps. "Damn him," she said under her breath. She heard the door open behind her and ignored it as she stalked toward the river and the trail. Tuck came bounding up behind her.

"You want to walk with me, little man?"

Tuck pranced ahead, looking back to make sure she was coming. He found something under last year's fallen leaves and eyed her for signs of disapproval as he gulped it down, but she made no effort to take it away. Together they disappeared into the forest.

She made it as far as the cottonwood armchair before her anger dissipated and she didn't feel like walking anymore. She sat in the chair and rested her head back against the cool, smooth log.

"What in the hell are we going to do with him, Tuckster?"

What was she going to do, other than go crazy trying to deal with the old man? She couldn't keep running out the door and slamming it behind her every time he got her goat. Joan would have told her, as she often did when Agnes let her temper flare, to stop a minute: respond, don't react. She had done a good deal of reacting to Clayt so far, and it looked as if he would continue to toss her barbs until he drove her out. The apartment search had turned up nothing so far. She let her thoughts wander to things she might do in the meanwhile, other than seeking escape from him.

She sat up with an unexpected idea: what about the garden? She could lift the rhubarb and split its wads of root into a whole row of the stuff. Give it away to anyone who needed more, to perpetuate a small part of the old ranger station.

Agnes returned to find Clayt standing in the tack shed.

"What're you up to here?" she asked.

Socks and Agate and Jasper shuffled and snorted, curious as well. The tack shed looked as if the trail crew had spent the morning organizing—saddles in a row and blankets neatly stacked, halters and bridles on their hooks, each hook labeled with a horse's name. Clayt was shaking out a pair of canvas panniers.

He shot her a glance. "Checkin' gear, is all." He caressed the polished leather, the faded halter ropes, the pack saddles of the sawbuck style, the same ones that had been stored in that shed since it was built.

"Shall I fix us some lunch?" Agnes asked.

"Got another call while you were off," he said. "Boys found that lost hiker."

Agnes knew from his tone and expression that they'd found the man dead.

The telephone rang as she started up the steps, and she ran to pick up, assuming more news about the dead hiker.

"Hey, sport. How's it going?"

"Hi, Patrick. I figured you'd be checking in."

"I wanted to offer a bit of moral support."

"It's not going too well at the moment," Agnes said. "He's distracted by everything else going on around here—a lost hiker that just turned up dead, a grizzly bear in the mountains."

"Who cares about that? He's supposed to be moving."

"You don't say. He doesn't seem to know that's the goal here. When you talked me into coming, I was led to understand he would be ready to move."

"That's what he told me."

"Not only has he packed nothing, much less found a place to take it, he tells me he has no intention of going anywhere."

A melodramatic moan came over the line. "He was always good at giving everybody a different story," Patrick said. "Sorry to put you in this situation."

"Sorry enough to come help? He might listen to you, but he sure doesn't listen to me."

Patrick didn't respond immediately. Finally he said, "Let me get back to you—I'll see what I can manage."

"I need someone to deal with him so I can get around and find him a place."

After a few more minutes of unproductive haggling, Agnes hung up. Clayt was still in the tack shed and showed no signs of wanting lunch, and she wasn't hungry anymore. She grabbed her handbag and the shopping list that had been growing since she had gone to Helen's a few days before.

"I'm off to town," she said to Clayt as she headed for her car. "Grocery list's a mile long already. Maybe I'll pick up some pack trip–friendly items."

"You mind stopping—"

She paused. "I do mind. You're hitting the bottle too hard and I don't like being part of it."

He waved her off and turned his back, muttering under his breath.

Rion was turning around the wooden sign hanging from the door.

"Closing early?" Agnes asked.

"I'm not in the mood for chit-chat with tourists, and besides, nobody's stopped by in a half hour. But regulars—that's different."

"Am I a regular already?"

"I can see you're going to be."

"Thanks. I love this little place and you're great to talk to."

"C'mon in. You can help me finish a batch of lemonade."

"Know where I can buy some flowers?" Agnes asked as she sat down. "I'm going to plant a garden, something that can reseed and go wild after Clayt's out of there. And maybe some lettuce if anyone has starts."

"Kind of late," Rion said.

"I didn't plant until the first week in July one year, and that was in Helena—a couple thousand feet higher than here. The tomatoes and winter squash did fine."

"One place might still have some greens to plant." Rion paused. "I suppose you heard—"

"About the hiker, yes. Well, I surmised it, from what Clayt would say about it."

Rion performed a theatrical full-body shudder. "That's why I'm in no shape to handle customers. Getting anywhere with him?"

"He's not going to cooperate and I don't have the energy to keep after him. You were right about there being no rentals, even in town, which is the last place he wants to be. My brothers are useless. I tried to get some help from Patrick, and he promised to carve out some time, but one kid's going to camp and another has music lessons and his wife's out of town visiting her folks and he's alone with all the responsibility and is saving his time off for when the family's back together and can take a trip to Yosemite…"

"Shall I get out the violins?"

"You get the picture. So I said, okay, forget it. Asked him to check with one of the others."

"Will he do it, you think?"

"Who knows. I'm not holding my breath."

Rion poured the remainder of the frosty glass pitcher of lemonade into two coffee mugs and brought them to Agnes. She sat across from her and watched her until Agnes looked up, startled.

"You look exhausted," Rion said.

"Mostly what I feel is frustrated. I've been here a week already. I expected to be done moving him by now, and off on my own little vacation, seeing a couple of favorite trails and some places I've never been. Now I'm stuck on a hamster wheel chasing my father."

"What's the hurry? Give yourself a break, if he's not going to cooperate. While he stews in his juices maybe we can take off for a jaunt—up to the park, one of those trails you wanted to see. I'm a city girl, but I do like to get out and hike."

Agnes thought for a minute. "Hunter asked Clayt to help him find some old trails in the area where that bear might be. Clayt seemed pleased to be asked, but since Roger can't go—"

"His busiest time."

"Right. Anyway, I can pack, so I offered. Clayt would hear none of it and now he refuses to consider going at all."

"And what's that got to do with us hiking?" Rion sounded distracted and impatient.

"Hunter still needs a guide. Clayt knows that country like the insides of his eyelids, but I remember it just as well and know how to read a map. So I thought the heck with old Grumpy—I'll go myself. It would be great to have a cook. I can rent you a horse."

"Have you checked all this out with Hunter?"

"I plan to, of course." Not that she had the first idea how to find him.

"I'll give it some thought," Rion said. "But I'm no expert rider."

"We'll get you a gentle dude horse, you'll be fine."

As Agnes's enthusiasm grew, so did Rion's. "How long are we talking about?" she asked.

"I guess that depends on whether he finds this bear."

"I have to warn you, I'm nervous about bears. I can cold-cock some asshole who sorely deserves it—I've done it more than once—but I don't know about grizzly bears."

Agnes laughed. "I have no doubt you can take care of yourself under any circumstances. How about it? Can you afford to close the shop and let that income go?"

"The busy season doesn't start until after July fourth."

"Great. In the meantime, I'll try to find Hunter and ask what he thinks of this idea." It occurred to her that Hunter had no genuine need for a guide, but had asked Clayt only to take the sting out of his being left out. "For all I know," she said, "he'll tell us to take a hike."

"Which is what I suggested in the first place."

The trail climbed a steep-sided valley beneath a forest dominated by ponderosa pine, four feet thick and a hundred feet tall. Like exclamation points among the smaller white and noble firs, the understory of thimbleberry and heartleaf arnica, the pines stood straight and bold as if to announce: *This* is a forest. Agnes leaned forward to pat Jasper's neck as she breathed in the matchless perfume of the giant pines, their sun-warmed terpenes redolent with a scent like vanilla mixed with ripe apples. Central Montana grew stunted, droughty woodlands—tick-infested juniper and wolfy Douglasfir and endless stands of lodgepole pine. *Pinus monotonous*, Joan called it, after miles of hiking trails hemmed in by even-aged stands. Lodgepole was rarely of a size that made you stop and stare. Even the local ponderosas were rarely ponderous.

Agnes remembered bits of descriptions from the books that lined her father's bookshelf at the ranger station. Arthur H. Carhart, the first chief landscape architect of the United States Forest Service and known as a pioneering preservationist, had written about the personalities of trees. "The ponderosa pine is an aristocrat," he wrote. "...old ponderosas often stand alone, as if they insist on being individuals. Lodgepole is more like a member of the common rabble." *A perfect comparison*, Agnes thought as she followed with her eyes the jigsaw-puzzle bark of each giant ponderosa until the trunk disappeared into the branching crown fifty feet above the trail. She glimpsed the broken cliffs of dark metamorphic rock where the trail led,

SUSAN MARSH

the depthless blue of the sky beyond. For the first time since returning, Agnes felt completely at home.

The trail split and they took the north branch, into the canyon of Eagle Creek. It climbed beyond the pines into a closed forest of fir and spruce. At a switchback came the first tantalizing glimpse of the cirque basins where they would make their camp. Agnes began to recognize old landmarks—certain switchbacks and boulders and even some individual trees.

"Yahoo—is this beautiful or what?" Rion called from behind.

"I'm so glad you decided to come," Agnes said.

"Just keep the bears away from me, would you?" Rion grinned.

Agnes was pleased with the entire party, as it turned out, which included Clayt and Tuck. She didn't know what Hunter had said to him, but whatever it was got him out of the ranger station and into the saddle. Probably plied him with a spot of whiskey, she decided. Regardless of how he had gotten there, Agnes was glad to see the old man on a horse again, for it would be certain to improve his mood. Moving him out of the ranger station would have to wait regardless, since she hadn't yet found a place for him to rent.

Clayt took the lead on Agate, with Socks carrying the gear behind him and Tuck zipping back and forth as if Socks needed help staying on the trail. The old man sat high in the saddle, his back straight under a straw Stetson that had been part of his Forest Service field uniform. He also wore a faded cotton cruiser jacket—another uniform component—and a pair of darkgreen Wranglers. The only indication that he was a retired volunteer was the patch sewn onto his right shoulder.

Hunter spaced himself between Clayt and Agnes, slouching comfortably in the manner of someone who had spent his life on a horse. He rode a Belgian-Morgan cross named Rooster, sized to carry Hunter's substantial bulk along with a handheld antenna and bulging saddlebags. Rion rode a gentle paint rented from an outfitter.

"Clayt up there, doesn't he look pleased," she observed. "Short man on a tall horse. Wait till he sees what I have for lunch."

Clayt was more likely to pull a peanut butter sandwich out of a saddlebag and eat on the fly than stop for lunch. Agnes pressed her knees into Jasper's flanks, urging him ahead. If she knew her father, he would ride without a break until nightfall.

They caught up to him where he had stopped at a wide swath of jack-strawed timber, the aftermath of a winter avalanche. Agate and Rooster were tied together and Clayt was standing next to Socks, pulling the one-man crosscut out of its scabbard.

"Can't we go around?" Agnes asked.

Clayt looked up the slope, where the path of destruction led into the talus below a cliff, then at her.

"Dumb question—sorry," she said. "Let me help."

She slid out of the saddle. The first log was small and it didn't take long. She helped him secure the saw over Socks' load and they began to wind their way through the jumble of splintered trees and root wads. Agnes walked, carrying a double-bit so she could chop small branches free. It took an hour to reach the far side of the avalanche path, and when they did there was no sign of a trail.

"Don't this district have a trail crew anymore?" Clayt grumbled. "It's damned near July—where'n hell are them boys?"

"What can I do to help?" Hunter asked.

"Ride herd on the womenfolk so they stay out a trouble. With weather headin' this way I don't want t' waste any more time."

Agnes scanned what she could see of the sky between the spires of subalpine fir. Thin mare's-tail clouds drifted overhead, but it didn't look like rain was coming anytime soon.

"We must have gone too low," she said. "The trail is above us."

Clayt considered. "Let's get into the timber where the goin's easier. Damn it, did y' hear that?" He climbed onto Agate with a grunt.

Agnes and Rion exchanged glances.

"You all stay put," Clayt said, "while I head up an' check for the trail. I'll holler when I find it."

"Hear what?" Agnes said.

"Might have been rockfall," Hunter said. "Or thunder."

Agnes watched after Clayt as he steered Agate through the timber. A dead branch caught his hat and it fell to the ground. His face was florid, from embarrassment or exertion, or both. Agate was balky, and that had Clayt upset. Agate didn't look as if he'd been ridden much, and now the old soldier was being pressed into strenuous service.

"He's going to give that horse a heart attack," Agnes said. She slid off Jasper and passed the rein to Hunter, ran up the mountainside and quickly caught up. She handed Clayt his hat.

"Damn it, didn't I tell y' to stay put?"

"Clayt, for God's sake, let me help." She took the lead rope before he could protest and led Agate through the deadfall. Jasper whinnied and Agate responded. "Hang on and relax," she said.

"Dunno what got in t' Agate," Clayt said. "He never acts up. Think that bear might be around."

"I think Agate's picking up on your mood."

Agnes led the horse slowly, pausing often to let him blow. Clayt exhausted his pique and let her lead, but his mention of the bear made her more alert and she could see from the set of Tuck's ears he was vigilant as well. Ahead of them stood nearly impenetrable black timber, and she kept as close to the avalanche path as the need to zigzag over deadfall allowed.

Hunter and Rion caught up, leading Jasper and Socks along with their own mounts. No one spoke as they proceeded through the forest.

Clayt pointed. "Looky there."

On the bole of a blistered subalpine fir, a blaze. Neatly cut with a hatchet decades ago, it retained its crisp corners under a varnish of pitch, a square over a longer rectangle, the symbol for the heel and toe of a boot headed along the trail. They reached a break in the slope where a bedrock outcrop formed a bench, and were back on the route.

The forest broke into a long, moist meadow, where the white avalanche lilies and elkslip were so numerous their blooms resembled patches of snow. A bare spot at the edge of the forest held an old fire ring and shelter from Clayt's predicted rain.

Agnes checked her watch—close to five o'clock. She gestured toward the fire ring and shouted ahead to Hunter. "Camp."

"If I know His Nibs he won't want to stop, but this campsite looks perfect," she told Rion. "Especially if it's going to rain."

"My ass hurts," Rion said. "I'm glad I didn't have to be the one to call it quits."

A clap of thunder echoed off the crest of the Sawtooth.

"Didn't take long for the flippin' weather to settle in," Clayt said. "Drier'n a popcorn fart since April and as soon as I saddle up here she comes." He turned his back to the meadow beyond camp, shrouded by dense fog and drizzle that soon gathered into rain. "Time t' get a fire put together."

The others found flat spots for tents and began to assemble the kitchen. Past campers had left cut poles stacked against a tree, and two of the longest ones were put into service as supports for the canvas tarp.

"I'll get that," Clayt said.

He was no longer strong enough to keep the crossed poles vertical while he tied off the rope to a tree, but that didn't prevent him from shooing Agnes away when she tried to help.

"Leave it be," he snapped. "You don't know how t' do it right."

"Well, let me take the dumb end, at least." She held the poles and the canvas taut while Clayt grunted over the tie-off, securing it with the perfect hitch that only he could throw.

"All right then, I can get the rest myself."

Agnes caught Hunter watching the exchange and laughing. "Every old packer is that way," he said. "Only one way to do it—their way."

"That's my father."

With camp in place, Rion sequestered herself in the kitchen area. Clayt fed the fire and tended the horses while Hunter studied the map and jotted in a pocket-sized waterproof notebook. Agnes assigned herself the task of scouring the forest floor for more firewood.

Clayt laid a dead fir branch on top of the fire and the dry needles crackled, sending a swarm of sparks into the cold, damp air. Perching on the upturned block of a sawn log, hunkered in his oiled duster, he watched the flames as they wrapped the fresh wood. Coals were beginning to settle at the edge of the fire pit and Rion raked them into place with a stick before setting two Dutch ovens over them.

"Fire feels great," she said. She ran her hand through her hair and pulled a ragg knit cap over her head.

Agnes agreed. Down vest zipped over a wool turtleneck, slicker draped over her shoulders, she soaked in the penetrating heat. Brightness bathed the packed earth around the fire and reflected off the sides of the tents sprinkled among sheltering trees. A layer of opaque cloud pressed into the cirque basin like a cold damp rag, wiping the talus slopes and snowfields away. The only thing that could drive off that rain-soaked chill of the mountains was the heat of burning wood.

Even Clayt let the pleasure of the campfire warm his mood. He tilted an aluminum fuel bottle into his battered tin cup.

"Anyone care for a slap?" He held out the bottle.

Hunter and Rion accepted a bit, but Agnes shook her head. "I'll have some in my coffee later," she said.

Hunter sat on the log beside Agnes and smacked his lips with satisfaction. "Don't spoil this with coffee," he said, and held his enameled cup toward her.

She took a tiny sip, felt the burning of alcohol on her lips, let its sharp sweetness wash over her tongue, and swallowed.

Hunter watched with amusement.

"She's got enough bad habits," Clayt said. "Don't get her started on expensive hooch."

"Look who's talking," Agnes said as she pushed the cup in Hunter's direction. She ignored Clayt's glare and watched the fire, waiting for its mesmerizing dance to calm her. *Pretend you're here alone*, she told herself. *Enjoy this place, if not the company.* At least the rain had abated, leaving only a drizzle that could not penetrate the dense crowns of spruce and fir surrounding their camp. She turned her attention toward Hunter.

"Where do the bears shelter up in weather like this?" she asked.

"Come down t' to see what smells so good," Clayt put in.

Rion lifted one lid and poked at the contents. "Some of this was supposed to be your lunch," she said. "It's ready if you are."

"That bear'll be down here for sure," Clayt said. "If it's got a decent sniffer and half a brain."

"I don't imagine we'll leave her much," said Hunter as Rion filled his plate with lamb and vegetable stew.

Under Hunter's questioning and the influence of more whiskey, Clayt began to open up. Stories, most of them featuring himself, of summers fighting fire, smoke jumping, pack trips into the wild backcountry, and, once he had moved up to the position of district ranger, building a team of talented and dedicated men.

"It was somethin' to be proud of," he said. "Before they gave half th' district to the park service and the other half to Twisp."

"Hard to believe they plan to tear down that ranger station," Hunter said. "It's in great shape from the look of it."

"Damn right it is. I've been seeing t' that."

Rion passed a tin plate stacked with warm brownies. "How cast in stone is this thing?" she asked.

"The concrete's dry," Clayt said.

"That sucks," Rion said.

Before she could say more, Clayt unfolded a topographic map and traced a creek drainage with his finger. "Gonna be a son of a bitch gettin' up here if them rocks are wet. Been needin' rain all right, but now I hope t' hell it takes a breather."

"It sort of is," Agnes said. While the group was focused on dinner, the drizzle had quit.

Rion watched Clayt studying the map. "Where'd they find that hiker?" she asked.

"Never heard," Clayt said.

Hunter stood behind Clayt and leaned over the map. "Up here," he said, pointing to the far corner of the topographic quad. "Looked like he might have been climbing the Camel's Hump."

"How's it you knew an' I didn't?" Clayt asked.

"You've heard the rumors going around," Rion said.

Hunter nodded. "None of this is official, so please don't pass it on." He looked at Agnes and Clayt, whose expressions showed they had not heard the rumor but certainly wanted to. "I was called in by the coroner's office—only reason I know anything about it." He gave Clayt a significant look, as if to apologize for being in the information loop when Clayt was not. "I'll leave out the details, but the body had been partially eaten."

"I knew it," Clayt leapt in. "Soon as them boys started up th' road I was sayin' to myself, that damned bear. Poor son of a bitch."

"Not quite, Clayt," Hunter said. "The evidence I saw clearly indicated the man was scavenged, not killed. One leg was badly broken at the ankle. I think it's likely he was injured in a fall and died of exposure. Then something found him. Could have been a bear. More likely coyotes."

A stunned silence fell over camp. Clayt broke it with a whispered *Goddamn*.

Agnes excused herself and went to her duffle for a warmer jacket, wondering how on earth she would sleep that night. Rion would no doubt stay up keeping the fire stoked and listening for the slightest noise, and she expected to join her. She stuffed her hands in the pockets of her jacket and felt the plastic bag. After settling onto the log beside Hunter, she fished the bag out of her pocket and handed it to him.

"I've been meaning to show you this."

He gave the bag a shake and held it out in the firelight.

"What in God's name is that?" Clayt asked. He and Rion leaned forward to see and Hunter passed it around.

"Looks like an old cigar," Rion said. She pulled a real cigar out of her vest pocket and lit it. "Smoke will keep those bears at bay."

"I know what it looks like," said Clayt as he handled the bag. "A big ol' turd."

"I got that far with it," Agnes said. "I wondered what kind."

"It's not exactly fresh," Hunter said when the bag returned to him. He opened the seal and sniffed, felt it with his fingertips, and produced a flashlight from his vest pocket. "Hang onto this," he said, and handed the flashlight to Agnes.

He spilled some of the loose bits into his palm. Agnes leaned in close to see.

"How old?"

"Let's see—thirty-six minus twelve, that would be about a quarter century."

"Looks like it."

"Keep it if you want."

He rolled the dried maggots under a finger. "These are pine nuts," he said. "Probably whitebark."

Agnes knew that whitebark nuts were favored by grizzly bears in Montana. Hunter put the bag and flashlight in his pocket and gave no indication that he considered it further.

Rion scraped the brownie crumbs into the fire. "You don't think that bear is going to come around," she said.

"Long as we don't leave anything to attract her," Hunter said. "That means toothpaste—it goes in the pannier too. Sorry to have brought up that gruesome story. As I said, please keep it under your hats. The investigation isn't over."

"Tuck'll warn us if there's a bear around," Clayt said.

"A few years ago, where I was working near Yellowstone, a bear pulled a guy out of his sleeping bag," Agnes said. "Right in a campground. He was doing everything right—food hung, all the rest of it. The same summer another—"

"That'll do," Clayt said. "Last thing we need is t' sit up all night tellin' bear stories."

Hunter talked about the usual circumstances of a grizzly attack: someone hiking alone, making little noise, surprising a sow with cubs.

"I can see it happening on the trail," Rion said. "But hitting some guy in a campground who was supposedly doing everything right? That gives me the major willies."

"Bears have personalities, like people. Some are mellow, some are hotheaded, some go off their rockers."

"I've always loved bears," Agnes said. "How did you get into studying them?"

Hunter took his time answering, started to speak then stopped. "Want the truth? I've probably had just enough whiskey to tell you."

Clayt drained his cup. "Not exactly our business, now, is it."

"In graduate school I took summer jobs with the state, tracking collared black bears. A few of them had been hitting orchards and it was my job to track the ones in the mountains who were minding their own business, try to find out how they made a living when they didn't have a steady supply of fallen apples. I got to know those bears pretty well—we were friends. One in particular, an older boar. He was shy at first, but he let me get fairly close a few times. He seemed to accept me, for whatever reason."

He paused and held his cup toward Clayt for another snort.

"So this old boar got blamed for breaking into an empty cabin. He was miles from that cabin at the time, I had the telemetry to prove it. But I was just a field grunt, couldn't convince my bosses to stand up and use the science. I let myself get talked into helping to trap him on the promise that he would be relocated, but as we were packing up with the bear in back of the truck I learned that they meant to put him down—easier than taking him somewhere else. Smart animal, a beautiful, healthy bear that hadn't caused any trouble. Treated like vermin.

"I looked into the bars of that little cage and the bear looked back at me. Those eyes…I'll never forget them. He seemed to ask what he had done to deserve this, and why didn't his so-called friend and defender help him out of this jam. He's haunted me ever since, and I made up my mind to do what I could to help people respect bears, or at least understand them."

Hunter abruptly stood and walked away from the firelight. Agnes saw him reaching for his slicker as he set off along the edge of the meadow. The drizzle had stopped, leaving thin mist hovering in the darkness.

Clayt gave the group a gruff goodnight. "Bedtime," he said.

"I'll say," Rion said. "Good luck sleeping, everyone—I'm sure I won't." She took her flashlight and headed for her tent.

Agnes remained next to the fire, staring into the pulsating coals. She fed it twigs and dried cones and it sputtered back to life. She loved the snap and glow of pine pitch igniting, the sparks that rose and blinked off in the darkness, the incense of the smoke. The intimate glow of the campfire and the penetrating silence of deep night in the mountains that lay beyond the glow. And now there was a grizzly sow out there somewhere, and a man who loved her.

The whiskey bottle was drained and her backside was chilled. Agnes figured she had sat alone for nearly an hour, but Hunter never returned. She imagined him wandering somewhere along the edge of the forest and meadow, searching for answers to unutterable questions, for hope where none could be found, for a trap door into the past through which he could exonerate and free the falsely condemned.

CHAPTER SIX

Agnes opened her eyes to daylight and stretched like a cat, all the way to her toes, before unzipping the tent's front flap. Her stiffness from hours in the saddle was the kind that Clayt would call *a good kind of sore*, obtained only from mountain travel on foot or horseback, going farther than you planned or thought you could. She saw from the way sunlight struck the tent fly that the weather had cleared, and that she had slept late.

She craned around the tent flap to see what was going on in camp. Three horses stood with Socks at the highline, shaking their nose bags for the last bits of grain. Rooster was not among them. Rion and Clayt attended the smoking fire with coffee mugs in hand, both smiling as if sharing a joke. How easily Rion brought him out with her forthright spunk and confidence, and Clayt seemed to genuinely like her. Agnes lay back and felt for her socks in the sleeping bag. It occurred to her that if Clayt and Rion hit it off, it would help him more than anything Agnes could offer. As far as she knew he hadn't been with a woman since her mother left.

"Here comes Sleeping Beauty," Rion said, and fetched another coffee mug—metal with speckled enamel coating. "These are fun. I might get some for the shop."

"You must of slept fine," Clayt said. "In spite a' them stories."

"Guess I did this morning," Agnes said. "You?"

"Like a rock. Best night's sleep in years."

Agnes glanced toward Clayt's bedroll, beside which Tuck was curled. Clayt and Hunter had opted for an open-air tarp instead of using tents, though Hunter had brought his. When he saw Clayt stringing up the tarp he'd gone to help and asked if he could use it too. There was plenty of room for everyone. It was the way Agnes was used to camping in the Rockies. A tent gave the illusion of security from the elements and bears, but she felt safer in the close company of others and their dogs, able to hear and see what might be going on beyond camp. If a bear was nearby one of the dogs would be sure to bark or growl, and the prone, apparently sleeping bodies would stir in unison, flashlights and pepper spray at the ready. Maybe she would suggest striking the tents for the rest of the trip.

Hunter appeared from behind a patch of forest, leading Rooster.

"He started early," Agnes said.

"Jes' letting the horse graze. Th' rest've got their bellies fulla grass."

"I don't know how you men do it," Rion said. "Up all night drinking whiskey, then all the chores are done before dawn. I'll plan on having the coffee ready sooner tomorrow."

"Soon as I hit the woods I'm on mountain time," Clayt said. "An' this time a year, the dark time's pretty damn short."

"I noticed," Rion said. "The night they had that bear meeting was summer solstice. I left early so I could do something more fun—a little group of us stayed up all night by the river and counted the hours of darkness. Less than five, total, and even then the stars were so bright you couldn't call it dark."

"I should have gone with you," Agnes said.

"Glad you didn't." Hunter stood beside her with a fresh mug of coffee.

"Time to make more?" Rion asked. She checked the pot steaming beside the campfire. "Looks like it."

Agnes looked at Hunter. "Why? I didn't even get a chance to say hello."

"It was nice to see a friendly face in that crowd," he said.

She took his remark as truth, but wondered if he had meant something more. She glanced toward Clayt, expecting a disdainful sneer. But he was poring over the maps he had brought, deep in study.

After breakfast Hunter and Clayt took off to check a lake basin for signs of the War Creek sow.

"What about that hike?" Agnes suggested. "I don't expect to see those two before dark."

"Sounds great," Rion said. "Pack a lunch?"

"I haven't got anything but a saddlebag to carry it in."

"Well, I do."

Rion went to her tent for the small daypack she'd worn while riding the day before.

Ready to go, she hesitated for a moment.

"What about the stock?"

Jasper, Socks, and Rion's little paint stood at a highline in the shade, their eyes half closed, each with one hind hoof resting on its toe, full of grain and sweet mountain grass.

"They'll be fine," Agnes said.

From camp, there were two choices: head back down the trail where they had come the day before, or turn west, toward the mountain crest. One choice, in Agnes's mind. She took the lead as they followed the horse tracks left in the damp earth by Clayt and Hunter an hour before. The trail continued to climb as the glacial valley of upper Eagle Creek widened at its head. The day was bright with sun, the last of the mist from the night clouds evaporating off the forest like scarves tossed into the sky. The meadow where they camped was part of a series of lush green carpets spread among the uppermost stringers of forest. Soon enough, both forest and meadow gave way to alpine wildflower parks, snowfields, and sky.

"Wow," said Rion. "Look at that."

Agnes turned. Rion stood facing away, toward where the ridge on the far side of Eagle Creek erupted into rocky peaks. They poked up above slopes blanketed in continuous deep snow. Even in the high June sunlight, the snow was protected by intermediate crags and pillars, flying buttresses of dark metamorphic rock that shielded it from heat and light and wind. If Agnes came back in September, she knew there would still be a few patches lingering among those crags and talus slopes.

As Rion marveled at the scenery that had been invisible the evening before, Agnes recounted trips to the mountains when she never got to see the peaks at all.

"We'd spend a night in the cold and rain, come back down the trail, and go home to look at photos from the last time so we knew where we had been."

Rion laughed. "You must know this place so well."

"Etched in my mind, but we'll see how accurately. C'mon, let's go for the pass."

With the forest far below and only a few patches of trees scattered in the meadows, they crossed a wide, flat basin, the floor of an old cirque.

"Imagine—a glacier once sat here," Rion said. "In the town where I grew up, a continental glacier once planted its behind, a few thousand feet thick."

"What town?"

"Detroit."

"Twisp must seem like an outpost on the frontier compared to that."

"Well, it is, isn't it?"

Agnes pointed out a narrow line angling upward between a remnant skirt of snow and the bedrock rib of the ridge above.

"We're going up there?" Rion asked. "Looks steep."

To Agnes, the pass looked close and easy to reach. But she noticed that Rion had started to slow down. She considered the age difference between them, Agnes in her prime and used to hiking, while Rion, though plenty strong, was a decade and a half older and used to standing in a coffee shop. Rion was a formidable presence at the Raven's Roost, the picture of competence. In the mountains, she was more like a little kid, pointing out every wildflower and asking Agnes to name it.

Fearful of things that struck Agnes as ordinary—a log creek crossing, a slippery snowbank.

Agnes stopped to run her hands over the branches of a tree no taller than she was. Its bright green needles were flexible and silky to the touch, and the bark was dark gray like the rocks on the mountains above. Each branch and twig was dotted with knobs where the clusters of needles grew.

"Alpine larch," she said. "Feel how soft."

"They look like cactus spines. How's that possible?"

"The needles are new, just opening. Larch is the only deciduous conifer."

Rion nodded. "Now I see why it looks familiar. It's like tamarack. We have those in Michigan. It must be just a seedling."

"I'll bet this tree's older than you and me combined. Larch is my favorite tree in the world—I have one in my yard in Montana, but other than the ones people plant, there aren't any on the east slope of the divide. I always make a pilgrimage to the mountains north of Missoula in October, just to see the larches."

"Pilgrimage," Rion said. "I like that. Today we're making a pilgrimage to Eagle Pass."

They continued on to the final switchback leading to the divide. The snow they crossed was soft and had begun to melt on the upper third of the slope, where sandy soil from disintegrating granite turned gold under the sun's brilliance.

"How high are we?" Rion asked.

"I think the pass is around 7,300. Look how dark the sky is."

Overhead, the sky took on a shade of deep indigo. Off to the east it faded into a pale, dusty blue, nearly white on the horizon. The ridges wrapping Eagle Creek spread toward the lowlands. Agnes pointed to one of them.

"Snowshoe Ridge," she called it. "Wouldn't that be fun to ski."

"I don't see any lifts."

Agnes laughed. "You put on skins and climb it. Backcountry skiing is such a blast. The mountains in winter—it's a whole different place."

"You ski stuff like that?"

"Not when I was growing up, except a little alpine at Loup Loup. But since moving to Montana, it's what people do. We have ski areas too, but the best powder is the snow you have to work for."

Rion was watching her as she talked.

"What?" Agnes asked. "Do I sound so bizarre?"

"You're one of the most remarkable women I've ever met."

Agnes continued, slightly embarrassed. "We're almost there," she said. "Just wait—the view will knock your socks off."

"You've already done that," Rion said. "Most of the people I knew at home have never seen a mountain. To you, it's nothing special."

"It's special, all right. But it's also home."

The last few hundred feet of the trail steepened, leading into a narrow chute between protruding cliff bands. Agnes could see the pass and knew it was nearly flat on top. It would only take a few minutes. Looking behind her, she saw that Rion had dropped back.

"Doing all right?" she called.

"I've just got to take it slow. Go on—I'll see you in a minute."

Agnes couldn't do much to help her friend walk faster, and she could hardly contain herself as she approached the pass. Unconsciously she started climbing faster in spite of being winded. She had always reacted this way when approaching a summit or col along a ridge. The anticipation of reaching it lent her an extra dose of energy, and she nearly sprinted to the top.

The view made the breath catch in her throat. A sea of peaks broke to the west like ranks of whitecaps, snowy Glacier Peak hovering like a ghost above the core of the North Cascades. Deep forested valleys and bare ridges, shadowed snowfields and sun-bleached talus slopes spread from north to south. She felt the silence that abided only deep in the mountains, a silence so complete she could hear the distant roar of a river cascading through an invisible canyon, miles away.

With no sign of Rion coming up behind her, Agnes started along the crest of the Sawtooth. It dropped off steeply on both slopes but was rounded on top, an easy stroll. Battle Mountain stood to the north about a mile away, one of a dozen named peaks along the ridge. Cols and minor peaks stood between Battle Mountain and Eagle Pass, and Agnes opted for the closest of the peaks, about two hundred feet higher than the trail. On the windswept ridge, bare of snow, alpine wildflowers had begun to bloom: cushion phlox with its masses of white flowers and sweet floral scent; sun-yellow draba, another low cushion plant that favored dry, rocky summits; silky phacelia, with spikes of deep purple flowers and stamens sticking out like hair gone wild. Flowers she remembered from these mountains, the same flowers that would now be blooming in Montana. She sat on a boulder dark with lichen and ran her fingertips over the stamens of phacelia.

To the west, mountains stretched to the horizon and beyond. To the east, the valley of Eagle Creek flowed into the Twisp River, which then flowed into the Methow. Lost in dust and distance and the curvature of the earth was Montana. For a moment, with their shared wildflowers and lichen-encrusted rocks and darkblue mountain sky, the places she had called home blended in her mind, all part of the same vast region.

But they weren't the same. No place was like this one: Agnes was sitting on Sawtooth Ridge for the first time in a quartercentury. On the far side of Eagle Pass, somewhere beyond a pyramidal peak that had no name, Clayt and Hunter searched for signs of the War Creek sow. There was no other place on earth where these two things were happening.

One thing had not yet happened: Rion's appearance at the pass. Agnes scanned the trail below and thought she saw her daypack hanging from the snag of a subalpine fir. Agnes stood and took a final look along the ridge before starting down to Eagle Pass and the wildflower parks below.

—

She caught up with Rion next to a tiny rivulet of snowmelt. Rion was studying a garden that bloomed between meanders of the deep melt-water creek: buttercup and elkslip, the first blooms of heather on a bank overhanging the water.

"Hey," Rion said.

"What happened, Ri? Are you okay?"

"I'm not used to steep snow," Rion said. "I got a little dizzy so I decided it was best to turn around."

"Sorry I didn't wait." Agnes noticed that Rion had put on her riding boots for the hike, not the best choice for negotiating steep, slippery surfaces. "I wanted you to see the view."

"You're the one who needed to see it, not me. Besides, this is just fine—what could be more beautiful?"

Rion laid lunch on a rock—sandwiches, a bunch of grapes, pumpkin-raisin cookies. Agnes surprised her by lying on her stomach on the spongy earth to drink from the creek like a horse. She sat back and wiped her mouth.

"That is the coldest, sweetest water you'll ever drink," she said.

"Aren't you worried about giardia?"

"Here? This water was snow five minutes ago."

Rion shook her head and passed grapes to Agnes. "I've had giardia twice," she said. "The second time I was drinking out of a spring." She drank from the water bottle she had brought, filtered in camp. "I know I must seem like a damned pussy," she said. "Scared of bears, heights, the water. Look at me."

"Whoa—such whining. That doesn't sound like you. It's not your fault you didn't grow up in the mountains. If I went to Detroit I'd be so worried about what to do or not do, I'd be a total basket case."

"I'd keep you out of trouble," Rion said. "Thanks for making me feel better about being a babe in the woods."

"You'll be an old hand by the time we get home. I think we ought to get back to camp, though, and let the horses graze."

They followed the trail slowly, engrossed by the wildflowers. Rion was a quick study, learning more names in an hour's time than Agnes thought she could have managed. Perhaps Rion was trying to take the edge off her embarrassment. She had grown self-consciousness since morning and Agnes wondered why. She watched Rion move, with occasional small hitches in her joints, as if she were in pain. Arthritis wasn't something Agnes worried about, yet, but maybe Rion did.

When they reached camp, Agnes took Socks and the horses to the meadow for an afternoon of grazing. She didn't know Rion's rented paint, so she picketed him and hobbled Socks, knowing Jasper would stick around the mule. She caught Rion watching her—wistfully, it seemed. It was easy for Agnes to forget how naturally it came to her to buckle hobbles onto a horse, bending at the front feet of a thousand-pound creature while trusting completely that she would not be stepped on, kicked or otherwise injured. Rion kept watching and Agnes thought she might be worried about her. She caught her eye and waved, and Rion turned away.

Agnes ran her fingers through Jasper's shaggy mane, picking burs. By the time she returned to camp, Rion had taken her sleeping bag and pad out of her tent and into the shade. She had gotten little sleep after the bear stories, and Agnes concluded that was why she seemed off today. With nothing to do, Rion asleep, and the others gone, Agnes decided to take a nap herself.

Clayt showed up with Tuck mid-afternoon.

"Everything all right?" Agnes asked. "Where's Hunter?"

"Your Goddamn boyfriend's outta his mind. Left this old buzzard in th' dust."

"I wish you'd stop calling him that."

"Took him down to Oval Lakes an' showed him th' way over the ridge, but he wanted t' see Fish Creek Pass. So he went thataway and I came home. Too pooped to pop."

Agnes took Agate, unsaddled him, and led him out to roll in the meadow and graze with the others. Roused by Clayt's arrival, Rion came out to meet him.

Clayt sat on the ground against the trunk of a spruce. Rion made a batch of instant lemonade with cold filtered water from the creek and handed two mugs to Agnes.

"Join us?" Agnes asked.

"Need to get the grub started," Rion said. "Your old man's probably half starved."

Agnes took the lemonade to the tree where Clayt was sitting and sat on the ground beside him.

"This will perk you up."

Clayt sipped his lemonade and smacked his lips with pleasure. "Nice t'be waited on by a couple a good-lookin' women."

"What we're here for."

"Way Swann's movin', he's gonna cover this country so fast we'll be goin' home tomorrow."

"I hope not. I'd like to stay up here forever."

He glanced at her appraisingly.

"Not because of Hunter—will you stop with that, please?"

Clayt watched the stock grazing. "Where'd you learn t' wrangle nags like that?" His way of approving her choice of placing picket pins and hobbles.

"I told you I've been working for the Forest Service every summer. Plus, where do you think I first learned it?"

"Didn't know you was payin' that much attention." After a moment he added, "Couldn't teach them boys a damn thing."

None of her brothers had opted for the mountain life as adults, which surprised Agnes since they seemed to enjoy it so much growing up. "Well," she said. "You wanted us to go to college and get real jobs, right? I guess that's what we did."

"An' nobody ever looked back. Funny how things work out."

"I went up to Eagle Pass today. What a view."

"Boyfriend was impressed."

She chose to ignore the comment. The more she asked him not to do something the more he would persist. "I'll bet you were glad to see Oval Lakes," she said. "Remember that trip with Roger and the twins? I couldn't have been more than ten or eleven."

"What I remember was you carryin' on like a banshee until I let y' come."

"That was my first pack trip—it meant so much to be included. I've loved being in the mountains ever since."

"Helena must be a letdown, in that case."

"Montana has mountains, but not right out your back door. And not like these. I about cried when I started seeing alpine larch—Rion thought I was a bit nuts."

Clayt grunted in reply and drank the rest of his lemonade.

Rion carried a plastic pitcher to where they sat. "More?" She poured some for them both and left them to their conversation.

"She's somethin' ain' she," Clayt said. "Bundle a energy."

"You should see her scurrying when the shop is full. She taught me how to make coffee. Sometimes I get the scones and sweet rolls out of the oven when she's busy with customers."

"Hear Roger's in there every day after one a them rolls. Must be pretty damn good for him t' show his face in that hippie joint."

Agnes laughed. "It has character—and great coffee. That's more than I can say for the places you like to go."

"I go for the talk, not the Joe." He sighed and leaned hard against the tree. "Could damn near take a nap."

They sat together without speaking for a while, then Agnes asked him, "Why'd you come to War Creek in the first place? Weren't you in Colorado before?"

"I was lots a' places before here. Job I wanted come up an' I needed to get th' hell outta Colorado."

Agnes wasn't sure if she was being given permission to ask why. He seemed to want her to, but she didn't. After a silence he went on as if she had.

"Buddy a mine, he got killed on the fire line. Wind come up an'the top of a dead lodgepole broke off. Hardhat don't do you much good when that happens. It was hard t' take—an' since we was pals, I got to tell his widow what happened."

"How awful," Agnes said.

Clayt swatted at a mosquito. "Them little bastards'r out

already, now. Anyhow, it all ended up okay—for a while. That gal I broke th' news to…" He swatted and cursed again.

Agnes waited. "What about the gal," she prompted.

"Yeah," Clayt said, as if he had completely lost his train of thought. "Turned out to be your mother. Time we got together, we'd both had enough a' memories and all that. So we come here."

Agnes took in the information. Had she ever heard this before? She knew her mother was from Colorado and that her parents had met there. Their wedding photo: she had never asked, but it must have been taken in Denver.

"You think that's where she went?" Agnes asked. This was a topic she was pretty sure she wasn't being asked to talk about.

He closed his eyes to indicate the conversation was over. "Dunno."

"I know you don't want to talk about her, but don't you think I might want to know?"

"An' what about that kid a yours? Think it might be wonderin' where its mamma is?"

It. That's what the nuns had said, not he or she. "Clayt, don't go for the jugular as usual. 'It' happened to be your grandchild. You know as well as I do that the baby died."

He opened one eye and pinned her with his stare. "That what they told ya?"

When she had gotten back to War Creek after giving birth, nothing was said about the baby. The unexpected departure of her mother overwhelmed both Clayt and Agnes, and that cataclysm shunted any chance of discussing what had happened to the child into the background, where it stayed.

"It's what they told me and what I believed," Agnes said. "You sound like you know something more about it."

"I think that kid got adopted out like the rest of 'em."

Leftover lasagna stayed warm in one of the Dutch ovens, in case Hunter returned before dark. Agnes could not keep herself from checking the trail on the far side of the meadow for movement, as if one more glance would cause him to appear.

"Told y' he was gonna scour the whole damn country today," Clayt said. "Man's got no sense."

"I just hope nothing happened," Agnes said.

"Got a couple hours to cool yer heels before it's time to start worryin' about—"

"Here he comes." Rion pointed.

Clayt and Agnes followed her finger downstream, in the opposite direction that Agnes had been watching. Hunter pressed Rooster into a trot and slid out of the saddle before reaching camp.

"Whaddya do, go back t' town for more booze?"

Hunter laughed, but Agnes saw the weariness in his eyes.

"I'll get Rooster squared away here and join you in a second," Hunter said. He led his horse toward the others.

"Ya need t' picket him, there's an extra pin in one a them panniers," Clayt yelled. He turned back to the campfire. "Christ. Glad I bailed when I did, or I'd be dead by now."

"Yeah, well, he's half your age, Clayt," Rion said. "Another cookie?"

"Why not?"

They looked up at the sound of water splashing. Hunter emerged from a deep pool in the creek and shook himself like a dog. "Yeeeoow!" he yelled. "Is that cold."

Rion laughed as she watched him racing for his clothes. "Let's get that man some supper," she said.

Hunter sat next to Agnes and Rion handed him a plate loaded with lasagna and French bread.

"Sorry it's a little dried out," she said.

"Does that look good or what? I think Rooster must have smelled dinner, he started getting antsy on me."

"Where'n hell'dya end up?" Clayt asked.

"I took the trail you showed me, over that low spot on the ridge. Came out right above Silver Lake, then hit the trail."

"Get up to Fish Creek?"

"Sure did. I let Rooster hang out near Star Lake and tromped around on the other side for an hour or so, went up Gray Peak hoping to catch a signal. Found some bear scat, but by then it was getting late. I should have just come back the same way we went over, but I wanted to see those woods down below."

"Y'covered some country, all right."

"I feel like it."

"That last piece of lasagna's got your name on it," Rion said.

"Thank you. I can't remember the last time I was out in the field with such a crew to look after my ass."

"Now that everybody's fed, I'm ready for a nightcap," Clayt said.

"Assuming there's any left," Agnes put in.

"Had t' save a wee dram for the bear hunter, didn' I?" Clayt leaned forward to stand.

"Stay where you are," Rion said. "I can find it."

He sat back with a smile. "Ain' nothing like bein' in the mountains."

Agnes watched him, glad he was contented. But she could see how much he had exerted himself to manage this trip. The elevation might be getting to him. The flush on his face was not sunburn.

"Where are you heading tomorrow?" she asked Hunter. "Maybe he should stay in camp and rest up."

"I was thinking War Creek Pass. With Rooster, I'll have to stay on the trail most of the way."

"That's like a twenty-mile ride," said Agnes. "Not counting all the ups and downs."

"About the same as today, then."

She lowered her voice. "Clayt shouldn't go."

"I can handle it alone. Though I like his company." He nodded in Clayt's direction. He had pressed his back against a tree trunk and was lightly snoring.

"It's not just the distance," Agnes said. "If he starts getting too far north, he's going to be looking at a lot of his old district. He's never gotten over losing it to the Park Service."

Hunter nodded. "I guess I can see why. Maybe I'll bag that part of it and come back another time. Thought I could pick up a signal from Gray Peak, but there were too many other peaks in the way."

"Sorry you didn't find her."

"She could be anywhere, so I'm not that surprised. But I was sure hoping to place her well away from the Camel's Hump, where that hiker was found." He set his empty plate on the ground beside him and sipped the whiskey Rion had brought. "Looks like old Clayt is tuckered out. We better get him home."

"This is the best thing that's happened to him in a very long time," Agnes said. "Because of you. Thank you, so very much."

Hunter moved closer and wrapped her in one arm. "The pleasure was entirely mine."

Agnes glanced in Clayt's direction, but he was sound asleep.

"That was a quick three days," Agnes said. She checked for loose tent stakes and tack that might have been overlooked. "Have fun?"

Rion nodded, but she didn't flash her usual cheerful smile. She poured herself a cup of coffee and sat on the log next to Agnes, keeping her eyes on what remained of the fire as it burned out. Hunter and Clayt were filling panniers, weighing them, redistributing gear, and weighing them again. Agnes knew that Clayt expected a perfectly balanced load before he would let Socks take a step onto the homeward trail, and therefore she knew they had at least a half hour to wait.

"I didn't get it that Hunter was actually your boyfriend," Rion said.

"Oh, Christ. Not you too."

"Couldn't help seeing the sparks flying."

"Don't be ridiculous," Agnes said.

Rion studied her uncertainly. "You're a sweet, guileless creature," she said. "You're probably telling the truth."

Agnes felt her anger coming on.

"See, now you're blushing."

"I turn red when I'm pissed off, just like the old man. My heart has not been going pitter-patter over a hairy, overweight man who smells like bear bait." It dawned on Agnes that Rion's heart might have been. "You don't have your eye on—"

"Not Hunter."

"I was kind of hoping you and Clayt—"

"Shall we change the subject, please?"

"I can tell something's bothering you, Ri—what?"

"Don't make me spell it out in bold block letters," Rion said.

At last Agnes comprehended. She pressed her fingers into her temples the way Rion did when she was most perplexed. "I had no idea," she said at last.

Silence settled between them as Agnes absorbed the information.

"I feel like an idiot," Rion said.

"If you think this is going to mess up our friendship, you don't have to worry about that."

Rion took a minute to respond. "It doesn't bother you."

"I couldn't care less. But I'm sorry I hurt you by being such a dunce."

"Enough said, then."

"One of my brothers is gay," Agnes said. "He's the one I get along with best."

Rion nodded as she continued staring into the fire ashes. "It isn't easy sometimes. But if that's who you are…"

"Let's walk over to the creek," Agnes said. "Clayt's going to be fussing with gear for a while longer."

Rion slipped into her vest and looped a pair of binoculars around her neck. Her stride was long and vigorous, as if a burden had been lifted from her. She opened her arms wide and lifted her chin to the warming mountain air.

"I am the luckiest woman on the planet," she said.

Agnes shared the expansive feeling that came from being in the mountains—but it was hard to imagine herself there for the first time as Rion was. The country was as familiar as her old bedroom at War Creek Station. The last bit of tension between the women dissipated like a bright mist retreating into the heights as Rion asked the names of plants and Agnes stopped to show her their details. The high country filled them both with a mordant mix of joy and melancholy, longing and inspiration. It was a feeling as close to magical as any Agnes had ever known, walking a well-packed trail that promised ever-higher terrain, alpine lakes, cols and passes and windy peaks. There was something about the light at that elevation, the way it shone on the dark metamorphic core of the range and the pale, honey-colored sand of peaks in the Golden Horn Batholith. Distinct in every way from the Montana Rockies that Agnes had come to know, where the forest was a narrow band of stunted pines between the plains and timberline, where glaciers were few and rivers the size of creeks, where the sky remained a pale and dusty blue from the top of a high mountain.

A shout brought her around. She turned to see Rion with her binoculars raised, waving her over.

"Hurry," Rion yelled.

Agnes ran back and Rion passed her the binoculars, pointing toward a jumble of talus. She scanned the north face of Oval Peak, looking for the dark object Rion described, moving across a snowy, timbered slope.

"It's her, it has to be," Rion said. "I can see her without the binocs." Rion stood behind Agnes and held her shoulders. "Straight ahead, hurry now, she's about to disappear into the woods."

Agnes alternated between scanning with the binoculars and squinting without them. Oval Peak, two miles away, was too distant for her to pick out an animal walking through the timber. Rion dropped her hands and softly cursed. The bear had disappeared.

CHAPTER SEVEN

Even before Clayt and Agnes reached the compound at War Creek, Agnes had a feeling that someone had been there. Tuck leapt out of the truck when she opened the door and began investigating unfamiliar scents along the pathway. While Clayt saw to the stock Agnes stood regarding the new metal sign screwed to the front door: GOVERNMENT PROPERTY NO UNAUTHORIZED ENTRY. An envelope was stuffed into the doorjamb. The lock had been replaced. Agnes took the envelope and read the notice within.

Mr. Bradford Clayton:
Reference is made to the four certified letters delivered to you since June 1988. As you are aware, the due date for your departure from these premises was March 31, 1989. This notice serves to convey the need for removal of any belongings that you wish to keep within one week. You may contact the Twisp Ranger District for entry and assistance. The demolition contract has been let and the contractor wishes to mobilize…

Hands shaking, she let the notice fall to the porch.

Clayt was heading her way. "I'm gonna need a hand wi'them saddles…whassa matter? He stopped short, his eyes moving from the sign to the newly installed lock to the notice lying at Agnes's feet.

"The sons a bitches," he said quietly. A deep breath later, he yelled, "The miserable sons a bitches!"

He kicked the notice away and went for the door as if to pull it from its frame. Agnes stood back and Tuck headed for the barn.

"Bugger-fuck all th' Goddamned shits," he shouted, and rammed his fist through the glass.

"Clayt!"

His hand turned slick and scarlet and Agnes yanked off her bandana. "Wrap it," she ordered. "And for God's sake, sit down."

She raced to the back of the house where she had left her bedroom window cracked, slid the frame open, and climbed in. She barreled through the house and flung open the front door, grabbed his shoulder, and pulled him inside.

"First-aid kit's hanging on the wall," he said from his prone position on the floor. Anger spent, his voice defeated.

"You're going to need stitches," she said as she cleaned his wounds.

He did not respond and she knew that meant she could forget getting him into the clinic before morning. She poured whiskey over the deepest gash and closed it with a row of butterfly bandages before wrapping his hand in layers of gauze.

"That'll do," he said, holding up his bandaged paw.

"You get on the sofa and keep that elevated," she said.

"I'm fine. Don't need t' run around actin' like Florence Nightingale."

"Go lie down, Clayt."

"Since you got that bottle out," he said. "It might help take the edge off."

Propped on pillows, arm raised, he swore himself into silence. Agnes made an ice pack from the few cubes left in the freezer and heated some canned stew. She could not make him eat, though he was glad to have more whiskey. By evening he had had enough to start getting mean. His hand was swelling and the pain of it made him angrier and all Agnes could do was sit and listen as he raved about the dirty sons a bitches.

"Get that bastard Flintstone on the phone," he ordered.

"You ought to wait until morning on that."

He lurched to the telephone and punched keys.

"Who in hell's hell do you think it is, you miserable…I'll have your sorry ass." He slammed down the receiver.

"That's not going to do you any good," Agnes said.

He swung around and faced her with a fierce look, the kind that had once made her shrink. *Let him take a swipe at me*, she thought. *I'll deck him.*

"I'll talk to Flintstone tomorrow," she said. "After we're done at the clinic."

"Ain't goin' to no bugger-fuckin' clinic."

"My dear father," she said. "You need to calm down."

He slumped on the sofa and looked at her with misted eyes. "Since when was I your dear father, now?"

She straightened. "For at least as long as I have been your darling daughter."

Overnight Clayt's hand had doubled in size and turned lurid and frightening colors. He wouldn't let her touch it for the pain. Agnes barely slowed at the four-way as she hurried Clayt to the clinic.

"Nice stop, missy," he said.

"This is an emergency vehicle." To distract him, she broached the question she had been wanting to ask since they broke camp in the mountains. "You never told me whether you got a look at the War Creek sow."

"He's got ya callin' it that now, then."

"Her. And it's better than 'number fifteen' or something—as if she were a rock."

"All I saw a that bear was a pile a shit, before Swann scooped it into a bag."

He groaned and rested his elbow against the window to elevate his throbbing hand.

Agnes wondered what it was about the basic functions of biology that disgusted him so. He could field dress a deer carcass in half an hour, but whenever one of the kids got sick before reaching the bathroom he would blanch and leave the house until Mary cleaned it up.

"Your Rion was the only one saw it, then. Less she was jes' dreamin' it up."

Agnes felt this wasn't fair, somehow—the one who was afraid of bears, the one who wanted least to see one. She was certain Rion had seen something, though it might well have been a marmot.

Clayt shuddered, not from the pain in his hand.

"Are you doing all right? It looks like you're short of breath."

"I'm an old man. You'll find out what it's like someday."

"Got a regular doctor?"

He nodded to the clinic just ahead. "You're hauling me to one right now."

"I assume, given a choice, you would prefer to keep that hand."

He closed his eyes to shut out the world.

"Take a deep breath for me."

"What for?"

"I want to see you do it."

He responded with a brief, audible huff.

"Please."

"For Christ' sake."

"In spite of what you might believe," she said as she swung into the clinic lot, "your children wouldn't mind having you around a while longer."

He opened one eye and pinned her with his icepick gaze. "If that ain't th' biggest line a horse manure I ever heard."

Agnes felt her color rising to match his, but she held her tongue. The way her brothers had responded to their father's need for help thus far, he might be right. She held the door for him and filled out papers. He couldn't sign his name so he took the pen in his left hand and scrawled an approximation of his initials. A nurse swept into the reception area, took one look at his bandaged hand, and hurried him to the back.

"Listen to his heart while you have him," Agnes called.

"Mind your own business, missy."

When the nurse appeared again it was to tell Agnes it might be a while.

"I have plenty of errands," Agnes said.

First on her list was to buy a piece of glass at the hardware store so she could replace the broken window before the Forest Service got wind of Clayt's misadventure and fined him for vandalism. Then to the local ranger district to intercede on his behalf. Perhaps if she explained her mission to get her father settled elsewhere, he would be granted another week or two of reprieve.

At the ranger district office she was greeted by a prim and businesslike woman dressed in a Forest Service skirt and blazer. A pickle-green version of Agnes's schoolmarm outfit, she thought with some chagrin.

"He's out," the woman said, in a voice that made Agnes want to sneak into his office to make sure.

"I'll leave a note for him, then."

The woman passed her a ballpoint pen and a tablet with a slogan printed across the top of each sheet: *Have you been a good host today?*

"What is this supposed to mean?" Agnes asked, jabbing at the slogan with the pen.

The woman shrugged. "The SO sends us boxes of them." She passed a fresh tablet across the counter to Agnes. "Keep it," she said.

"What happened to Smokey the Bear?"

The woman bent to rummage through a cabinet, came up with a cardboard coaster and a plastic ruler. Both bore Smokey's flat-hatted visage.

"This is more like it, thanks," said Agnes, and dropped the gifts into her grocery tote.

The pen skipped and left blobs of sticky ink, so she gave up with the message and asked for an appointment to see the ranger. Tuesday morning he could give her thirty minutes.

"That's almost a week away," Agnes said. "But fine, I can make it."

"May I tell him the topic?"

"Clayt's daughter needs to have a little chat."

The woman studied her with a puzzled look before asking Agnes for her phone number. "I'll call you back to confirm."

"Thank you very much," Agnes said, scolding herself for being so polite. *Well*, she told herself, *a bit of courtesy wouldn't hurt at this point.*

"You're not going to want to hear this," Rion said as Agnes walked into the Raven's Roost. She brought coffee for them both and sat down. "Hunter was in here first thing this morning. Somebody's gone and blabbed about that hiker being eaten."

Agnes frowned. "I'll bet he was pissed."

"Got a lot of damage control in front of him. I hope Clayt didn't—"

Agnes cut her off. "He's in no shape to cause trouble. Rammed his fist through a window last night. He's being sewn up at the clinic as we speak."

Rion listed with concern as Agnes described what had happened. "I wish there was somewhere you could take him," she said. "Get this whole thing over with, and he might settle down."

Agnes knew Collins would probably take him in. One old man in a large ranch house, the children grown up and gone, his wife in a home for the demented. No wonder she had lost her mind, living with him. Agnes would take Clayt back to Helena with her before turning him over to Collins.

"I've got to run," she said. "Did Hunter say where he was headed when he left here?"

"I'm not his mother."

Agnes stood before finishing her coffee. "Later," she said. "I'm going to find him."

She buckled herself in, started the car, and realized she had no idea where to look for Hunter. She drove around town hoping to spot his pickup or a likely looking office, a blandly painted single-wide with a temporary Fish and Wildlife Service sign tacked onto the door, but she saw nothing of the sort before it was time to return to the clinic and collect her father.

She helped him into the car and went back to settle the bill. The nurse gave her bottles of pain pills and bullet-sized antibiotics for Clayt to take three times a day for as long as they lasted.

"He needs to see a specialist." She pressed her hand against her chest to indicate she did not mean the cut hand.

"I was afraid of that. It was hell enough to get him here."

"He could be in grave danger, as I tried to make him understand."

"Any recommendations?"

"If he were my father, I'd make an appointment with the cardiac unit at the Mason Clinic."

"Thank you," Agnes said, and turned away. A trip to Seattle to see a heart specialist—she could imagine the reception that idea would meet.

Clayt slept for two days, waking only to fight her when she tried to give him his medications. He chewed the antibiotics as if they were children's vitamins and washed them down with coffee. He would not touch the pain pills. The third morning he finally wanted solid food. She waited until he finished his eggs, then sat across the kitchen table from him.

"Why didn't you tell me you were supposed to be out of here by April?"

"You didn't ask."

"You know what, Clayt? It's impossible to help you. Why do you insist on keeping secrets from your allies?"

"Allies. Where on God's green earth do I have allies?" His eyes softened as Agnes stirred cream into his coffee and sat down across from him again. "I know you mean well."

"Glad you noticed," she said. "I'm not going to stand by and watch you get tossed out on your ear."

"Fuckers'll have to burn the place down around my Goddamned ears."

Agnes marveled at the way he tossed around profanity, using words she had overheard while growing up only when he thought he was alone with Roger. Now they sprang from his tongue as naturally as if he was an aging bachelor. Which, she supposed, he was. Too many years of bitterness, children grown and tossed to the winds and living their lives far away while he stayed on at War Creek, alone except for Tuck, the aging stock, and a barn full of six-toed cats. It was good for him to allow himself the small luxury of no longer giving a damn what he said.

"For now, let's take care of that hand," she said. "And we need to talk about your heart condition—"

"What heart condition."

"You can sure play dumb as hell when you want to."

He gave her a sharp look that quickly softened into resignation.

"Don't tell me you were about to give me shit for saying hell."

"Not as if I haven't been swearin' like a sailor."

"Spouting off a bit when you have to is good medicine."

"Always tried t' set an example." He closed his eyes.

"You did fine. I know—and so do you—who to be civilized with. I hope we can be ourselves around family."

"Guess family's what we are, like it or not."

Agnes sucked in a breath and held it. The minute her heart softened toward Clayt he was sure to show it the back of his hand.

"I hope you get around to liking it, Clayt," she said. "Because for the moment, you're stuck with me."

"You can help me to the sofa and bring me a wee dram," he said. "I'll read for a bit while I digest my breakfast."

Agnes tucked him under a wool throw but neglected the wee dram. Nine in the morning, after all. Soon he was asleep with a magazine open on his chest, one arm hanging off the sofa, his good hand curled on the floor. Agnes cleaned up and went outside to grab the paper.

The ranger in Twisp had not confirmed her appointment. She hated to call the Good Host woman and inquire, as if she were a supplicant seeking an audience with His Excellence. She tossed the rolled newspaper against the front door and it rolled across the porch back to her.

Clayt stirred at the noise made by the flung newspaper. "Bugger off," he snarled.

She unrolled the newspaper and the *Weekly Nickel* on the table, where she saw the same advertisements for high-priced rentals she had circled and then crossed out the week before. She wasn't in the mood for a walk or another drive to town. The lettuce starts and flowers had stayed tucked in the shade for the few days she was in the mountains. It was time to plant.

She fetched a sharp-nosed fire shovel from the toolshed and stopped to exchange soft breaths with Agate and Socks and Jasper while slipping them each a piece of horse candy. Breathing the wheaty exhalation of horses as the soft hairs along her jawline brushed against their velvet muzzles—what could be more comforting? Since childhood she had shared breath with horses as her own form of Holy Communion. *Take this air, for it is my life. Take this thin, bright mountain air, for it is my joy.* When she was with the stock, their native sweetness could overcome her darkest mood.

She took the shovel to the site of her mother's garden, still discernible under crabgrass and dandelions, a faint rectangle of darker soil between bent fence posts and buried concrete blocks. She tried the shovel but the ground was hard after weeks without rain. She stood with the hose nozzle leaking down her arm and sprayed the imagined rows of lettuce, flax, and Johnny-jump-ups.

She clipped spent flower stalks from the decades-old clump of rhubarb and found beside it some dark, straight leaves, erect as a mule's ears. Horseradish. She could taste her mother's cabbage rolls, filled with leftover corned beef and barley and cooked until they yielded at the touch of a fork. Clayt used to pile her homemade horseradish sauce on his cabbage rolls while the boys turned up their noses. Agnes had always spooned a dab of horseradish onto hers, out of consideration for her mother's efforts in shredding, boiling, and puréeing the tough root to make it edible. She decided to harvest the thick old horseradish plant and make a fine sauce for Clayt to slather on a piece of corned beef. Minced horseradish, ground mustard seeds, a dash of salt and a cup of cider vinegar—the concoction would keep in the refrigerator for months. Each time Clayt tasted it he would be eating from the sacred soil of War Creek.

CHAPTER EIGHT

Agnes worked her jaw, suddenly aware of having driven with it clenched tighter than her fingers on the steering wheel. She saw her speed and eased off the accelerator. Outside the ranger district office, she had left a spray of gravel as she jerked the car into gear to get away. Maybe she would drive to Okanogan and barge in on the forest supervisor, since there seemed to be no advantage to making an appointment with the ranger. Maybe she would keep going and drive into British Columbia, drive until she ran out of gas and then leave her car by the side of the road and hitch a ride back to Helena. To hell with this entire enterprise—how could she do anything about the mess her father had gotten himself into? She banged the steering wheel with her fist and bruised her hand.

The ranger had never intended to give her an audience, hadn't even been thoughtful enough to tell the receptionist to call her and cancel. It had come like a blow to the stomach when the Good Host woman greeted her that morning with a perfunctory smile. "He's not in."

"He better be. I have an appointment in five minutes."

The woman's eyebrows knitted as she flipped through an engagement calendar. "My goodness, he does have an eight fifteen." By way of apology she added, "He left early, before I came in."

The Good Host woman eyed the white board mounted on one wall and Agnes followed her gaze. The ranger was signed out for a fun-sounding place called Hornet Draw, back at five o'clock. The woman turned to Agnes with a practiced vacant smile.

It wasn't her fault, stuck in the office on a beautiful July morning. All the men at the district were signed out and the only employees who remained were the receptionist and a young girl sorting papers in the back.

"I can put you down for next week," the woman offered.

"No thanks."

After driving for a few miles north of town, Agnes had calmed down enough to consider what to do next. Abandoning her car in Canada no longer topped her list. She turned at a junction with a gravel road that felt familiar and her face relaxed as she remembered why—a secret place where she and her brothers used to look for fist-sized nodules weathering out of a volcanic outcrop. Sometimes she would break one open with a rock hammer to find rainbows of banded agate, clouds of smoky quartz. Thunder eggs, they called them. She had been going somewhere after all when she took off in a blind rage.

She left the car beside the logging road where a gate had been placed, barring vehicle access to the thunder eggs. Her long legs took her the remaining quartermile in a few minutes, and she scrambled up a rough trail at the edge of an open slope where blocks of lichen-blotched basalt unraveled into rubble. Among the dull, lumpy rocks lay petrified gas bubbles that had become suspended in the lava as it cooled. Over the millennia, dissolved minerals filled the bubbles and gave them solid skins, like eggshells made of stone. Gradually they weathered out of the crumbling volcanic rock around them. Her eye knew the size and shape to look for and her hand knew the heft. She found a likely candidate, laid it on a slab of basalt, and dropped a boulder onto it. Heard the grainy crush of it breaking into pieces.

The thunder egg was mostly empty, but one corner held a cluster of dwarf quartz crystals, fine and pointed as sewing needles. Beside them, laminae of agate had formed a smooth, globular mass. It looked like a naked child curled in sleep with a tiara on her head. Agnes saw it all at once—a child indeed, an infant, crowned by the rarest of jewels, protected from the world's unforgiving stare by the dark encasement of basalt. Until she came along and broke it open.

In an instant she was seventeen again, her body tented under sheets, frightened into a rigidity that resembled that of the stone that now lay in her hand. She had cried out once in her labor and was brought around by a sharp slap and someone hissing *Stop that!* into her face. How she had longed to die, to escape that place of misery and astringent odors where her body had been commandeered by people who condemned her for her sins.

Deliverance had come in the form of a bear.

She had evacuated her pain-racked body and backed away from the delivery room until all that remained was a distant pinpoint of light. The light began to waver and grow, as if someone with a flashlight moved toward her through the deepest forest. The beam strengthened and diffused into sunlight slanting through the trees. It penetrated to the forest floor, where a bulky mammalian form floated along the ground. Its silver guard hairs formed a halo, glowing as if the bear itself were the source of light. Slowly it approached, its luminosity increasing.

Agnes was not afraid. She reached out toward the bear but it melted into the forest. In the lingering radiance Agnes fell into a scoured, depthless sleep and woke the next day, childless.

"Just missed th' boyfriend," Clayt said as she walked in. "Where th' hell you been?"

Agnes made a noncommittal sound, surprised at her disappointment over not seeing Hunter.

"So how'd it go at th' district."

"The ranger stood me up."

Clayt chuckled. "Why'm I not surprised, now. You didn't give that gal your real name."

"Why shouldn't I?"

"I guess I didn't mention who th' hell the ranger is down there. Remember Fred Flintstone?"

The range tech who used to work for Clayt, who had reminded Agnes of the missing link, with his hairy forearms and deer-in-the-headlights expression. "You're not serious. Ranger?"

"Like I said, they don't make 'em like they used to. Couldn't teach that kid a damned thing an' now..." His voice broke.

Agnes knew what came next, the thing that Clayt could not say because it galled him into silence. War Creek was now under the supervision of Flintstone.

"What did Hunter want?"

"Heard about my hand an' stopped to check in."

"Nice of him."

"I 'spect he came to see you."

"Did he have any news?"

"Some boys're takin' a pack trip over the weekend," Clayt said. "Maybe do a little early summer bear hunting."

"Collins. You can't let him."

"I'd go along if it weren't for this damned hand."

Baiting her now, but she wouldn't take it. "I've decided to pay the forest supervisor a visit," she said. "What's her name again?"

"It won't do you any good."

"It'll do me a world of good to give her a piece of my mind regarding Flintstone. I'm the public, damn it. I'm going to give her this..." She flapped the *have you been a good host* notepad at Clayt. "And tell her where to shove it."

Clayt laughed with genuine cheer. "That's the girl," he said.

Agnes arrived at the Raven's Roost as Rion was reversing the sign in the window and locking up. She waved at Agnes and twirled in the parking lot, showing off her brimmed felt hat, a broad-shouldered tweed jacket and matching vest. Pressed jeans, polished boots. At the collar of her crisp white shirt hung a braided leather bolo tie.

"Do I look like a country lawyer or what?" she asked.

Agnes laughed. "You look fabulous. And intimidating."

"Good."

Hunter's pickup turned into the lot and he eyed the closed sign in the door.

"Looks like double trouble here," he said. "Out of coffee?"

"There's plenty for you," Rion said, and lifted a Thermos out of her bulging satchel. She filled his travel mug and jiggled her keys. "Best be off," she said.

"We're on our way to Okanogan," Agnes said. "To meet the supervisor."

"Make it a threesome? I'll bet my appointment is right after yours."

He offered to take them in his pickup. Agnes slid into the seat first, rearranging clipboards, notebooks, and Styrofoam cups while Hunter tossed bundles of field clothing into the back.

"Sorry about the mess," he said. "This is my office."

"Been busy lately, I imagine." Agnes leaned toward him so Rion could fasten her seatbelt.

Hunter whistled. "Shit's hitting the fan. A vigilante posse is promising to take care of the War Creek sow themselves."

"Collins is in the middle of that one," Agnes said. "Clayt as much as said so."

"The headlines haven't helped," Rion said, picking up the newspaper. "'Hiker Killed, Eaten by Bear.'"

"I'd like to know who started that one," Hunter said.

"Why don't these newspapers talk to people like you?" Agnes asked.

"I wouldn't be allowed to say anything; it all goes through public affairs. It does piss me off, though—I know that guy was dead before the coyotes got to him. The state guys agree with me, but won't say so in public."

Agnes remembered Hunter's story of the black bear, how everyone above him knew the bear was innocent of mischief but they were willing to sacrifice him anyway. Hunter read her silence.

"They put down that bear because the cabin belonged to a state senator—only reason. He promised to dispatch every furry beast he could find until the Wildlife Department caught the culprit."

Agnes mulled that for a while. "The break-ins must have continued if they killed the wrong bear."

"I suspect the good senator did what he promised."

"So now the state's afraid of Collins and the boys," Rion said.

"The last thing Collins said to me was that he'd carry that bear's hide down Main Street on the hood of his pickup." Hunter pressed his foot to the accelerator.

He turned onto Highway 20 and drove in silence for a while, past drying alfalfa fields and bunchgrass hills. The road passed a national forest sign and patches of scrubby pines and junipers began to dot the hillsides, the trees gathering into an open forest with the approach of the small resort where Agnes had learned to ski. In July, it looked like a cut lawn, and about as steep. Beyond the summit, the road left the national forest for state land, where tall ponderosa and lodgepole pines grew in narrow between clear-cuts. Gravel roads snaked through the hills, aprons of castoff dirt spilling from their fill slopes. As the highway lost elevation, the trees became sparse again, and farms appeared along the roadside, some green from irrigation, some pale with the stubble of harvested hayfields. The Okanogan River Valley opened in both directions and the road left the mountains behind.

Except for the band of willow and cottonwood along the river, the valley was golden-bronze with cured grass. Lawns were going brown, a sure sign of watering restrictions. Down-valley, the view was obscured by dust and the smoke of range fires burning in many places across the Columbia River Plateau.

"Would it be nosy to ask what your business is with the supervisor today?" Rion asked Hunter.

"I need a place to relocate the bear before she gets shot. If they take her into the park she'll be back before sunset, so I'm looking at the Pasayten Wilderness."

"Good luck," Rion said.

"Appreciate it. Dry years are hard on bears. If the berries don't come on, she might wander into the valley."

"Oh, great," Rion said. "Just what we need: a shot-up, pissed-off bear."

Hunter dropped his passengers off in front of the supervisor's office and made plans to meet them for lunch. Agnes hesitated before sliding out of the bench seat, wishing she could think of something encouraging to say.

"I should wish the two of you luck as well," he said. He squeezed her hand.

"We'll compare notes," Agnes said. "I hope we all have something to celebrate."

Old man Collins was getting into his truck when Agnes returned from Okanogan.

"That you at the bear meeting last month?" he asked.

"I wanted to say hello but no one seemed in the mood."

"Now look at the mess we're in. That feller running the meeting about had me convinced after drinking half his whiskey, but not now, by God—not after what happened up on that mountain. No goddamned grizzly bears for me."

Agnes didn't answer right away and Clayt prodded her. "Tell him about your friend Hunter. She thinks the sun rises on his behind."

Collins laughed and lit a cigarette.

"I think you ought to investigate the facts before you make up your mind," she said, addressing them both.

"I saw the pictures of that poor son of a bitch," said Collins. "Nothing besides a bear leaves such a mess of a man."

"Hunter said it looked like he had broken a leg and died first."

Collins shook his head, piled into his truck, and smiled.

Hung his arm out the open window and said to Clayt, "Got your hands full with her again, I see," and started to drive away.

Agnes felt like a child, raging and helpless, wanting to shout at Collins: *You and that dickhead son of yours.* Instead she looked him in the eye and approached the cab.

"I know what you're referring to. It never would have happened if not for your angelic little boy."

Collins looked as if he might fling the truck door open and throttle her, but she stood her ground.

"You lying bitch."

"Ask him sometime."

He stepped on the accelerator and Agnes stepped aside. She turned to her father.

"Do you want to hear how it went with Sara Lee? Her name is Mary Lynn, by the way."

"If y' want to tell me, I'll listen. What'd you say to Collins?"

"Don't worry about it."

Clayt sat on the bottom step with his bad hand elevated. Agnes noticed a tremor in his arm.

"How long's your hand been doing that?"

"Doin' what?"He put it down and clasped it with his other hand. "Whaddya want to tell me?"

"I want to look at your hand."

"Y'had something to say—spit it out, damn it."

Words poured out of her like water behind a breached dam, but not the ones he waited for.

"Why do you hate me so much? I've been here for longer than I planned, cooking, cleaning, running your errands, taking you to the clinic and out for a bit of fishing…"

"Settle down, missy. Y' get yourself too wound up tellin' yourself all this malarkey. I ain't saying I don't appreciate what you're doin' here."

"I can't talk to you for five minutes without being yelled at."

"Who's yellin' at who, now?"

They fell quiet for a moment, neither of them sure where

this conversation was headed. Then Clayt took it somewhere unexpected.

"When's th' last time you went to Mass?"

"Mass—you can't be serious."

"I raised you kids to be reverent and observant. But you've lapsed beyond redemption."

"I thought redemption was God's line of work. When did he delegate that duty to you?"

"Don't get smart with me, missy."

"I'm not getting smart. But I've had about enough of this self-righteous Christian crap from people who don't know how to forgive. I thought you might be mellowing out as far as your religious high horse goes, but I can see I'm wrong."

"That's about enough a that talk, missy. 'Thou shalt keep holy the Sabbath.' I didn't make that up—read it someplace, can' remember quite where…"

"Now who's being the smartass. I try to keep holy every day. To act right, be kind. Isn't that what Christians are supposed to do? Charitable deeds?"

He raised his good hand to swat at a horsefly and she saw the tremor again. She realized it wasn't caused by his wounded hand or his balky heart. He and Collins had been sharing a wee dram.

"Faith's what matters, givin' your soul to the care of th'Redeemer. Faith. An' you ain't got none."

"You know nothing about me and my faith. How dare you judge me."

"All the dark ones," he continued. "Bad omens, bad news. I could see you weren't mine th' minute I laid eyes on you."

"I sure as hell inherited your temper."

Clayt went on as if he hadn't heard. "I saw it in the distance in her eyes, th' way she busied herself with music an' gardening. Should of seen it coming—did see it coming but couldn't stop it."

His anger spent, he fought the tears of a drunk that had turned to feeling sorry for himself. "I was away too much back then, three weeks at a time on fires then turn around and go on another one. Livin' in tents and bunkhouses, no place for a family. My boys grew up without me, then you came along—years after Mary would lie with me."

He raised his head and grazed her with red eyes.

"Do me a favor now," he said. His anger had dissipated into melancholy.

"And the favor is…"

"Get out of my sight for a while."

"The pleasure would be all mine." She got up and went inside.

She pulled on a pair of riding boots and tried to absorb what he had said. Those old half-joking comments about her looking different from the rest of them. The family resemblance she saw with her father could have been her imagination, or the result of long association, the way dogs and their owners resembled one another. What if he was right about her not being his flesh and blood? At the moment, she might have considered it a blessing.

She passed Clayt without a word and strode to the barn with Tuck at her heels. He had been pleased that the dog didn't warm to her right away, but now Tuck seemed to prefer her company. Clayt went into the house and let the screen door slap behind him.

Agnes saddled Jasper and rode blind up the War Creek trail until she reached a sunlit meadow surrounded by ponderosa pines. She slid from the saddle and withdrew the bridle from Jasper's mouth so he could graze more freely on the tall summer grass and wildflowers. He chomped at the meadow and chewed with his eyes halfclosed, his rhythmic grinding the sound of pure contentment. How little he needed to find joy, and how difficult it was for her to do the same. She sat cross-legged in the grass, her mind aflame.

If Clayt couldn't find anything else to criticize, he would be sure to dust off religion. His hackles had been raised on that subject since her rebellion against the Church began as an adolescent. After her treatment at the hands of the Sisters of Charity, her doubts would no longer allow her to pretend in a belief she did not have. He lambasted her for refusing to go to

Mass. She countered by asking him what loving deity would let a mother leave her youngest child, never to return? Clayt didn't have an answer for that, other than to mutter that she was risking the salvation of her immortal soul if she heard Christ's good news and chose to ignore it.

It had never been church, but the tantalizing mystery of creation that stirred Agnes, manifest in lunar eclipses, starlit skies, blood-red sunsets, and the green iridescent beetle now crawling over her knee. Such wonders, such beauty—at her feet and everywhere for all to see, if they would only take the time to notice. She had found refuge beside the river during her darkest hours, and beauty in the wild since leaving War Creek twenty years before.

She watched the beetle ascend to the summit of her kneecap and perch for a moment, as if taking in the view. She touched it with her fingertip and the beetle climbed aboard, the tiny hooks in its legs clinging to her skin. A warm breeze slid along the back of her neck and the beetle opened its elytra, shell-like forewings protecting the delicate flight wings. From under the metallic car-hood elytra the flight wings unfolded and the beetle sailed into the air with a barely audible whir. Agnes watched until it disappeared beyond the meadow. Her finger held the memory of the touch of the beetle's feet, as if the creature had been sent by the divine to remind her that her beliefs were as legitimate as those of her father. She believed in the beauty and power of the earth, and she knew that Clayt believed as well, or else he would not have become a forest ranger.

One fundamental trait she had in common with her father was their shared affection for wild places, for the earth that nurtured their souls, for places they held dear. How could they be at such odds with each other when they both loved the same things? She didn't care if Clayt was her biological father or not— he had raised her and imbued in her a deep regard for the same things that mattered most to him. They were related in a way far deeper than genetics, yet they could not be in each other's presence for an hour without starting to spar and bicker. Every time she told herself to let it go when he baited her, and every time she found it impossible to do so.

Honor thy father and mother—that impossible commandment. She wanted to, tried to, yearned for another chance to do so. She wept with frustration. Did she not also deserve some measure of honor from them?

She rolled over onto her belly and spread her arms out to hug the ground. The flattened grass beneath her was warm and moist, the sun on her back hot and dry. She felt grass blades and flower stems pressing their impressions into her face. Soon her mind stilled and contentment seeped from the damp earth into her thighs and chest and outstretched arms. She must have fallen asleep for a minute, for suddenly she noticed Jasper's gentle cropping of the grass, his sweet, horsey scent inches away. She sat up and hugged Tuck. The companionship of animals and the wild beauty of the world brought her the good news she needed. Hot sun, thunderheads beginning to raise a stronger breeze, the incense of pines, the brittle, dry grass and solid earth beneath her.

She lay back on the meadow and watched the clouds forming and unraveling overhead. Tuck watched her with curiosity and she laughed.

"I think I'm going to survive," she told him.

He stood and stretched, the tip of his tail wagging.

"Ready to go," she said. "I guess I am too."

She gave Jasper his head as they returned. The day had grown uncomfortably hot in the time she had been sitting in the meadow. Fields of heartleaf arnica wilted under the sun, leaves folded together like the wings of butterflies. The trail was dusty enough that Jasper raised a dense cloud. Tuck stayed ahead, small puffs of dust following each step as his brisk trot urged them all home.

When Agnes returned she rubbed down Jasper, watered Tuck, and went to work on the garden. She saw her mother working the same little plot, wearing a broad sunbonnet and an apron with pockets full of trowels and snips and paper bags to hold the produce. Mary sang out loud when alone, in a strong, clear voice, but she hummed under her breath when anyone else was around. Sometimes when Agnes arrived home from school, the afternoons belonged to her and her mother. Other times Agnes would hear Mary lost in music, the notes from her piano drifting through the open windows. She would wait outside, petting the horses, throwing a stick for Brownie until she heard the quiet that meant her mother was ready for the first of her evening's interruptions.

Mary played on winter afternoons, usually on a Sunday, the one day of the week that could be counted on for weather fierce enough to keep the family indoors. Agnes always wondered why they didn't call it *No-sun-day*. Mass and early dinner dispensed with, only Mary remained in her church clothes. The boys glanced with longing out the windows as they tried to read. Clayt dozed on the sofa. Agnes remembered herself tucked into a knitted afghan as she listened. Her mother sat upright on the piano bench and played tentatively at first, as if made timid by the unaccustomed audience. But soon she gave herself to the music, and her perfect posture softened as she leaned into the keys. She always kept a foot on the mute pedal, damping it down so as not to interrupt the reading she hoped her sons would learn to love, and she chose sweet and unobtrusive melodies among the familiar hymns. Agnes smiled at the memory, knowing that Mary's favorite was an Anglican hymn one never heard at Mass. She usually sang along when she played it, but only when was alone in the house.

Once on a Sunday, she built up her courage for the twenty-third psalm. If anyone wondered what it was, they didn't ask, but Agnes knew, for it was her favorite as well. *The Lord is my shepherd, I shall not want; He maketh me to lie down in green pastures: he leadeth me beside the still waters.* Mary would close her eyes and rock gently with the cadence, laboring at the piece though she had it memorized, caressing her beloved piano with its quarter-sawn walnut panels, painstakingly trying to coax magic from the keys.

"You play that so beautifully," Agnes told her, but Mary shook her head.

"I can play the notes," she answered, "but I don't know how to make them sing."

Mary had taught her scales and basic chords. When Agnes was six she received a child's keyboard for Christmas, a toy organ she would sit on the floor to play. On warm spring evenings she would take her instrument out to the porch while her mother played the piano inside, leading her through the scales and simple songs that Agnes knew. Their duet took them into the dusk when Clayt was late coming in from the forest and the boys were all off somewhere.

The boys were always off somewhere—in town, at the rodeo grounds. However reckless with their trucks and rank horses, they could not get into the same kind of trouble that Agnes could. Named for the Gospels, the ones who followed Will: Matthew, Mark, Luke, and John, twin to feckless Patrick. She followed the twins eight years later.

She had been a better shot than John and a better rider than Patrick, but they pretended otherwise. *Just luck*, John said when she knocked a coffee can off a fencepost at fifty yards. She did it again to prove him wrong. He winked at her, knowing she wouldn't brag about it later or protest when he said in front of others that girls couldn't shoot, for if Clayt knew about him letting her try, they both would have been in Dutch.

She wondered what had become of that old toy organ. It must have been sold or given away after Agnes outgrew it and asked for a guitar.

She pulled her attention back to pulling the old horseradish. She replanted some of it in manure Clayt had raked into the corner of the corral. The silence within the house intruded on her pleasure. Clayt could hold a grudge, could nurture his anger like a glowing ember for days. Years.

Back when it was Agnes and her mother on those quiet afternoons, both were content with the other's company. The cloud that loomed over the family as Clayt's drinking became more frequent, his moods darker, lifted for a while. The rugged exterior of the house and compound faded into a general place called "outdoors" when Mary opened the screen door for Agnes and held it so that it would close gently behind them. Inside, the floors were polished, the walls and ceilings dark with the patina of decades. It was a cozy, comforting darkness when Clayt was not around. Bright spots stood out: the white lace tablecloth, a bouquet of lilacs, an open sheet of music on the piano. Mary and Agnes were at peace in the presence of each other, until her mother lost her peace with everyone and everything.

CHAPTER NINE

Agnes straightened at the sound of an approaching vehicle. A Forest Service green rig turned onto the bridge, a man in uniform at the wheel, alone. Tuck growled under the porch. She watched from under the shade of her broad-brimmed hat as the crew cab passed between the garden and corral. A glimpse of the driver's dark, kinky hair, receding and going gray, along with the profile of his wide face, was all Agnes needed to tell that Clayt was about to receive a visit from Flintstone.

He returned Agnes's stare with a nod of acknowledgment and parked beside Clayt's old Dodge one-ton, a surplus green fleet truck he'd bought for nothing and used for hauling firewood. Agnes turned her back on him and finished tying a long strip of woven wire fence to the stakes surrounding the garden, a necessary precaution against nightly visits from mule deer.

Clayt stepped down from the porch. No handshake, no invitation to go inside. The two men stood facing each other a few feet apart, Flintstone in his ill-fitting pickle suit—pants too short and too tight in the butt, belt buckle askew, shirt buttons straining to stay closed around his belly—while Clayt gripped his suspenders and executed his agitated pacing. They began to walk toward the barn as if to inspect it. Then out of sight and earshot on the far side.

After some time the men emerged, following the narrow path beside the corral with Socks and Agate and Jasper trailing them along the rail. Flintstone patted Socks' forehead and returned to his pickup. Clayt lumbered up the steps and closed the door behind him without a word. The mule and horses stood at the corral with disappointment in their eyes. The green rig rattled over the cattle guard, crossed the bridge, and turned onto the river road.

As she finished with the deer fence, Agnes heard no sound from within the house. Hardly a word exchanged since their row. All week Clayt had picked at the food she offered him, pushed his chair back, and gone for the whiskey and the sofa. His hand was better now, the stitches out, and he worked it with a tennis ball, squeezing, relaxing, squeezing again, to bring the muscles back. Agnes wondered if their relationship would heal as well as his hand.

They did better together when they were in the mountains, reveling in places they both loved. Perhaps their shared love of this rugged quarter of the Cascade Range would spin some threads of affection between them. They were already there, Agnes knew, but both she and Clayt had given themselves decades to coat them in layer after layer of resentment. Since reading his old work logs and paging through the photo albums, she had begun to see him as a person, with a past before she was born. A past that he considered the best part of his life.

The afternoon was over and she had little more to do in the garden, so she took her tools back to the shed—every rake and trowel in its place, the way Clayt liked them.

The phone was ringing when she returned, Clayt asleep on the sofa. "Hello," she said.

Rion's voice, wound up, stumbling over itself. "Can you meet me here tomorrow morning? Sure you can, you don't have anything else going on. I want you to meet a gal from the historical society I've been talking to. She's going to be here at 6:30."

Agnes smiled, surfing on the breaking wave of Rion's energy and enthusiasm. "If you insist," she said.

"You sound tired," Rion observed.

"I've been working in the garden."

"You're a slave to him, you know."

"See you tomorrow."

"Hey, I'm serious," Rion said. "When you first walked into my place, I thought, 'Man, who's that saucy gal?' A mite timid, but the confidence showed through with your big old smile and the way you walked. I knew I was in the presence of someone special. Then when you could name where all the pictures hanging up were taken, when you knew all the flowers we saw... hello? Are you still there?"

"I'm listening, Ri," Agnes said.

"Good. Because here's what I see now. Hunched shoulders and bowed head, someone who's been cowed into submission. You're stressed out and not sleeping and busy, busy, busy doing shit for your old man who only expects more. You need to tell him to fuck off—or I will."

Agnes felt her insides hardening, not in defense but rather with intention. Rion was telling her what she had been thinking herself, but until she heard it from someone who cared about her she had chosen to push it aside. She had convinced herself she was beyond her fear of the old man, yet she hadn't mustered the courage to confront him about family secrets. Perhaps it was her fear of the truth rather than of her father that kept her from asking.

"Message received," Agnes said. "I'm working up to it."

"I'll expect a full report."

Agnes turned from the phone, grateful for something to look forward to other than Clayt's silence. He paid no attention as she fed Tuck, rinsed some lettuce, and headed for the bathroom. *This is what it would have been like for Mary*, she thought. The silences, the expectations, the hidden traps waiting for a misstep. Interludes in the garden and at the piano interrupted by his orders, resentment building like a thunderhead.

Maybe Rion could put her up for a couple days. Agnes could not continue tiptoeing through Clayt's house, nearly choking on the tension in the air. *You're a slave to him.* No, she wasn't. She could pack her things and walk out the door and drive back to Helena that afternoon.

If she was a slave to anything, other than her own stubborn nature, it was War Creek. She had felt its pull on her when she first drove upstream along the Twisp River Road. Her love of the place had been buried by her dread of seeing Clayt and her anger at her brothers for putting her into this painful situation. What kept her here now, a month after she arrived, was that love, more evident to her each day. The pack trip into the mountains had brought back remembered moments of pure joy when she stood alone on a summit, surrounded by forests and peaks and glaciers. She needed to fill her lungs with the scent of ponderosa pines and her fingernails with the dark earth of her mother's garden. The life she had made for herself in Montana was satisfying, but it had not helped her find her true and deepest self. Only War Creek could do that.

Agnes arrived at the Raven's Roost just as another car pulled into the lot. A slight, brown-haired woman in a plain blouse and dark slacks approached her, and she immediately recognized Helen, who had run the local grocery since Agnes was a girl. Helen wrapped her bird-wing arms around Agnes's shoulders and kissed her on both cheeks. She had been all business when children were in the store, on the lookout for shoplifters of candy bars and jawbreakers. Agnes guessed that with her brothers on the loose, Helen had reason to be wary of the Claytons.

"What a fine-looking lady you've become," Helen said. "Why haven't you come to see me?"

"I go to the store at least once a week."

Helen laughed. "You won't find me there these days. Rob and Jilly run the place now."

"No point in making introductions, I see." Rion waved them inside and brought an insulated jug of coffee to the back table.

Helen did not waste time with chitchat. "Your dad has never said a thing about this business with the old ranger station," Helen said. "We could have helped him."

"Glad to know I'm not the only one he keeps in the dark. Apparently he was supposed to be out of there months ago."

Helen looked at Agnes through her reading glasses, and Agnes realized how old she must be. Her magnified eyes reddened at the margins, and a slight tremor made her look as if she were shaking her head in disagreement.

"The Forest Service came by while we were in the mountains," Agnes said. "Changed the lock and gave him one week to vacate the premises."

"It's been two weeks and he's still there," Rion pointed out.

"Flintstone's blowing smoke. But he's not the one who makes the decisions."

"Then we need to find whoever does and talk to them," Helen said.

A tap on the front window turned their heads. A man stood with a travel mug in one hand, pointing with the other at the sign hung in the door's window that still read CLOSED from the outside.

"Shit," said Rion. "I forgot I had a business to run."

"There is one thing I need from you," Helen said. "Clayt has some old photographs that I think would be essential for what I have in mind."

Agnes knew what she was talking about—a large-format portfolio Clayt used to bring out to show important visitors. The kids were not allowed to touch it, but once in a while he was willing to turn the pages for them and talk about the men whose faces looked out from the past. She hadn't seen it since returning.

"You want Clayt to give you that folio? He'll never go along with that," she said.

"I assume he cares about the ranger station," Helen said.

"I think he does. So do I. But I can't see him willing to give up something he wouldn't even let us kids touch."

Her kind brown eyes held Agnes for a moment before she glanced at the wall clock and stood. "You leave that part up to me," she said.

"Helen wants me to retrieve Clayt's history of War Creek," Agnes told Rion. "I'd prefer to eat a plate of horse manure, given the choice."

"I'll give you some cinnamon rolls to take back to him." Rion squeezed Agnes's shoulder and turned at the jingling of the door bells. "Told you the busy time was starting up."

A buzzer went off behind the serving counter and Agnes stood. "I'll get those for you," she said.

Rion greeted the man walking through the door. "Honey Badger himself."

"Hey, Roger," Agnes said. "Fresh muffins of some kind here."

"He won't eat those," Rion said. "Too healthy. " She pointed to a cinnamon roll and Roger nodded.

Roger stood with an elbow on the counter and nibbled at the cinnamon roll. His face was tanned and freckled, his eyelashes as pale as his hair. When he worked for Clayt on the trail crew he was in his twenties, and he didn't look much older than that now.

"You look like something the cat drug in," he said to Agnes. "Fighting with the old man?"

"He's mad at me—I can't even remember what for. And Helen expects me to ask him for some old photos he's guarded with his life."

Roger listened with sympathy, agreeing that Clayt would be intractable.

"You know him better than I do," Agnes said. "Any suggestions?"

Roger ran a hand through his hair and stared at the counter. "Never been much good in the idea department. 'Specially when it come to your old man."

"Well, it's not your problem. I want to hear what you're up to."

He ducked his head shyly.

"Got that tractor running," Rion said.

"When did you quit the Forest Service? I can't imagine you doing anything else."

"Who said quit?" His eyes flashed. "I got shit-canned."

"No way."

"When Clayt retired, I knew things'd change," he said. He took a long, slow sip of coffee while Agnes arranged the muffins on a plate and Rion waited on a gaggle of tourists. "When the outfit combined us with Twisp, half the folks had to go. I was safe, the only one who knew how to keep the station running." He gazed across the room with unfocused eyes. "Went all right for a while, until I got saddled with a new boss. They had to find jobs for all them extra people and gave me a washed-up timber beast. Didn't know shit from peanut butter about trails and didn't want to learn. We was oil and water from day one. He couldn't'a cared less how things run before he came—didn't matter what it was, the stock, the tack, the saws, he knew better. I had to ask his permission to take a piss in the woods and then he'd want to tell me how to do it."

"Flintstone put up with that?"

Roger shook his head. "This was way before Flintstone. Blake never saw for hisself what was going on at War Creek; he never come up to the station, let alone the woods. Didn't take long to figure out that Mitch had Blake convinced I was a bad apple."

Roger paused for an enormous bite of the cinnamon roll.

"Anyhow," he said, wiping his mouth, "the final straw come when they tried to sit me down in front of a computer."

"The Forest Service never had a more dedicated employee," Agnes said.

"Excepting your father, and look at what they done to him."

"Sad story."

"Not on my end," Roger said. "I'm my own boss now. Miss the hell out of the old days sometimes, but the old days is long gone."

Agnes stopped at Helen's grocery to scan the public notices for rentals. One looked like a possibility and she jotted down the phone number. She checked the produce section and found Rion had been correct about the local goods. One aisle had been set aside for greens and early vegetables brought in by growers in the area. Each bundle of chard, radishes, garlic scapes, and mixed greens was labeled with the name of its producer, from commercial farmers to backyard gardeners. There was a tub of Thompson seedless grapes from someone down in Entiat, and a row of Ziploc bags full of dark red cherries. She gathered more than she needed and headed for the door. By the time she returned to War Creek she had eaten two pounds of cherries.

She picked a bouquet of wildflowers and arranged them in a pint canning jar, set it in the center of the old pine table. They made the ranger station look like somebody lived there. *Like a woman lived here*, she thought, for the first time since her mother left. She felt the old room around her smiling its thanks.

She turned toward her bedroom to change and saw Clayt standing there, so still she hadn't noticed him when she came into the house. The faux-mica ceiling fixture produced a feeble glow, dimmed by one dead bulb. Its amber light rendered his jaw in craggy shadows that made him look spectral as he stared down at a frayed rug. A strand of cobweb dangled off the light fixture and swayed toward his silver hair.

Agnes stepped toward him. "Are you all right?" she asked.

Clayt turned to face her, his eyes shining.

She gripped his shoulders. "Talk to me."

He shook his head.

"How about some coffee," she said, steering him around. "You need to sit down."

"I got somethin' to say," he said.

She felt her stomach tighten.

"Come on then," he said. "Before I lose my nerve."

He led her to the kitchen and pulled the lid off the trash can under the kitchen sink. An empty bottle, that good Scotch he'd asked for.

"You didn't finish that already," she said.

"It went down the sink."

She said nothing as she took in his words.

"It was time."

She stared at him. Nodded slowly as she comprehended his resolve. "Well, good for you. This will make everything easier."

"Guess we'll see about that."

They took their coffee onto the porch steps and sat together as they had the day of her arrival. Tuck sat between them, accepting scratches behind both ears.

"You should know that the historical society is taking up your cause."

"Helen warned me you'd be wantin' that book a' mine." He set his coffee on the step and slapped his thighs. "An' I just remembered where it is." He started to get up.

"Let me." Agnes was on her feet.

"My journals," he said. "Back a' the file cabinet."

"The ones you had out that day."

"There's more. The safe…" He pushed himself up. "Let's take a look."

They pulled the chairs back from the kitchen table and Clayt arranged the envelopes, folders, letter boxes, and albums Agnes carried from the tiny office that had once been her bedroom. She watched his shaking hands and urged him to drink more water. He had opened the safe, and inside she found the large portfolio album that Helen wanted to see, bound with leather between covers of carved wood. The front panel held a mountain scene with trees and river and a cloud-stacked sky, depicted in a mosaic of local species of wood, the trees and receding hills cut precisely and perfectly inlaid. Laid open, the portfolio covered half the table.

The frontispiece was a hand-drawn map covering both pages, mountain ranges hachured in India ink, lettering done in white to contrast with the dark neutral-gray pages. A circular inset flew to one corner of the sheet like an inflating balloon. War Creek Station, a gabled cabin bearing a flag, professionally rendered. Clayt poked at the initials at the edge of the drawing—*AHC/1938*.

"He did this map 'specially for us. One of a kind."

Agnes studied the perfect architectural rendering of the War Creek ranger's house when its paint was still drying, the ground around it newly cleared. The larger map resembled a crisp aerial photograph, each peak and ridge in its proper place, each creek coming off the Cascade Crest carefully named with hand lettering. It finally dawned on her who "he" was: AHC—Arthur H. Carhart, the Forest Service landscape architect who had assigned personalities to trees.

Clayt pointed out Bridge Creek, at the far northwest corner of the map. "Used to be part a my district," he said. He had never forgiven Congress for conveying part of his district to the National Park Service.

"Don't you think it honors the place to include it in a national park?"

He rubbed his whisker stubble. "Good a way as any to look at it. Now turn the page."

She lifted the heavy gray sheet and the binding squeaked like saddle leather. Under a protective leaf of crinkled tissue was a faded photograph of important-looking men standing in stiff poses in front of War Creek Station or perched astride horses nearby. Handwritten directly onto the photo paper were their signatures. Dwight Eisenhower stood front and center wearing a smile that did not belong to a careful politician—it was open and genuine, the wide smile of a child released for the afternoon into an endless forest to play. Clayt had insisted on bringing the chief executive and his entourage to War Creek after the ceremony at the jumper base at which Clayt and the other smokejumpers had been honored for their service during the Second World War.

"Ranger roster," Clayt said, turning to another sheet. "There's me at the tail end." The sandy crew cut, the jutting jaw, chest thrust forward, one hand on a Pulaski. As she remembered him.

Clayt continued to direct Agnes, reminding her more than once to turn the pages gently. He could name everyone whose faces smiled or frowned out of the photographs. Pockets held maps and documents, floor plans and elevations for the house and barn and bunkhouse. Working drawings used by the Civilian Conservation Corps, and records—who built the arching bridge and laid the foundation for the house, cut from local rock.

Clayt sat back in his chair, his face flaccid. "I'm tired of remembering," he said. "Now when you run off with this…" He pointed at the portfolio. "Make damn sure t' wrap it up good and don't give it to nobody but Helen."

"I'll have her come get it, Clayt. And I'll tell her to bring whatever kind of archival box she can lay hands on."

He grunted and she took it for assent.

"I'll have her stop by tomorrow, if she's free. Before you change your mind."

"Ain' changin' it."

"Some lunch might perk you up." Agnes brought bowls of grapes and cherries to the table. "How about a sandwich or something?"

"Not hungry," he said. But he couldn't resist a handful of inch-long sweet grapes.

She realized that by noon he would have had a nip or two. She hoped he wasn't in bad enough shape to develop a case of the DTs. She worried over how to keep him busy and distracted, but he solved the problem for her by announcing it was time for a nap.

While Clayt dozed, Agnes settled in with the portfolio. Its pages recorded the history of War Creek from its beginnings in the late 1930s through the '60s, though not in precise chronological order. One page held a large photograph that Clayt would have railed about, making Agnes glad he was asleep on the sofa: a team of high-level officials, at War Creek after a survey of the proposed Ice Peaks National Park. Clayt was not in the photograph but Agnes recognized the names of those who were, conservation luminaries of the early twentieth century—Robert Marshall and Aldo Leopold standing beside Interior Secretary Harold Ickes and Forest Service Chief F. A. Silcox. Thirty years later, the efforts of these men would result in the formation of North Cascades National Park. Agnes smiled at the thought that, other than the original drawings by the famous Arthur Carhart, this photograph was the most valuable in the entire collection.

She set the portfolio aside and glanced through boxes of photographs and negatives, location and date unknown—except to Clayt, who apparently had kept the information entirely in his head. The bottom drawer of the file cabinet had yet to be explored, but Clayt had not asked her to look there. Agnes knew he would not neglect a record to go with all the pictures.

At the bottom of one box she found a square envelope tied with a frayed yellow ribbon. Something about it made her pause—it was not her business to investigate. Curiosity prevailed and she gently worked the knot loose. Clayt's snoring assured her she would not be interrupted.

Inside was a cracked leatherette billfold. A newspaper clipping folded into a tight square fell onto the floor. Her older brother Will gazed sternly out from the yellowed sheet, a young corporal in a starched uniform. Agnes read its single column paragraph. *Survived by...*the sibling names rolled down the page in a litany, her name at the distant end.

The obituary, if she could call the tidy paragraph such a thing, included an odd turn of phrase: *passed away.* Agnes let her gaze drift over vague forms and shadows, focusing on nothing. Had journalistic euphemism become that obscure near the end of the Vietnam War? Perhaps reporting the dire news to a citizenry fed up with hearing the words *killed in action* one more time had urged the writer to reach for something different. But why had there been no mention of the platoon in which he served, the medals he had earned? She looked at another photo in the wallet, Will in his high school picture. There she saw his effort to look grown up and serious. A few years later, when he posed in his military garb, his face had hardened—whether into anger or resignation she could not tell. Will was Clayt's pride, his hope for a successor worthy of the family's glorious, if imagined, past.

Passed away. Agnes thought she might pass out. She slid the wallet back into the envelope and tied the ribbon and replaced it. She went to the front room and banged her coffee cup down on the table, angry at the obituary writer who couldn't think of more to say about her eldest brother, who had fallen in service to his country, whether or not one thought the war had been worth fighting. His image brought back the arguments, her mother's perpetual grief and increasing periods of silence. Will had died, Agnes learned she was pregnant, and soon the Clayton family disintegrated. She knew this much, but she knew there was much more to the story. It was easy enough to understand why some parts of the past had been buried, but her desire to unearth them would not rest.

She went into her bedroom, not planning to sleep, but she drifted off and woke with a start, feeling an oppressive heat against her side—the breath of an animal in her face, thick fur under her hand. She pulled her hand back and sat up with a stifled shriek. Tuck leapt off the bed.

"Oh, Tuck, I'm sorry," she said. The dog eyed her with bewilderment and she collapsed onto her back.

The dream was still vivid in her mind, up to the point where she had mistaken Tuck for the silver bear. Instead of ambling peacefully away, the bear had walked up to Agnes and stared into her face, its breath close and steamy and rank. The bear had been close enough to touch and Agnes moved her hand toward it. In the past, the dream ended with the bear dissolving into the mist like a mirage, but this time she had felt warm, thick fur under her hand.

CHAPTER TEN

Clayt wouldn't eat breakfast. All morning he shuffled around the house in a mood he called "do-less." Finally he sat at the table and watched Agnes eat a piece of toast. He stared into his coffee cup for a minute, then lifted his eyes. They skimmed the familiar walls around him and landed on his daughter.

"What in hell's hell am I going to do, missy? My life's been behind me for years now."

"It's been one day since you went off the booze. Give yourself a break." She pushed the bowl of grapes toward him. "First thing you need to do is get some decent nutrition. Fresh fruit and veggies and none of that damned Vienna sausage out of a can. Ugh."

"Don't knock it—stuff'll keep ya goin' on the trail."

"What if I cut one up and scramble it with some eggs?"

"Sounds all right."

She pushed her chair back and refilled her coffee cup. Three local eggs from Helen's, one daintily sliced Vienna sausage, a handful of chopped chives, and the only kind of cheese they could agree on—medium cheddar—went into a mixing bowl while her favorite blend of olive and peanut oils heated in a cast-iron skillet.

"Clayt," she said. "I've been thinking about a lot of things since coming back."

He shot her a look of warning mixed with worry.

"How about a little ride after breakfast?" she asked.

"I've ridden enough for ten lifetimes. Been everywhere."

"It's a fabulous day, not too hot—"

"Damn sure gonna be." Clayt left the table to pour the last of the coffee into his cup. He took a sip and made a face, tossed it into the sink. "All right," he said. "Just to shut you up. But that ain't what you wanted to talk t' me about."

"Who said I wanted to talk? Been thinking, that's all." She looked at him and smiled. "You aren't used to my sense of humor. I was kidding you, Clayt."

"Didn't know y' had a sense a' humor. I sure as hell don't."

"It's time we both got one, don't you think? Life's too short for arguing, slamming doors, giving each other the silent treatment. We have more in common than either of us will admit."

"Sense a' humor included."

"See? You do have one."

"That ain't what you been thinkin' about either."

"Let's discuss it on the trail. We seem to be able to talk about things in the mountains that we can't manage here."

"Not your mother again."

"I was scared to death to come here, you know."

"Scared a what?"

"What do you think? You. We didn't exactly part on the best of terms."

"I got y' off to college an' on your way—that was my end a' the bargain."

"So maybe I've come to pay you back. You've been stewing in your own juices for long enough, as Rion would say."

"I s'pose the two a' you get a charge outta talkin' about this old fart."

"Not at all. We'd both like to see things get better for you."

"I'll get them nags saddled, then."

"Your eggs are done."

Riding with Clayt was a lot like riding alone. He pressed Agate into a fast walk and it was only Jasper's desire to keep up with his corral mate that allowed Agnes a glimpse of the back of Clayt's Forest Service cruiser jacket. She was just as glad to be left to ponder the brief but unusually disturbing bear dream. Each episode had been different, like chapters in a long narrative, and each seemed to carry a specific message, however densely coded. Why had the bear allowed Agnes to touch her this time? Was she getting closer to the meaning of this dream? A bookstore clerk had once told her that in a dream every character represents the dreamer in some form. Agnes assumed this information had come from one of the books in the store, and she had dismissed it at the time. What did it mean that she became a lit-up disappearing bear as she slept? She knew only this about the bear: she was definitely female, and over time she had become more distinct. In each dream the bear had moved closer, as if she wanted Agnes to come with her. In each dream Agnes had longed all the more to touch her, but now that she had—or had at least touched Tuck—it left her unsettled and perplexed. If she could understand what the dream bear had to do with the one whose scat she had given Hunter, she might unravel the significance.

The dream concerned her less than what she'd found in the leatherette billfold. How would she broach the subject with Clayt when Will was primary among the family taboos? He was killed in Vietnam and had died a hero's death, and there was nothing more to say about it.

The demands on her time during the years she'd taught school had distracted her from unanswered questions about her family. Now that Clayt was in the mood to open up a bit, she saw her chance. While she had kept in touch with her brothers, they all were busy with their lives. They managed to send a card at Christmas, most of them bearing a printed greeting and stuffed with photos of children she'd never met. On the rare occasions when she called, she had little time to say more than hello before she found herself talking, instead of to the brother she had called, to one of those children.

Matt was the only brother who had not married. In a long and surprisingly candid letter that had come with last year's

Christmas card, Matt wrote to her about his decision to move in with a male "friend." Agnes didn't question why she had been singled out among the siblings to receive this information. A fellow outsider, Matt knew he could trust her. She had called him not long after receiving the letter to assure him that he always had her support; one of her hoped-for destinations, after she had Clayt moved and settled, was Matt's house north of Seattle.

Clayt stopped at the trail junction and slid off the saddle to fix a crooked sign. The effort winded him and he sat on a log to rest. Agnes dismounted and sat beside him, urging him to drink some water.

Clayt removed his hat and wiped his face with a bandana. "I was a ranger, I'd have level-three restrictions in place—no campfires, no smokin', no drivin' off the road."

They rode through a meadow thick with grass, purple lupine and scarlet Indian paintbrush. A fire did not seem imminent here, but the distant valley held fields of curing pasture grass, looking more like August than July. Agnes had watered the garden that morning, knowing that when she got back to the station she would water the wilted greens again. Why was she even doing this, now that she could buy fresh vegetables at Helen's, and knowing she would soon abandon her little plot? Another bit of ritual, she supposed. Like the bouquet in the canning jar, it brought back her mother. Mary, if she could see Agnes laboring over a row of spindly baby lettuce that had already begun to bolt, would probably laugh at the futility of it.

Clayt interrupted her thoughts. "I tell you about the time Roger and I damn near burned up the North Fork? We parked where the grass was good'n beat down but she went up before we were half outta the truck. We stomped it with our shovels until it played itself out."

Clayt put a boot in a stirrup and paused for a breath before pulling himself into the saddle.

"Won't be long before I can't do this," he said.

"You're doing fine," Agnes said as Agate fell back into his fast, steady pace.

In spite of his shortcomings, Clayt commanded respect, and Agnes couldn't help admiring him. In the days when he was a junior forester and Roger was barely out of his teens, the two of them had lived outdoors—clearing trails until the first fire assignment and rarely seen again for the rest of the summer. Clayt was the grinning smokejumper from the old photographs, clowning and making faces for the camera with the rest of the boys: full of fun and energy, loyal to the agency down to his undershorts, and bursting with well-deserved pride over the work he did. He had been ready to get up at five in the morning to do it all again, years before his transformation to a strict and humorless father of seven.

They had ridden only a couple of miles before Clayt guided Agate from the trail and started up a brushy crease in the mountainside, below a long, dry slope of scree. A fissure in the bedrock on the south face of War Creek Ridge angled upward in a nearly straight shot from the tumbling creek to the ridgeline. The approach to a feasible route would not have been noticed by anyone on the official trail, other than Clayt, who had long ago memorized each tree and shrub that obscured the way. Agnes knew where they were headed as soon as he left the trail—a gap in War Creek Ridge that Clayt called Panorama Pass. She understood why he had left Tuck at home, for it was a long, exposed south slope with no water. The horses had drunk their fill at the creek, but a dog needed a mud hole once in a while to cool his belly.

Panorama Pass was one of the first places Clayt had taken Agnes when she was old enough to ride for half a day, and she remembered the thrill of riding a horse off trail to a place she imagined no one had ever been before. From the pass there was a view of the entirety of War Creek—Snowshoe Ridge wrapping the South Fork, with Oval Peak standing tall beyond it to the south; the South Fork valley, with no maintained trail and mantled in deep forest; Black Ridge, separating the forks of War Creek and culminating on top of Sawtooth Ridge at Sun Mountain; and a view straight up the main fork to the headwaters and War Creek

Pass. The creek threaded its way down the long, straight canyon, thick with forest on the south side, bright with glacier-polished bedrock on the north. She remembered Clayt pointing out War Creek Ranger Station, barely visible in the forest below, and the winding valley of the Twisp River running toward the Methow under buckskin-colored hills. Clayt had loved that view because from there he could see nearly all of his district, and very little of what had been turned over to the national park.

More than all of this, she remembered the pleasure in her father's gaze, the uncharacteristic gentleness of his hand as he held hers, taking care of her as they stood above a thousand feet of loose talus. He had looked tall in his weathered chaps and cowboy hat, standing on a boulder. He'd often stood on boulders, especially when someone had a camera out.

They approached the wide gap and that well-remembered view surrounded Agnes. Off to the east a yellow-brown haze settled over the Columbia Plateau from wildfires south of Wenatchee. The distant peaks faded like a watercolor wash of weak blue into dim outlines on the skyline.

They dismounted and Clayt tied both horses to a wind-flagged pine—expertly, but with small, sharp grunts of effort. A solid knot, a good short lead, horses in the shade and out of the breeze.

"That hand is on the mend," Agnes said. "Not to mention your health in general."

"Being in the mountains improves it."

"I'm glad to have gotten somewhere with Mary Lynn, at least. A little breathing room." Agnes had found the forest supervisor open, sincere, and sympathetic, if not particularly encouraging. At least she was willing to override Flintstone's decree and give Clayt a few more weeks to move. Middle of September, she had told Agnes, since they would have to turn the water off by then.

"So far what you got were promises," he said.

"We'll see. I understand Helen's talked her into a public meeting about the future of the ranger station. They're calling it a listening session."

Clayt barked a sarcastic laugh. "The last thing that's going t' happen is listening."

Agnes didn't respond. More listening might be possible if Clayt wasn't there.

"I could stand a bite," he said.

They sat on a table-sized boulder with a flat top and ate their lunch—a scrambled egg sandwich for Clayt, baby carrots and melon cubes for Agnes. The view across War Creek was muted with the smoke, but inspiring just the same.

"No wonder you're so skinny, that's all y' eat," Clayt said.

"We had a big breakfast, remember?"

"Always a picky eater. Took after her that way."

"I take after you in the ways that matter, Clayt. But why won't you talk about her? Why don't families talk?"

"Figured that was on your mind this morning."

"I asked if you ever heard from her. Whether or not she's still alive."

"An' I said I didn't know. Haven't heard squat in a long time." He paused. "You don't know the half of what went on."

"Because nobody would talk about it and I was afraid to ask. It always seemed like everybody knew things I didn't."

"Some things aren't meant for a child t' know."

Agnes looked around at the boulders surrounding them. "See any kids here?"

"Don't be smart."

"When will I be allowed to understand my own family? How will I ever know who I am?"

"Y'make your own self into who you are. I sure as hell had to."

"What about your folks? They were my grandparents, and I don't know a thing about them."

"Not much t' say. Dad was a mean old bastard, swatted us around most of the time. Mum kept' er mouth shut and made us eat everything on our plates."

Agnes realized she didn't even know her grandmother's first name. Clayt was named after his father.

"Sounds like an unhappy childhood," she said. "I don't mean to drag you through it."

"I put it behind me an' went on with life. It's what I recommend."

"Which of your boys are you closest to now?"

"None a' them kids're what I'd call close."

"I don't mean where they live. Any of them visit?"

"Used to."

Clayt fell quiet. His face was shaded by his straw hat so Agnes couldn't read his expression, but the quality of his silence told her she'd struck a nerve. *Used to*—she guessed that his drinking and rages had driven away protective fathers like Patrick, who would not have wanted to expose his children to Clayt's temper. She felt sorry for him in a way she never had before, and not knowing how else to express it, she put her hand on top of his.

"So, missy," Clayt said. "You said you been thinkin'. If it ain't your mother, what is it?"

Agnes weighed her desire to learn about her family against Clayt's pain in having to answer her questions. "Will," she said. "I hardly knew him."

"What about 'im?"

"I found a copy of his obit in your records. There was no mention of his time in the service, no memorial planned. It said he simply 'passed away,' as if he vaporized or something. There must have been a Mass, but I can't remember it." She stopped herself there, realizing there were other things that didn't make sense. His grave—where was it? The silence about Will was so complete she had never allowed herself to wonder.

"With your situation and your mother takin' off I didn't have time t' write no obituary."

Matt certainly would have—or any one of the older boys. But she could sense in Clayt's flat tone the need to drop the subject of Will. He flexed his hand to let Agnes know it was time to move hers.

She felt an unexpected pang of empathy for Clayt. She shared with him the loss of a firstborn child. How much harder had it been for Clayt to lose his first and favorite son, the one in whom he had placed his expectations for greatness? A son he had known and loved for years, not a baby that had not been named nor even seen. Though Agnes thought Clayt's sorrow must be deeper than hers, a day had not gone by since she was seventeen when she failed to think about her little child. At the bottom of the pit of loss, they shared the same inconsolable grief.

Clayt grunted as he stood. "Damn. Older y' get, the harder it gets to stand up."

He wadded up the paper bag that had held his sandwich and a sliced apple, and walked over to Agate and Jasper.

"Here ya go, boys," he said, as he passed each a slice of apple. "I see you got somethin' on the calendar for next Sunday morning," he said abruptly.

"Hunter's taking me bear-watching."

"Now that's a good one."

"I'm serious. I want to see how telemetry works, and I want to see that bear."

"He work seven days or what?"

Agnes shrugged. She suspected he was giving up a free weekend morning on her behalf.

"No Mass for you again, then," he said.

Sunday Mass had been the last thing on her mind when she made plans with Hunter.

"If your mother knew, it would break her heart."

Agnes doubted it. Her mother had a heart beyond breaking. "I'm sorry it bothers you so much," she said. "But why are you singling me out and not the rest of them?"

He shot her a look. "They go, all of them."

"If you say so."

"You heard this, then. Which one?"

"It doesn't matter who does and who doesn't go to Mass every Sunday of the year," she said. "It's too beautiful a day for us to argue about it."

But Clayt was now in pursuit of information. "Patrick and that cheeky woman of his. Ain' she a Buddhist or some damn thing?"

"She grew up Buddhist the way we kids grew up Catholic. And I'm not about to tattle on my brothers."

"Brothers, is it, then? Who else—Matt? He was always a corker. Couldn't a been the others. Mark clings to it, you know. Gives him great comfort."

Mark was staunch in his practice, and a strict disciplinarian. His children stood at attention for their holiday photographs with fear on their faces.

"I hope so," Agnes said.

They both knew which brother had jettisoned his vocation, complete with an admission to the seminary, in favor of Army boot camp. But the bright silence of the mountains lifted their spirits above the heartbreaks of the past, and for once Clayt let it rest.

"Are we not close to the divine right here?" she asked.

"An old man ought t' know better'n to ask questions if he don't want the answer."

"I'll go to Mass with you next week. Now come on." She stood.

"Where are you taking me?"

"Heaven."

They left the horses tied where they were and Agnes led the way from the gap to a high point on the ridge, three hundred feet higher than the saddle. A thin sliver of snow left from the previous winter's cornice garlanded the north side of the ridge. Agnes followed a line of buttercups hugging the damp edge of the snow, pausing frequently to let Clayt catch his breath. Near the top she spotted the compact cairn Clayt had placed years before.

"Look at that," she said. "I was hoping it'd still be here."

"Son of a bitch. You helped build it, remember?"

"Of course I remember."

"Put that little bitty one right on top."

From the high point on the ridge they could see mountains not visible from the gap below. The wind had shifted, and the haze of wildfire smoke rolled back like a curtain. Ranges and ridges receded in imbricate ranks into the distance, like breakers disappearing into an ocean of snow and ice and stone.

Clayt stood beside the cairn, wiped his eyes on his sleeve, and shook his head.

Agnes kept an eye on the horses and left her father to his thoughts. She saw in his face, the way he pulled himself up, that his chronic anger had been lifted by the wind that freed the mountains of their haze. His shakiness abated and he stood tall, the way he had done as a younger man, regarding the world with penetrating eyes, hat in hand and hair blown back from his proud, high forehead, backlit by the summer sun and framing his face. He was the fearless smokejumper, the wielder of axes and Pulaskis, all that he had been before she was born.

Clayt was struggling to remain sober and his hands still shook, but Agnes knew he meant to pull it off. She felt his resolve and determination, and as it grew she found the sixteen-year-old inside herself retreating into the past. For a change, she was in charge, leading him up a mountain he didn't believe he could climb, and she knew that he was grateful.

After a night of thunderstorms that brought little rain, Sunday morning broke cool and still below fog-shrouded mountains. Hunter's pickup slowed as he turned onto a logging road. Through the windshield Agnes saw a silver slice of creek. The logging road abruptly ended at the creek and the trail began on the far side of a shallow ford. Hunter turned the truck around and parked at the edge of the road.

Agnes rolled her jeans up to her knees and tied her boots together and slung them over one shoulder. "God is that cold!" She squealed like a child until she heard Clayt's disapproving voice in her head—*trying to get his attention, have him notice you.* She pressed her lips together and headed for the other shore, the way she would have as a girl when she was trying to impress Roger. Though Agnes was becoming more assertive with her father, his teasing about Hunter was one thing she couldn't respond to with a snappy comeback.

Hunter followed her across the creek, burdened by pack and boots and the tracking antenna he carried. Agnes, hurrying and upset by her father's imaginary scrutiny, slipped on a black mossy boulder and landed midstream on her rear end. Hunter was beside her, pulling her up, laughing as she struggled to stand. She sprinted for the far shore.

"Wait there," he said. He laid down his pack and the antenna and returned to his truck.

Great start, she told herself, *falling on your behind*. Clayt would have loved seeing her get her comeuppance. Agnes sat on a rock and held her feet, pale and rubbery from the icy water, and watched as Hunter opened the toolbox in the truck bed. He held up a pair of olive-drab rain pants with bright yellow suspenders. Agnes nodded.

She ducked into the forest to change, the coated rain pants stiff and cold against her bare skin. Determined to maintain some decorum, she followed Hunter in silence as he plunged into the forest.

The old Crater Creek trail was strewn with debris and fallen logs, all but abandoned. Hunter paused to turn the antenna in various directions, but he picked no signal out of the air. Dawn turned into day and the sun's heat burned away the morning mist. Two hours passed as the trail took them into higher country, where ponderosa pine gave way to lodgepole, western larch to subalpine fir. After the final switchbacks, the trees abandoned their efforts to grow straight and flattened into Krumholtz no taller than Agnes. The bare mountainside swept into the sky like a wing, strewn with boulders and the dry heads of wildflowers gone to seed. Cured clumps of rough grass crunched under her footsteps, brittle as glass.

Hunter stopped and lowered his daypack to the ground and Agnes did the same. Her jeans, having ridden on the top of her pack exposed to sun and wind, were still damp around the waist, but wearable. She ducked into a patch of Krumholtz to change.

She need not have bothered with the display of modesty, for Hunter seemed absorbed, hardly aware of her at all.

He was jotting in a notebook when she returned.

"Anything promising?" she asked.

His brows creased and he gave a slight shake of his head, not looking up. She sat beside her daypack and picked at a granola bar and tried not to add her disappointment to his. Sara Lee—Agnes promised herself she would never slip and call the supervisor that to her face—had given permission to move the sow before the locals caught up with her, but that would not be possible unless Hunter found her first.

He finished writing and put the notebook away. "I finally had a chance to look at that bear scat," he said.

It took Agnes a moment to realize what he meant.

"Where did you find it?" he asked.

"In the back of a chest of drawers."

"All right, smarty. Where was it before that?"

"Clayt buried the family dog near War Creek," she said. "The bear must have found him, because I went to visit his grave a week later and there wasn't anything there. I found that pile full of maggots—about made me gag. But then you said they were pine nuts."

"Full of calories. The grizzlies raid squirrel caches in the fall and chow down on them just before hitting the sack for five months."

"If that bear didn't eat my dog, what could have happened to him?"

He reached into the bottom of his shirt pocket, and after a moment of fumbling pulled out a tight packet of tissue paper.

"Thought you might want to keep this," he said, handing it to her.

She unwrapped the tissue to find a few strands of long, dark hair, brittle with age but clean, and clearly those of Brownie.

"Jesus," she said.

Hunter watched the horizon while Agnes quietly placed the dog hair in her own shirt pocket.

"Somehow 'thank you' doesn't seem like the right thing to say. But I'm glad to have these."

Agnes stared across the smoke-shrouded land. Dust rose in rooster tails behind trucks passing on the logging roads below.

"I think I know that bear," she said. "Or one just like her."

"Her?"

She told him about her recurring dream: the way the bear had changed over the years from a suggestion of shadows and light to the one who stood nose to nose with her a few mornings past. The dream had come infrequently at first, every few years and usually precipitated by some kind of personal crisis. Since she returned to War Creek, she'd had three visitations from the bear.

"I'm trying to understand it," she said. "There has to be a connection between all these dreams and…" She patted packet of dog hair in her pocket. "This."

"Maybe Clayt's the bear," Hunter suggested. "Even though you said she."

"Clayt…" In her dreams the bear had been a comfort, the opposite of Clayt. "I don't think so," she said.

"This bear seems to be after something, like you said."

"Thanks for not laughing."

"Why would I laugh? I take dreams seriously. They usually mean you have something to work out."

"I have plenty to work out, all right."

Hunter was quiet for a moment. "I was impressed by the way you handled the stock on that pack trip," he said. "Learn all that from the old man?"

"Some. I worked for the Forest Service myself—just seasonal work. I did a fair amount of packing then."

He watched the smoky horizon, nodding slightly. "There's something different about you," he said. "You're serious, like me. None of that silly girl stuff. But sad. Not my business, but it's something I notice."

"What's silly girl stuff?" she asked.

"I don't picture you and Rion sitting around talking about shopping while you paint your toenails."

Agnes laughed out loud.

Hunter dug in his pack for a sandwich and began to eat without commenting further. Agnes mulled his mention of her sadness. She was not aware of being sad, especially at that moment, but he was able to see it. Hunter didn't know about the child she had borne or the mother she had lost, but since she had returned to War Creek her mind kept drifting back to the deep hole they had both left inside, as if her womb and all the organs around it had been ripped out. In Helena, at Joan's urging, she had spent a year in weekly therapy in search of what her counselor called closure, but no matter how much she talked in that quiet, beige office, the dull pain remained. And it remained with her even in the mountains, on a beautiful summer day.

To the west, puffs of cloud had gathered into cumulus that punched like boxing gloves into the sky. Agnes watched, fascinated by how quickly the weather could change. Another thunderstorm was working itself into a fury.

She felt the old man looking over her shoulder again. "It feels as if he's here right now," she said.

Hunter glanced at her. "He who?"

"Clayt. Listening in on our conversation. Looking for anything he can give me a hard time about."

"He has a powerful presence, but I doubt he followed you up this mountain. What would he give you a hard time about?"

"He thinks I'm flirting with you."

"Are you?"

"I don't think so. Don't mean to, anyway."

"I'm sorry to hear Clayt wouldn't approve."

"It's me he disapproves of. I guess I've given him reason enough."

Hunter didn't answer. This wasn't what she meant to talk about—the flirting business and all. It had to make him uncomfortable.

"We didn't come here to talk about Clayt," she said. "Want some grapes?"

"No thanks—fruit and I don't agree. I wouldn't mind hearing more about you, though. What was it like growing up?"

She told him about the activities she most remembered: how Clayt and the boys would go select a tree for Christmas and drag it over the snow behind a horse; how she caught a rank colt that had bucked off one brother after another, and slid onto his back with no further mishaps. "Of course," she said, "by that time he'd pretty much bucked himself out."

"Sounds like a picture postcard," Hunter said.

"Not exactly. My parents were strict. Catholics—I guess you can tell from the number of kids. My mom…"

He didn't prompt her to continue, but she felt him waiting.

"She left. I was seventeen."

There. She had said it. Now he would have more questions and give her the chance to tell him all of her secret stories. As suddenly as the urge to tell him had come over her a few minutes before, it now passed.

"That had to be tough," he said. "My folks split up too, but not before I was out of the house. They actually started liking each other again, once they lived apart."

She was grateful to Hunter for redirecting the conversation. Perhaps he sensed that her desire to open up had slammed shut. Perhaps what she divulged allowed him to say something about himself.

He told her he had grown up on the Montana highline. "Pop was an ag agent," he said. "So we moved around a lot while he went off to look at people's wheatfields. That got to Mom—she could never make friends for long because they'd up and move again. I couldn't either. I guess that's why I've been a rambler, too."

"Where all have you been?"

"You name it. I thought I would like Alaska, but Southeast was too damn rainy and I couldn't take that closed-in forest feeling. I get pretty claustrophobic when I can't see what's going on around me—especially in bear country. I went to Denali to follow up on some of Adolph Murie's work with wolves. More rain. I need sky, and a little bit of light in the winter doesn't hurt. And not too many people. Cities give me the willies."

"I'm with you there."

He pointed to the rank of thunderheads, moving slowly over the mountains. "Did you catch that lightning?"

Agnes hadn't seen the lightning, but she now heard the thunder that followed.

"This area suits you," she said.

"It's great. I'm sorry I won't be here long."

Agnes felt her chest fall. "I didn't know you planned to leave."

"I leave when the job ends. They haven't told me exactly when."

They sat without talking and watched the streaks of lightning.

"Where's your mom now?" he asked.

Agnes held her breath. He wasn't finished asking questions after all.

"I don't know where she is. I haven't seen her since I…I'm not sure I want to tell you this. I got pregnant when I was sixteen— by somebody I didn't even like that much. He pressured me and…I don't know why, it seemed easier to just go along. That sounds terrible, even to me."

"It probably was terrible."

"Anyway, they sent me to a home to have the baby. When I came back to War Creek, my mother was gone."

"Not even a note?"

"Not even. I had the baby between my junior and senior years of high school. I don't know what line of malarkey my father gave everybody, but I was spared the shame of having to face my high school friends when I got home. The baby came in the summer, but the whole previous winter and spring the nuns kept us busy studying so we wouldn't fall behind. They did a good job, I guess, because I went to college that next fall. I remember a miserable few weeks at War Creek with my father, with him hardly speaking to me. All I did was study for the test I had to take so I could start school a year early. At least I had something to do."

"You had a hell of a time," Hunter said. "I'm sorry to hear about it."

"I didn't mean to blather on."

"I'm the one who asked. And I hope you'll tell me more next time you have a chance. But right now we have a bear to find."

Hunter stood and pulled on his heavy daypack. Agnes folded his rain pants and started to tie them to hers.

"I'll carry those," he said.

"You have enough to lug around," she said. "I'll take them."

His face held a mix of genuine gratitude that she was willing to carry the heavy pants, surprise that she would not have it otherwise, and something like affection.

They hiked to another high point from which he might pick up a signal before Hunter gave up looking for the War Creek sow.

"Not too productive today," he said. "I'll keep trying on the way down, but we ought to call it quits due to the weather. I hope you weren't too disappointed. Or worse, bored."

"No such thing as being bored in the mountains. I wish we could find your grizzly bear, though. The longer it is, the more I worry."

"Don't fret. If I can't find her, that bunch of yahoos wanting to take a crack at her won't either."

Agnes considered the building thunderheads. "What do bears do in a forest fire?"

"They know their home range, all the places where they can move or hole up."

"The War Creek sow is new to hers."

"A forest fire's the last thing she has to worry about."

Agnes stared at the closest thunderhead, now darkening and sending strands of virga toward the parched grass below. "I wonder if she's lonely," she said.

Hunter glanced at her. "She...the bear?"

Agnes nodded.

"They're solitary creatures, unless they have cubs."

"She would at least expect to find a scent mark or something."

"I wouldn't be surprised if she did. It's not that far to Canada, where there's a few griz."

"Maybe that's why you can't get a signal," Agnes said. "She heard about old Collins and his gang of vigilantes and took off to join her pals."

Hunter chuckled and squeezed her shoulders. "You have quite an imagination. Let's hit the trail before we get rained on."

She fell into a brisk pace behind him as he headed down the switchback trail. Her steps were light, as if a great weight had been lifted from her. She had told another human being some of her darkest secrets. Joan knew, but Agnes couldn't think of any of her other friends who had heard the story she'd shared with Hunter. She felt she could trust him, and he had told her a bit about himself as well. But there was something distant about his easy friendliness, as though he had a few closed-off walls of his own. His story about the black bear in a cage had stayed with her, a small glimpse into the heart of a man who shared little about himself. It felt liberating to have a potential confidant, and Agnes found herself liking him more and more.

"I'll let you know next time I go out," he said. "You're good company."

"I want to see the bear," Agnes said. "I want to know she's all right."

He turned and gave her a reassuring smile. He looked to be a half-decade younger than she was, but he had the authoritative manner of a long-seasoned professional. "We'll find her," he said.

They dipped through the lowest bands of Krumholtz and into the timber as the first raindrops began to peck the dry granite soil. They were the last to see that part of the country before it burned.

CHAPTER ELEVEN

The driest July in thirty years wilted toward its end under the ruddy glow of the sun. Smoke in the air from wildfires to the south turned the shadows beer-bottle brown. The fires were closer now, fueled by lightning strikes that came without rain, what the Forest Service forecasters called dry lightning. Agnes wiped fallen ash from the picnic table and benches every morning, and lately she had been doing it again at noon. Clayt raked loose straw from the corral and picked up fallen twigs while Agnes stood on the porch roof sweeping pine needles into a pail. The fires brought Roger to War Creek every few days to report on their progress and talk old times with Clayt. As the smoke intensified, hikers and campers went elsewhere and Clayt had scant visitors.

The few who came were regulars, groups of old friends who hiked the same trails every year, fishermen who hit the same high lakes. With no inkling that Clayt would soon be gone, they sought him out as they always had. He was their accustomed source of information, conversation, and a sense of belonging to the place. Anyone who considered himself a member of the North Cascades cognoscenti claimed to be friends with old Clayt.

A hale and energetic older couple paid a visit. They told Agnes they made an annual backpacking expedition to the Copper Pass area, and never missed a chance to visit with Clayt with offerings of smoked salmon and fresh cookies. Agnes had never been to Copper Pass; by the time she was old enough to ride into the mountains, the pass marked the boundary with the newly formed national park, and Clayt had refused to look over the Cascade Crest into what was no longer his district. The couple brimmed with anticipation as they described their favorite haunts. Agnes wished she could go with them.

"Not a good time for a backcountry trip," Clayt said. "Red flag alert."

The man laughed. "Where we're headed, the snow's barely off. If the rocks catch fire, we'll hop onto an iceberg in Stiletto Lake."

"All well an' good long as you're up there. But y' might not be able to get out."

"We almost canceled, Clayt," the woman said. "But we couldn't miss a chance to see you."

"Might be your last chance," he mumbled.

The couple looked at him with alarm.

"Not him," Agnes said. "This place. Soon as I can get him moved out, War Creek's history."

"Why in blazes didn't you—?"

"No point in it," Clayt said.

"Clayt." The man's voice held a tone of long-accustomed authority. "I know you better than that."

Agnes watered the garden while Clayt sat down at the picnic table with his old friends. She knew well enough how the conversation would go, the couple offering suggestions while Clayt told them why each would never work. The plate of cookies took a hard hit while they talked, and Agnes reminded herself to keep the place well stocked with sweets. Clayt's resolve to quit drinking was strong, but he struggled, and sugar seemed to help. If the cookies ran out, sheer orneriness would keep him going.

The couple took their leave with assurances they would be in touch. Agnes watched the Volvo wagon slide over the bridge and turn downstream toward town, rather than toward the trailhead.

"Looks like you talked them into changing plans," she said. "Who are they?"

"He used t' be the big boss—regional forester."

"Seems like he might have some influence."

"What about? He's just an old retired fart like me."

Agnes shook her head. "You act like you have no interest in keeping this place from being torn down around you. Why?"

Clayt ignored her question and started for the house.

"Clayt," she said. "Are you telling me that if you can't live here anymore you don't care if it gets bulldozed?"

"Just too damn old and tired to give a damn," he said, and went inside.

"I don't believe you," she called after him.

She noticed the quality of the air as she stood looking at the house, for it had changed in the past hour. Another forest fire was burning, and not very far away. The daily buildup of cumulus had begun before noon that day, and a dry wind rattled in the cottonwoods, their leaves still green but faded and tired-looking, as if they were ready to call it a summer. Agnes's amber shadow splashed across the drying lawn like a stain. She picked some lettuce for a salad, moving as though sleepwalking through some strange, thick medium other than air, a steamy broth that sapped her energy. She washed the lettuce and left it in the sink and lay down on her bed.

Her thoughts drifted to Hunter. He had responded with an understanding that surprised her when she told him about her past, and since then she had felt closer to him. Under his bear-rug persona beat a kind heart. They had begun to meet at the Raven's Roost on mornings when he wasn't in the backcountry. In spite of his upbeat conversation, she knew he was increasingly worried that something had happened to the War Creek sow. Rion continued to insist that what she had seen that last morning of their pack trip had been a bear, and a large one. But why had Agnes failed to spot her, then?

An idea occurred to her: she could pull Clayt away from War Creek for a few days, to the Mason Clinic in Seattle, away from the smoke that wasn't good for him to breathe. Her brother Matt lived north of the city, and she might be able to squeeze in a visit with him after all. The notion bloomed into a plan as she imagined exploring the west side of the mountains, with cool salt breezes instead of the ominous dry clatter of torn-off cottonwood leaves blowing down the river road.

A thunderstorm descended the next morning before dawn, accompanied by gusts of wind and fingers of dry lightning snapping across the sky. A scant spatter of rain hit the bedroom window where Agnes lay awake, watching the storm. The room was lit for a moment by a brilliant flash. The mountainsides danced in an eerie electric glow.

Smokes were reported everywhere by noon. Clayt sat beside the radio and Agnes watched helicopters trailing canvas buckets the size of watering troughs. The choppers were followed by four-engine slurry bombers, flying low with their heavy cargo of flame retardant. Protecting Collins and the few other small farms in the valley, Agnes guessed, herding the fire deep into the backcountry. She watched the air traffic and wondered where Hunter was, out amid the forest fires looking for the War Creek sow. She worried about both of them.

The fire took off a few days later. It made a run up Fish Creek from Lake Chelan to the top of Sawtooth Ridge and by sundown it had grown to over five thousand acres. A Type 1 team was called in, and when the team arrived, Clayt learned it was the same crew he had spent summers with in California, Arizona, and Glacier National Park. The team set up an incident command post in a pasture a mile down the Twisp River, and Clayt went to offer his knowledge of the country. He found his energy returning in the company of Forest Service men who spoke his language, and for most of the following week he left for the post right after breakfast, returning well after dark.

Agnes gave the house a thorough cleaning and kept the windows closed to keep out the heat and dust and smoke. She bought a box of pickling cukes and canning jars from Helen's and put up her version of Kosher dills. In the smoky blue of the evenings, she sat on the porch steps with Tuck as the slurry bombers droned overhead between the airfield at the smokejumper base and the fire.

She was not worried about what the fire was doing to the mountains, having witnessed larger ones in the dry forests around Helena. Hiking a trail outside of town with Joan after one such fire, she had been encouraged to see wildflowers and young aspen sprouts breaking through the scorched duff while it was still warm. The fire at hand remained on the west slope of Sawtooth Ridge, slowed by a lack of timber near the mountain crest. If the wind came up and the fire leapt the ridge, it would certainly consume the dense old-growth forests in War Creek, and probably the ranger station as well. Ironic, she thought, that her mission for coming in the first place would be accomplished if the station burned—ironic, since it had been some time since she'd abandoned her mantra to get him moved and get out. Clayt might be too old and tired to give a damn about War Creek, but Agnes wasn't.

One evening Clayt returned home early from the incident command post, his face set in a fiercely determined frown. He was breathing hard, having left his old pickup on the far side of the bridge. The day had been so smoky that noontime looked like dusk, and now a swollen sun dropped toward the treetops, red as a bag of blood.

"What's up," Agnes said, surprised to see him there in time for dinner.

"Y' better come with me."

He strode to the shed where his truck was usually parked, fiddled with the lock, and started pulling out lengths of garden hose. Handed her one end.

"Hook this up to th' frostless," he ordered.

Agnes did what she was told. Clayt returned to his truck and lowered the tailgate, waving her over.

She struggled to keep up as he lifted his side of an irrigation pump borrowed from Roger. They set the pump beside the road and Clayt sidestepped down the riverbank with the intake hose. It reached the water with a few feet to spare.

"Let's get started on a rock dam for this thing," he said. "Just in case."

Clayt clambered up the bank and Agnes began arranging river rocks, setting them in imbricate rows so the pool would be deep and stable as it filled. She worked alone until Clayt returned. He inspected her work with approval and scrambled down the bank to steady some of the rocks.

"This'll do," he said. "Do just fine." His tight-lipped smile expressed his thanks. "Now get your car over here."

Agnes ran to the house for her keys, pausing only to kick out of her wet shoes and let them drain. Clayt had started the garden sprinkler on the roof and back side of the house. He had laid two-inch-thick fire hose across the yard, ready to connect to the pump as soon as the pool filled. Agnes let Tuck out and drove across the bridge.

"What's going on up there on the mountain?" Agnes asked. "Did it jump the divide?"

"Just precautionary," he said. "Fire'll lay down tonight, may not be any trouble at all by tomorrow."

Agnes took her sleeping bag and pad out to the porch that night. She lay awake, watching for the first signs of a red glow in the forest above the ranger station. The sprinkler ran, now behind the barn. The reassuring *slap-slap-slap* of water on wood lulled her to sleep.

Clayt stepped over her and let the screen door slam behind him, waking her to the gray dawn. He was off to move the sprinkler. Agnes quickly dressed and ran to help. The smoke was dense and close to the ground after the cool night allowed it to settle. Charred pine needles were falling from the sky.

"The stock," Clayt snapped. "Take 'em up to Collins's place."

Agnes jumped onto Jasper bareback and led Socks and Agate along the river road, clip-clopping in their new shoes, the only sound in the silent morning. Collins's was the only ranch upstream of War Creek, and its hayfields had been cut and baled, offering a decent firebreak.

Collins had set his sprinklers overnight and she helped him move them. He offered to take her home.

"It doesn't look good," Agnes said as they drove the two miles back to War Creek.

"Looks like hell," Collins said. "When you two goin'?"

"Going. Where?"

"Young feller stopped in before five," Collins said. "Evac orders."

Agnes thought for a moment. Clayt had been up before five. "He didn't stop at our place," she said.

Collins parked behind Clayt's truck and shouted over the rumble of the generator. "Clayt, time t' get our asses out."

Clayt was using the heavy fire hose to soak the house while the sprinkler continued slapping at the side of the barn. He turned the nozzle down so he could hear what Collins was shouting about.

"Come again," Clayt said as Collins walked up the sloping lawn.

"I said they've issued evac orders. We need to git."

"Horse feathers."

Agnes gave Collins a pleading look and he shook his head. "I got my place buttoned up," he said. "What if I stick around a bit and give you folks a hand?"

"Appreciate it," Clayt said. His breathing was labored, his face drained of color.

Agnes had never heard her father accept help so easily, nor had she heard Collins offer. Crisis brought out the best in people, she decided.

"Did some young guy come here this morning?" she asked Clayt. "Would have been four thirty or so."

Clayt shook his head. "What about them damned cats."

Agnes went into the barn to gather the six-toed clan of felines, most of them docile enough to be picked up and deposited in the house where they had never been allowed. She enlisted Tuck's help to snag the wilder ones. When she picked up the last of them and carried him toward the steps, his claws sunk into her shoulder.

"Ouch, you little shit," she said, and tossed him inside.

The phone. Agnes ran for it.

"I was afraid someone would answer," Hunter said. "What in the hell are you still doing there?"

"Clayt won't leave."

"You need to, whether or not he will. I'll meet you at the gate."

She could hear shouting outside. "I need to go," she said and hung up. The phone rang again but she was out the door.

Clayt and Collins were working the stiff fire hose toward the far corner of the barn, where Agnes saw a rising ribbon of smoke. She ran to help, dragging a piece of hose to give Clayt some slack.

"Take this," he shouted, thrusting the brass nozzle at her. "Sweet Jesus."

"Sit down, Clayt, I'll handle it."

Agnes aimed the water, surprised by the strength of the stream. It chased wisps of smoke that seemed to skitter across the roof. She ran the water over it like a paintbrush, back and forth, but smoke kept rising from between the barn's shingles. The hayloft.

"Collins—" she yelled.

"I'm on it," came Collins's voice from inside the barn. Spray from the garden hose shot out the opening above the loft—nearly empty now, thank heaven, and ready for this year's hay. Not that there would be a delivery this year.

They worked in grim silence, but Agnes could see the damage, a corner of the barn charred and steaming. She directed a fountain of river water over the hot spot until the hissing ceased.

Clayt came around the corner. "Probably not out," he said. "Keep an eye on it."

Morning passed as Agnes and Clayt and Collins kept watch and watered every surface on the compound that they could see through the heavy smoke—buildings, bare ground, the lower trunks of the pines. The slow passage of hours reminded Agnes of Clayt's old summary of firefighting: hours of boredom and moments of terror. With the terror of the burning barn past, boredom threatened to distract them from their necessary vigilance. Agnes did what she could to stay busy, hauling lengths of hose, monitoring the barn, making and serving coffee with the lemon cookies left by the regional forester's wife, checking the depth of the pool in the river.

She was moving the sprinkler to the back of the tack shed when something made her stop. Radiant heat. The smoke went black and dense. She could hear crackling as the pines along the mountainside above them torched. She called for Clayt and Collins but the roar of a slurry bomber low overhead drowned her out. Blindly she cast around for her father.

"Let's hit the river," she shouted. "Clayt, where are you?"

Clayt and Collins appeared from the smoke, both with soaked bandanas around their faces. They looked more than usual like a couple of old outlaws.

"Flippin' pump crapped out," Clayt said, and tossed the limp, empty fire hose away.

"The river," she said. "Come on."

They floundered through the smoke to the river and found seats on rocks under the bridge. The concrete abutment would offer some protection from heat if the fire burned all the way to the compound. If necessary, they would join Tuck in the pool behind the rock dam. He lapped at the water and swung his shaggy tail, sprinkling them.

"Rate it's coming this won't take long," Clayt said.

"We did all we could," Agnes offered.

"I've always done all I could. Sometimes it don't matter."

Agnes looked over her shoulder toward the house. In spite of the soaked exterior, enough heat could cause it to start burning from inside. Her bedroom window was open a few inches and she saw the cat who'd clawed her shoulder leaping onto the ground. He took off for the woods downriver.

"Might as well polish this off," Collins said. He held up a flask.

"Don't you dare," Agnes said. "Or I'll grab it and throw it in the creek."

Clayt stared at the whiskey as Collins held it toward him. "I'd like t' toss back the whole shitaree," he said. "But I'm not in the mood."

"Well then." Collins took a long swallow. "That'll put lead in your pencil."

They settled in, no one willing to look at what was happening behind them. Nothing seemed to change in the density of the smoke, the roar of pine trees igniting on the mountainside, the prattle of the river and the silent generator, out of fuel. From under the bridge they kept their eyes on what they could see of the river road beyond the shapes of their vehicles.

Time passed as Collins sipped, Clayt sat with his eyes shut tight and his arms crossed over his knees, and Agnes splashed in the pool to entertain Tuck. They began to notice that the fire was passing also, up the river and not over their heads. The sudden roar of an air tanker flying close to the ground made them instinctively duck their heads. The plane left a long slap of fire retardant across the station, splattering the bridge and the people underneath with foaming red wash. Agnes tucked her head between her knees until the retardant settled.

"Bet that's Wink," Clayt said, cocking his head toward the sound of the aircraft. "Good thing the team doesn't answer to fuckin' Flintstone."

After the plane retreated the intensity of the heat began to abate. Another retardant drop came minutes later. The smoke thickened around them, then broke into a bright pink haze. Over the next hour the air cooled and the huddled group began to stir. Collins stumbled to the bridge and across to his pickup, where he tried without success to clear the retardant from its windshield.

"What do y' see?" Clayt demanded.

"Speak of the devil himself," Collins said.

Clayt and Agnes climbed the riverbank until they could see the road. Fog lights, then a Forest Service green rig, resolved from the smoke. Flintstone. Anxiety etched his face, but whether he was worried he'd find War Creek burned with Clayt in it or worried that he would not, Agnes couldn't tell. Either way he considered this trouble to be his.

Flintstone rolled down his window and frowned, his eye moving from Collins and the parked vehicles to the generator and finally to Clayt and Agnes.

"What a lost opportunity, now," Clayt shouted. "Damn near got rid a' me."

"I'd expect an old fire dog like yourself to know better than to stick it out in these conditions."

"It's a ranger's duty to stand and save his station," Clayt said. Meant and received as a swat in the face.

"Why don't you just get the hell outta here and let him be," Collins said.

Flintstone smiled. "This is government property, sir. It would be my place to order you out."

"Go fuck yourself, Freddy."

Collins was a tall and imposing man, with ropy muscles and big hands that made fists like boulders. He started for the green rig and Flintstone rolled up the window.

Clayt settled Collins down and approached Flintstone. He held a lungful as he turned to see the house and barn and shed all standing, unburned. When he let out his breath Agnes could tell that he was stifling a whoop of joy.

"So what can we do fer ya," he said to Flintstone. "As you can see, things're under control here."

Flintstone eyed the charred corner of the barn's roof. "Just checking on you, Clayt," he said. "Whether or not you believe it, I'm glad you're all right."

They regarded each other in silence for a moment before Flintstone began to turn the truck around. He paused.

"I'll have to inform the SO. They'll be sending an engineer out to inspect that barn."

"Ain't y' already decided to torch the bastard? What's the point of another damned inspection?"

"See you later, Clayt," Flintstone said as he started for the incident command post.

Clayt turned to watch the river. It slid among its dark boulders, clear and bright and oblivious to all that had taken place.

CHAPTER TWELVE

Clayt sat on the porch steps blowing on his coffee. He hadn't showered or changed clothes since the previous Friday when the forest fire nearly claimed him, and he was beginning to smell bummish. Even Tuck kept his distance.

His eye worried the charred corner of the barn while he tallied the price of shingles, lumber, and siding. Agnes joined him, taking her accustomed position on the far edge of the steps. A flicker in his eye acknowledged her, but he kept staring at the barn.

"He's testing me, y'know."

"Who—Flintstone?"

"Now, who d'ya think I mean, Agnes, my little lost lamb?"

By reflex Agnes rolled her eyes, as if someone were there to share her exasperation. In the aftermath of the fire, both she and Clayt had forgotten her promise to go with him to Mass. On the other hand, he had forgotten to go as well.

Clayt continued, talking more to himself than to Agnes. "He's testin' this old man, seeing how much I can take. Poor old Job—I know what y' went through, feller."

"Clayt, you passed the test. Here we are, sitting on the porch steps just like always. Instead of feeling sorry for yourself, you could look at things the other way—God spared you, didn't he?"

For a moment, this silenced Clayt. "Might be right, missy," he said at last.

The river road remained closed to the public, and only fire crews and support vehicles passed. A water truck sprayed mowed grass stubble in front of the bridge leading to the ranger station. A young man in a hardhat opened the passenger window and tossed a soft drink can onto the shoulder.

Clayt's eyes snapped. "See that? It was me driving, I'd…"

The water truck braked to a halt and a moment later the object of Clayt's scorn leapt to the pavement and ran back to retrieve the can.

"Damn well better pick that up, y' little snot," Clayt yelled.

The youth glanced up and quickly returned to the vehicle.

"Clayt, I'm going to call you on that lost little lamb crap," Agnes said. "I bet I went to church more times when I was teaching at Saint Vince's than you have in the last ten years."

"What's that got t' do with the price a' eggs?"

"You never miss a chance to beat me over the head about God and church and what I'm not doing right. May I remind you that you spent yesterday morning on the couch?"

"It's all right t' skip Mass if you're sick, missy. An' I was feelin' mighty rough."

For a moment Agnes thought he was going to tell her he had found some whiskey hidden somewhere in the house. He seemed to read her mind, and answered her unspoken worry with a smirk and a shake of his head.

"Instead a Mass, I was havin' my own private conversation with the Lord."

The next morning Clayt took a shower and put on fresh clothes.

"You look chipper," Agnes said. "Coffee's on the way."

"Little bit a rest goes a long ways. Tired a smellin' like them hippies down th' road livin' in a teepee."

Agnes didn't mention that she had been buying most of her produce from them hippies. "I'm proud of you, Clayt," she said.

"What for?"

"Refusing Collins's whiskey."

He nodded. His effort to save the War Creek Ranger Station the day of the fire was nothing more than the work he had been trained to do. Ordinary in such circumstances. But his passing on the drink had not been so easy, and it made him proud as well.

"I'm glad you're dressed decently," Agnes said. "I'm hoping to talk you into coming to town with me."

"I don't want to see nobody."

"You might be interested."

"You keep talking about your crazy-ass dreams. Well, last night I had one. God told me the same thing you did: to get off my ass and stop shittin' in my own damn drawers."

"I didn't put it quite that way," Agnes said. "I'm surprised to hear the Almighty uses such profanity."

"Got to talk to me the way I understand."

Agnes handed him a cup of coffee and he took it to the table. He stood and regarded her, those icicle eyes holding hers.

"I decided something last night," he said. "We damn near lost this thing."

She waited, returning his intense and earnest gaze.

"The old man upstairs had reason t' save it." He scraped his chair back and sat down.

"Let's say he did," Agnes said. "What do you think that means?"

"I been fallin' down on my end a' the bargain. Should of been on t' what you said all along with them old biddies at the historical club—"

"You've kept the place in top shape—that goes a long way. And you let Helen take that bunch of pictures and documents— just think if the place had burned with them in it."

His vague nod acknowledged the truth in what she said. "There's more that needs done. Hit me hard when you told me I didn't care about this place, just my bein' here. It ain't true but that's how I was actin'."

She sat at the table across from him. "Do you remember saying you'd never stop fighting to save this little ranger station?"

"Well, I let up, didn't I, now? Got waylaid. Ain' saying it's your fault, but when you showed up it took me off the tracks."

"You weren't the only one whose life was derailed this summer," Agnes said.

"Happened way before this summer."

"I know. Our job is to put things right, and we need each other to do it. Now let me tell you why we need to go to town. You get a private audience with Sara Lee." She checked the clock on the kitchen wall. "You'll have to be ready in about fifteen minutes."

"If you insist."

"Hey, it's up to you. This is your chance to give her an earful about why this station is important."

Clayt pushed his chair back and stood. "I don' know much these days, but I know this—if I give up now, the best a this old buzzard will die, and what's left won't be worth a damn."

He walked past her and she felt his fingertips brush her shoulder. One small gesture said more than words—at last, they were on the same team.

Clayt went outside and stood at the bottom of the porch steps looking at the charred barn. Agnes followed him out and sat down.

"You 'n Collins," he said. "You was quite the crew."

"And you were quite the crew boss. It's a good thing you had everything soaked."

"Yep." He lowered himself to the step and took the coffee from her. "Fire season ain't half done, though."

A Forest Service six-pack raced along the river road and braked to a stop across the bridge.

"More damn rubberneckers," Clayt said. "Ain't they ever seen an old man sittin' on his porch drinkin' coffee?"

"They may not have seen one as stubborn as you. We're still supposed to be evacuated."

"Interesting that nobody told us."

"Flintstone being a turd as usual," Agnes said.

The pickup's back door opened and Hunter jumped to the ground. After a few words with the driver, he turned and ran toward the house.

"Damn," Clayt said. "Just when I thought we were gonna have a little peace an' quiet."

Agnes met Hunter beside the garden. He wrapped her in a hug and she hugged him back.

"I'd have come sooner if they'd let me through."

"I see you found a way."

He let her go and looked around the compound. "I can't believe the three of you managed this. The fire came down the mountain and skipped around like it was afraid of Clayt."

Agnes laughed. "It had reason to be. Come on."

Clayt nodded a hello to Hunter. "Damn phone's been ringin' off the wall between you 'n her."

"I've been worried about both of you," he said. "I wanted to see what I can do to help."

"Ain't it Monday morning?"

"Hard to go to work when your workplace is burning up. This was going to be one of those report-writing days anyway."

"I can see why you'd put it off, then. Missy, shall we offer the man some Joe?"

"You're drinking the last of it."

"I'm all set," Hunter said. "Mind if I have a look at that barn?"

"We're on our way to town," Agnes said.

"They'll let you through, but they might not let you back."

"Shit." Agnes hadn't thought about that.

"The bunch that gave me a ride up here said that if things look okay they might reopen the road, at least part of it."

"I'll chance it, then. Clayt, it's time to go."

She took his empty coffee cup and went inside for her car keys. Tuck lay on his side on the porch's cool planks, and his tail whacked them to indicate that he was fine staying where he was.

"I'll hang around if it's all right," Hunter said. "That driver was dropping off a crew and said he'd stop for me on the way back."

"Unless you want to come with us."

"It's okay. Since I can't get anything else done, I might as well help you two repair that barn. I'll make a list of materials."

He touched her hand as she started to turn toward her car. "It's good to see you," he said.

She met his gaze for a moment and he gripped her hand.

The Raven's Roost parking lot was full. Among the vehicles sat a bevy of Forest Service pickups. Agnes stopped at the front door and let Clayt out of the car.

He eyed the fleet vehicles with suspicion. "I wasn't expecting a crowd."

"Me either. Let me find a place to park and we'll go in together."

Rion had told her that Mary Lynn was in town for the listening session that evening, and Helen had talked her into meeting Clayt for coffee first. Agnes pictured Clayt, Helen, and the forest supervisor at a table talking about War Creek Ranger Station while she and Rion guided customers to seats that would assure the conference some privacy. Now it looked as if a retinue of brown-nosers and suck-ups had accompanied the supervisor. Agnes parked along the street and hurried back to the Raven's Roost.

Clayt was looking agitated as he stood beside the door. "Place is shut up tighter'n a boar's ass," he said.

Agnes saw the CLOSED sign hanging from the door, which was locked. She peered through the window and knocked, and Rion rushed to let her and Clayt inside. The shop was dark and empty.

"What's going on?" Agnes asked. "Did she stand us up?"

"They're all across the street at that greasy spoon," Rion said as she punched the keys on a cordless phone. "Jimmy," she said into the mouthpiece. "They're here."

Rion gave Clayt the seat of power at the back table, with the window behind him. "Coffee cake, anyone?"

"It smells divine," Agnes said.

"An extra dash of vanilla and a good dollop of sour cream—how can you resist? I had to get out my mother's secret recipe in honor of the brass. What's her name again?"

"Mary Lynn," Agnes whispered as the front door opened. "And for God's sake, Clayt, don't call her Sara Lee."

Mary Lynn shook Clayt's hand. "It's good to see you again," she said.

"I'll bet." The last time had turned into a shouting match at the War Creek Station corral.

She slid onto a chair diagonal to Clayt. "It's been an exciting summer on this district so far. From what I hear, you're the one responsible for saving that ranger station from the wildfire."

"I had help."

Agnes hoped he wouldn't clam up and act ornery, now that he had the ear of someone who could be useful to him.

"Your friend here," Mary Lynn nodded toward Helen, who sat beside her, "she let me have a look at that portfolio of yours. It's extremely impressive and I want to hear more about it. But first I need to ask what you know about this bear situation."

Clayt looked up from stirring his coffee. He had taken to dumping enough sugar in it to make syrup.

"Fish 'n Duck guy's been up in the mountains tryin' to find her," he said. "I guess you gave him the okay to get 'er moved."

"She still hasn't turned up, then. Not good news. Apparently the biologist is not the only one looking for this bear. I would very much like to prevent a media circus, and that's what we'll have if someone runs off and shoots her."

Clayt nodded. "Wouldn't want t' be the one handlin' that."

"I read a draft report about that man who was killed. The evidence is strong that no bear of any sort was involved. Next thing I see on my desk is a headline about a grizzly bear killing and eating him. It's very irresponsible, and I've already expressed my concern to the newspapers. Somebody's stirring things up. Can you help me understand where this is coming from?"

Clayt shifted uncomfortably. "Well, ma'am."

"Mary Lynn, please."

"There's a lot of folks unhappy about the whole thing."

"So if I were one of them, it would be to my advantage to

spread some rumors. And if I had a buddy working at the paper, I'd be having a heyday."

Rion brought a coffee refill to the table. "I don't mean to interrupt, but why won't the paper retract that story? They know it isn't true."

Mary Lynn cocked her head. "They can't seem to get any definitive word from the Fish and Wildlife Service. Since the investigation is ongoing, they won't release a draft report."

"How about an interview? With the truth locked up in a lab, the rumor mill flies. And I hear plenty of rumors around town."

"I'm sure you do. Not a day goes by without somebody from the Park Service calling about how we are mishandling 'their' bear." Mary Lynn turned back to Clayt. "Anything you can do to calm the waters would be much appreciated. You can tell the anti-bear people that we're doing all we can to keep this girl in the mountains and away from people."

"I 'spect she'll go where the grub is," Clayt said. "Th' orchards are gettin' watered and the mountains ain't."

A tentative rap on the front door made everyone turn.

"Can't they read?" Rion said. She went to answer it.

"I don't know why you have to keep your shop closed for us," Mary Lynn said.

Rion let the woman in. "She only needs a Joe to go."

Mary Lynn smiled at the slender woman with long blond hair tied into a ponytail. Her hiking shorts revealed the legs of an athlete as she stood on one foot among the bags of coffee beans. "Don't let us scare you off," Mary Lynn told her.

The woman smiled back. "What smells so good?" she asked.

The door opened again and a head peeked around in search of Rion. "You open today or what?"

Rion waved him inside. "Looks like I am."

Agnes went behind the counter and started a fresh batch of coffee while Rion cut the sour cream coffee cake into squares.

"That's more like it," Mary Lynn said. "The dark and quiet was starting to make me nervous."

"Sorry," Rion said. "I didn't want you getting interrupted."

"I appreciate it, but I've had lots of practice fending off interruptions. Where were we?"

"Bear rumors," Clayt prompted.

"I think I've said enough about that. Look, I need your help on this—you have the inside track on folks in this area. I'm still new, and people are wary. It's to be expected, but I want them to know that I am listening and—well, that's why I'm here. Are you planning to come this evening?"

Clayt shook his head. "I can only handle one trip t' town a week."

"I forget how far it is up there. What kind of a turnout do you expect?"

Helen answered that one. "Everyone will be there. They may not agree about bears, but they agree about saving that ranger station."

"What about bears?" came a voice from behind Helen.

It was Roger. He walked over and shook Clayt's hand.

"Told ya the grub's good in here."

Mary Lynn sat with a patient smile on her face while Roger and Clayt discussed the current fire situation. Helen was less patient. She had known Roger since he was a boy and knew how he loved to talk.

"Roger," she said, "you may not have anything better to do than stand around flapping your gums, but this is supposed to be a meeting."

His eyes widened in mock surprise. He noticed Mary Lynn's uniform and introduced himself. "I use ta work for ole Clayt here. Good ole days. You here to talk bears?"

"She's here to listen to us tell her why we want to save the War Creek Ranger Station. So far, the subject has barely come up."

"That's right—that meeting tonight. I'll be there." He started to turn away.

"So what do you think of the grizzly bear reintroduction?" Mary Lynn asked him.

He glanced at Helen to see if he had permission to answer. She propped her elbows on the table and threw both hands up.

"Well, ma'am, I have a farm," he said. "Apples 'n pears 'n beehives. So I ain't that fond of the whole idea. Long as she stays out of trouble…"

"Some people are looking for trouble with her. I'd like to prevent that."

Roger nodded.

A tall, sandy-haired adolescent with freckles that matched Roger's came to stand beside him. "I heard somebody's gonna shoot that bear," the youth said.

Roger tried to shush him.

"Who might that be, young man?" asked Mary Lynn. "If you don't mind saying."

He looked at his father.

"Not our business," Roger told him.

"Well, I shouldn't tell ya, I guess. I just know he's gonna. Maybe already did."

"How do you suppose your friend will find the bear?"

"He's not exactly a friend."

"Okay, got the picture. You tell him to keep his gun at home before deer season. Tell him the forest supervisor said so."

"Okay…but it's really this kid's dad."

"Think telling anybody to keep their guns at home is going to work, lady?"

This comment was shouted across the room by a sandaled man with a long brown braid.

"Some of the Forest Service's so-called customers happen to like knowing there's at least one wild bear back in the woods where she belongs. But the rednecks around here like to take matters into their own hands."

Clayt cleared his throat. "Enough, all of you," he said. "Roger, good t' see ya, but we've got other fish to fry. You, feller, thanks for the input—now skedaddle."

Mary Lynn laughed as the coffee shop emptied of people. "I guess this town knows who's in charge."

Rion wiped the counter after the ponytailed man left. "Thanks for the tip," she shouted after him as the door swung closed. She turned to Mary Lynn. "Now you know why I wanted to keep the place closed. It frosts me the way word gets around—the forest supervisor's over at the Raven's Roost, if you have an ax to grind…"

"Not a problem," Mary Lynn said. She turned her attention to Helen. "I'm sorry this conversation hasn't gone according to plan. What do I need to know before the meeting tonight?"

CHAPTER THIRTEEN

Agnes shook leaves of lettuce into the kitchen sink and laid them in a colander to drain. In spite of the recent heat, it had not yet gone bitter. With the cucumbers, cherry tomatoes, and green onions she'd bought at Helen's, she would make an exquisite summer salad. A loaf of crisp sourdough from Rion would make it a meal. The smell of roasting garlic, purchased from the teepee hippies, filled the house.

Handling fresh vegetables brought Agnes a measure of peace. They were still alive and warm after being rinsed, and she admired each rust-tipped lettuce leaf as she patted it dry. She arranged the lettuce leaves on a platter and started slicing the cucumber. Assembling the salad focused her attention and took her mind away from the raw emotions that had bloomed across town like a rampant growth of bindweed, choking off reason and cooperation, replacing friendly waves from behind steering wheels with grudging glances. The kid that Roger's son knew was apparently bragging around town that his father had shot a bear. With the local forest fire contained, Hunter had returned to the backcountry, looking for the injured sow. His bosses from the Fish and Wildlife Service arrived in town to comb the coffee shops for information about the circumstances that led a citizen to take it upon himself to eliminate what half the local population saw as an unwelcome threat. The other half, mostly newcomers from cities far away from grizzly bear habitat, claimed they did not mind sharing their apple harvest with the single representative of a threatened species.

Signs began sprouting in front yards: *Save a farmer, shoot a bear.* The next day the signs would be seen in the street, torn to shreds. Agnes, like Clayt, had avoided the listening session, but Helen had filled her in. The discussion of War Creek Ranger Station was entirely forgotten when a group of disruptive drunks marched in, carrying someone's bear rug that they'd stuffed with newspapers and hung by its paws from a long pole. "Where's the barbecue?" one of them shouted. Mary Lynn, whose long experience dealing with unexpected interruptions told her to let this one play itself out, sighed and gave Helen a resigned look.

Divisions deepened between the old guard—farmers and orchardists, ranchers, Forest Service employees and small businessmen—and the more recent refugees from smog and cities: summer people, many of them, weekend residents for a few warm months.

Agnes's mind played around the edges of what was really bothering her as she sliced the cucumber and scallions. She missed Hunter. They had recently had The Talk—the kind people have when both are contemplating the risks of embarking on a new relationship. Agnes was pretty sure it would be a bad idea and told him so. Hunter agreed. Together they listed all the reasons why—neither knew how long they would be in the Twisp Valley, and neither had a definite plan for the future. Clayt would give her an endless hard time. And neither Hunter nor Agnes had ever been willing to commit to someone longer than a year or two before finding an excuse to leave. Plenty of good reasons, they assured each other, to never find out if it would have worked.

In the afternoon light, the list dissolved into scattered bits of frail excuses. She and Hunter were flexible, not rudderless. Clayt's disapproval had simmered down once Hunter took over the barn repair. But it was always going to be true that Hunter spent as much time as possible in the backcountry, moving from one place to another. And Agnes always ended up preferring her friends, both male and female, who shared her love of the woods, to the men she had dated. Joan was a more compatible housemate than any of her handful of boyfriends would have been.

From the morass of feelings and denials, the truth seeped into her consciousness. The heck with everything—she knew what she wanted: Hunter. He had sounded as definite as she had when they concluded it would be best to remain friends, allies, and hiking companions. She knew his first love was the bear.

And she knew why. Slowly the War Creek sow had come to stand in Agnes's mind for everything she cherished: a family blown to the winds, a home that was more fundamental than anywhere she had gone since, and most of all, the chance for love and redemption. *Redemption*—she snickered to herself. It had been drummed into her mind that wayward girls were beyond such things. She had grown up cowed by household rules and expectations, by the church and her grade-school teachers. The one she'd had in first grade struck her as a sour old spinster, though she was probably younger then than Agnes was now.

She caught herself in the middle of a long, heavy sigh. *Stop feeling sorry for yourself*, she thought. She would see Hunter when he returned from the woods, and she hoped he would bring news that the War Creek sow was alive and doing well.

Agnes covered the salad with a damp towel and sifted through the pile of mail that lay on the table. She found a manila envelope forwarded by Joan and prepared to write some checks for the bills that had come in since the last batch.

When she opened the package, she was surprised to see a letter among the bills. She knew the handwriting on the return address, that of her friend—at the time they had called each other cellmates—from when she was pregnant. The little funny face Jaz had sketched next to her return address made Agnes chuckle. Spirals of hair sticking out in all directions, eyes crossed, tongue poking out from a crooked smile.

Agnes and Jaz had become instant friends at Mother Cabrini House, both of them scared to death of what the future would bring, both imagining the cruel gossip that whirled in the wake of their leaving school in the middle of the term. They would return with their bellies flat and pick up their schoolbooks, probably ahead of their classmates with the way the nuns made them study. But they would never be the same. They grieved for the lost children they had been, and for the babies they would never know.

Jaz had dropped out of high school to marry the boy who'd gotten her pregnant. Somehow she had made the marriage stick. Agnes opened the letter.

I got a letter from a convent, it began. *Remember Sister Baggy Crease?*

Agnes laughed at Jaz's nickname for the oldest nun in the place, whose real name was Sister Magdalene Cecilia—a mouthful. She had allowed the girls to shorten it to Maggie Cease and Jaz had taken it a step further. She had been kind, and a good listener—unlike the rest of them—and Agnes hoped she had never gotten wind of that moniker.

I guess the old gal's still kicking, Jaz wrote. *She said she remembered me, do you believe that?*

If anyone remembered the confused and frightened girls who had passed through that shelter, it would have been the old nun. Agnes read the rest of the letter quickly. A young man had contacted a series of convents in search of his biological mother. He must have done some serious research, since Mother Cabrini House no longer existed. Had anyone associated with Cabrini gotten the letter, they would have discarded it without reply. Unless the letter came into the hands of Sister Magdalene Cecilia.

Maybe someday I will meet my son, Jaz wrote. *I've already told them to give him my address and phone.*

Agnes fought tears as she folded the letter. Jaz had cried for days while she recovered from the birth, but at least she had always known her baby was alive. Agnes thought about what Clayt had said when she talked to him about it in the mountains. What if her child had been adopted, as he suggested? What if the nuns had not told the truth? She could think of no reason why they wouldn't—yet Clayt had planted a seed of doubt, and reading the letter from Jaz helped it grow.

"What the hell," she said. Putting the bills to be paid aside, she found some paper with which to write a letter to Jaz.

Thrilled that you might find your son. Keep me posted.

She followed with a summary of what she had been doing since they last corresponded around Christmastime, and ended with a question.

Can you put me in touch with Sister Baggy Crease?

The phone rang and Agnes cleared her throat before answering.

"Music tonight," said Rion. "Coming?"

Rion had initiated a Friday night open mike for local musicians—mostly single guys working for the Forest Service—and although she had no liquor license, someone usually brought beer. Agnes said she would see her there.

She drove down the river in the hazy August sundown. Forest fires continued to burn, though none locally. The horizons were pale with smoke and the air remained the same dim amber color she had been seeing for weeks.

When she arrived at the Raven's Roost, her insides leapt as she recognized Hunter, part of a halfcircle of people sitting on upturned logs and pickup tailgates, playing a banjo. For a minute she waited in her car, trying to talk herself down from the immediate sting of finding him in town, since he hadn't called her. Expectations were already worming their way into her regard for him, though she knew she had no reason to expect a thing.

She had a classical guitar back in Helena. She imagined standing up there with Hunter, entertaining the small crowd. But she had never played in front of people, even Joan, though her fingering was accomplished. Agnes played for herself alone, using the guitar in the same way Mary had the piano—to soothe herself with melody. She had taught herself some classical guitar standards and a decent rendition of Psalm 23. Probably nothing Hunter knew how to play.

She closed her eyes and pinched the bridge of her nose, aware of what she was doing to herself. *You've decided it would be a bad idea. Don't mess with it now.* As she stepped out of her car she warned herself to be careful.

Hunter saw her and smiled broadly. He turned the mike over to a small string band calling itself the Methow River Ramblers, found a beer in a cooler, and walked over to meet her.

"I didn't know you played," she said.

"Now you do."

"Didn't know you were back from the hills. Bear news?"

He shook his head.

They stood without speaking, Hunter listening to the music, Agnes wishing she knew what to do with her hands.

"I guess I'll go find a beer," she said.

Hunter looked at her as if noticing for the first time she was standing there without one.

"Shit, sorry," he said. "If I spend too much time in the woods I forget my manners."

He led her to a free seat and fetched a beer. She didn't really want it, but the cold bottle felt good in her hands. Rion stopped to chat as she made the rounds with customers, offering trays of homemade baklava.

"How's it been going?" Hunter asked. He slid onto the bench beside Agnes and sat close.

She tried to remember how they had left their last conversation, for their agreement to be no more than friends was nearly squeezed out of her thoughts by her reaction to Hunter's presence. Her pulse, her tingling skin. *Damn it*, she told herself. *Don't do this.*

"All right," she answered. "I tend to be a worrywart."

"Worrying about…"

"You. With all the fires burning. I wish you'd called when you got home."

"I know better than to ride into a forest fire. But I appreciate your concern."

"Not that I had any reason to expect you to call."

Their eyes met and both looked down.

"At least we won't have to watch the bulldozers tearing down War Creek," Agnes said. "That listening session must have done some good. But they're making Clayt leave regardless."

"Doesn't make sense, does it? You'd think they'd want him around keeping an eye on the place."

"He's been feuding with the ranger. I suppose this is Flintstone's way of showing Clayt who's in charge now."

She didn't tell him the rest of her theory. Collins's name had come up in reference to the bear shooting, and Clayt had strenuously defended him, enough that Flintstone seemed to think Clayt knew more about it than he let on. Rumors to that effect were circulating.

It was after nine and fully dark when the music stopped and the beer ran out. Agnes poured hers onto a juniper next to the building and headed for her car.

Hunter was beside her. "Feel like taking a walk?"

She searched his face, surprised. "Sure, why not?"

"We haven't had enough chance to catch up," he said. He picked up his banjo in its case and nodded toward the dark street ahead.

"Tell me how it went," she said.

"I'm still hoping for the best. The collar might have fallen off and quit working. She might have headed back into the park."

Agnes listened, saying little, as they turned from the main strip and wandered through quiet neighborhoods. There were no sidewalks or streetlights, but no traffic either. She leaned into him as they walked side by side and he laid his arm over her shoulders.

Hunter turned onto a darkened block and indicated a prefabricated house across the street.

"Home," he said. "Want to stop in?"

He offered her some whiskey, which she turned down. He poured a splash into a glass for himself and Agnes wondered if he was more like Clayt then he appeared. If he was a drinker, it was a red flag as far as she was concerned. She perched on the edge of the chair he offered while he slouched across a sofa that looked as if it had been salvaged from a motel furniture sale. Decent quality and clean, but battered.

The whiskey opened him up and he began to tell her about his interest in folk music, what he might do next when the bear project was completed, the places he had been and might return to someday. Then he surprised her with a change in subject.

"I wish our talk the other day had ended differently," he said.

Agnes looked at her hands, her fingers clenched around each other. The surface of her body felt alive with an electric charge—her forearms, face, and scalp flushed with heat. She had not expected to see him at all that evening, so why had she taken a shower and dressed in a pretty cotton shift?

"Me too," she finally said. "What are we going to do about it?"

"It depends. I spent a good amount of time in the last week thinking. You're the first woman I've met in a long time that might be able to put up with me."

Agnes laughed. "Since I can tolerate Clayt, I could handle anyone—is that it?"

"Not what I meant. And you need to know another thing: I'm not looking for a little quickie. I have a lot more regard for you than that."

"If we got together I know it wouldn't be easy. For all the reasons we already discussed."

He sat up straight on the sofa and looked at her intently. "You're strong and smart and independent. Not to mention beautiful."

"I've never considered myself a raving beauty," she said. "But yes, I'm strong and smart. So why am I getting ready to do something we both decided is not a great idea?"

He stood and pulled her to her feet, wrapping her in what she called his bear hug. "What worries you the most?" he asked.

"How old are you?"

He laughed. "Forty. I know—why haven't I ever been married?"

Forty—she had assumed him to be younger than her by five years or more. "Thanks for not making me say it. Of course, I've never married either. I guess that's obvious."

"And you're…"

"Thirty-six."

"That's right—I remember that. Well then, here we are, a couple of middle-aged semi-geezers, neither of whom has found the right person. It's not that I haven't wanted to."

"It's hard to know if you've found the right person before you're waist-deep in the water," Agnes said. "But you know right away when you have the wrong one."

He took her by the shoulders and looked at her face. "And what do you know now?" he asked. "What's your belly telling you?"

"Part of me thinks I ought to be afraid of this. But I'm not."

They dipped their heads together and kissed. Kissed again, with more conviction and confidence.

"Let's put our agreement to stay friends on hold for the evening," Hunter suggested. "We need to gather a little more data before we can make an informed decision."

Agnes was disoriented when she woke in his bed, surrounded by the walls and windows of a strange room. Hunter was no longer beside her, and for a minute she thought he must have risen early and left while she was still asleep. As she came fully awake, she heard him singing from beyond the closed bedroom door and the aroma of strong coffee reached her.

"Greetings, sleepyhead," he said when she appeared.

"Smells good in here. How can I help?"

"Grab yourself a cup. Cream's on the table."

Agnes stood behind him and hugged his back as he stood at the stove. He reached around with one hand and pressed her close while he finished scrambling eggs.

"You were right," she said.

"I usually am. What about?"

"The need for further data. I think we need to continue gathering it."

"Can we have breakfast first?"

They walked arm in arm to the Raven's Roost to retrieve their vehicles. Rion served Agnes a coffee with steamed milk and filled Hunter's travel mug.

"See you soon," he said to Agnes, and they parted with a kiss.

Rion smiled from behind the counter. "Looks like things are moving along," she said.

"I hope I know what I'm doing." Agnes sat on a stool next to the counter and left the tables to customers.

Rion laughed. "You have a goofy look on your face," she said. "Like somebody in love."

"Let's not get hasty. He's awfully nice to me, though."

"Good in the sack, too?"

Agnes blushed. It wasn't something she was used to talking about.

"That would be a yes," Rion said.

"You could use a hand here," Agnes said, as the bells on the door tinkled.

"Appreciate it."

Agnes made coffee and change for the next hour, trying to pay attention to what she was doing instead of reliving the night before.

Clayt gave Agnes a look she recognized, and she wasn't surprised to see it. He didn't say anything when she greeted him, so she sat at the table across from him and asked what was wrong.

"What in God's name were you up to all night?"

"Who wants to know? I don't have to tell you everything I do."

"Long as you are occupying space under my roof you will conduct yourself like a lady."

Agnes refrained from mentioning that the roof did not belong to Clayt. "Have I failed to act ladylike while under this roof?"

"I figured this'd happen the minute you laid eyes on him."

"Clayt, it's none of your business. I don't get why you dislike him—he's helping repair the barn."

"Only reason he's blowin' smoke up my ass is to get at you. Guess it worked."

"Not true," she said. "He admires you."

Clayt mumbled to himself and got up to put his coffee cup in the sink. He stood for a minute leaning on the sink, catching his breath.

"Are you all right?"

"No." He turned to face her. "I haven't been all right in a hell of a long time."

Agnes stiffened. "Right now it looks like more than the usual. Why don't you sit down?"

He did as she suggested, and propped his elbows on the table, his forehead resting in his hands. "Just a little dizzy spell."

"It might not be a bad idea to lay off the coffee for a while. You still have done nothing about your heart problems."

"Ain't nothin' wrong with my ticker other'n bein' wore out." He stared at the table between his elbows. "My life was over when she left. Been a long downhill slide ever since."

"Join the club," said Agnes. "I'm not trying to be mean, but you act like you're the only one who took a hit when she walked out."

Clayt looked at her.

"But," Agnes continued, "I am trying to put it back together. Coming here is part of that."

"You keep wantin' to know where she is…an' I keep tellin' you I don't know."

"I believe you, fine. What I want to know is why she left in the first place. It couldn't have been Will—she would have needed the rest of her family around her after that. And I don't believe it was all about me."

The mother Agnes remembered would have met her at the front door of Cabrini House after she gave birth. She would have wrapped her in her arms and said how glad she was to see her. Then she would have taken her out for ice cream. Agnes's eyes welled and she didn't care if Clayt noticed.

"There was other things, too," Clayt said. "Wasn't just Will, or what happened t' you. But let's just say your situation didn't help none."

"I'll tell you a few things if you'll listen. If you haven't got your mind made up that I'm going straight to hell and it's all my fault. I've suffered plenty for what happened, so maybe I've already done my time in hell."

Therapy had helped Agnes see one thing: that she had been forced. Terms like "date rape" didn't exist when she was sixteen. When Mary questioned her, she couldn't say for sure that she had used every ounce of strength to fend the boy off. And she had to admit that after things had gotten completely out of hand she felt sensations that were frightening and painful, yet thrilling.

She wasn't the first girl in eleventh grade to succumb to hormones and pressure from a boy, but she had been the only one in her class to have consequences. Since then, she had been wary. Boys and girls, men and women, got together as a result of similar urges and for similar pleasures. When the girl or woman skipped her next menstrual period, she frequently found herself alone. Agnes had enjoyed the company of short-term boyfriends for a while, but when they began to pressure her for sex, she backed away.

Until she met Hunter. He hadn't pressured her; he had only opened the door to possibility, and she had eagerly walked through it.

"Well, here goes," she said. "It was at a Halloween party the first time."

"First time?"

"I said you'll have to listen if you want me to tell you this. Somebody spiked the punchbowl and we were all feeling a bit unsteady on our feet. We were going to spend the night at this girl's house anyway, but more people than we planned ended up staying over. Nobody wanted to risk a DUI. It was girls and boys all over the house in sleeping bags, half in the bag ourselves, and I ended up in the same room as Petey Collins."

"Petey Collins! You must've been shitfaced drunk."

Agnes wondered if he meant this as a joke, but he wasn't smiling.

"Anyway, we got together once more after that—I didn't even like him, really. And then he found another girl."

"If y' didn't like him, what the hell?"

"He pressured me. After that first time when we were half conscious, he said he wanted to experience it with all his senses intact or some such horse manure. I said no and no again."

"Could of told me about it. I'd a knocked his sorry little ass across the river."

"I didn't want anyone to know, especially you and Mother. I was ashamed of myself, couldn't look you or anyone else in the eye for a week. Anyway, he finally caught me in a place where no one was going to hear if I hollered for help. He pushed me, punched me, held me down. I went limp since it seemed better than getting hit, but I kneed him in the crotch when it was over. "

Clayt chuckled. "Good for you."

"I told Mother I'd more or less been forced into it. I'm surprised she didn't let you know what happened."

"We weren't talkin' much in them days."

Agnes pushed her hair behind her ears and sat straight, shoulders back. "It felt good to tell you all this," she said. "It helped."

Clayt nodded. "Wish I'd a known it then."

"I wish I'd been able to tell you."

He sat and thought a minute. "Collins know about this?"

Agnes shrugged. "Not unless that no-good son of his said something. Which I'm pretty sure he didn't, once word got around about my so-called condition."

"That must of been what you told 'im when he drove out here all pissed off."

"Something like that."

Agnes felt lighter as she understood that her mother hadn't left War Creek simply out of shame over an out-of-wedlock baby. Mary had left long before that, having created a separate life in her garden, at her piano, at church, and by joining every organization she could that would get her out of the house after her boys had grown into independence. Clayt had been jealous of his wife's beauty and charm, had unconsciously squelched it in his effort to keep it for himself, burdening her with children and the responsibilities of a ranger's wife. After bearing one child after another, a period of barrenness had come to Mary, and Agnes suspected she had resorted to birth control against the rules of her church. With birth control came another possibility: the company of other men. Agnes had no evidence that this had happened, other than Clayt's jealous eruptions when he'd had too much to drink.

Clayt stirred. "Better get back at it. Guess the boyfriend's coming by to help me finish that barn roof."

"He's a good man. Try to see that, even if you don't like what he does for a living."

"We jes' don't see eye to eye about that Goddamned bear, is all."

"You used to love animals. It didn't matter what they were, you said they were all part of God's creation."

"Bears being transplanted to where they don't belong is not the work a' God."

"Would you be glad if someone shot her?"

He didn't answer.

"Do you know who shot the bear?"

"Nope."

Agnes thought about the injured bear, perhaps dead bear, the single animal released as an experiment to see if the greater North Cascades ecosystem with its millions of acres of wilderness was big enough to allow one grizzly bear. Apparently not, thanks to a trigger-happy local. She excused herself and headed for the garden.

The lettuce had begun to bolt, and she turned it under near the far edge. That had been the place where Mary once grew gladiolus, meant only for the altar. The ones picked for the table at home were the imperfect ones, the ones unworthy of gracing the house of the Lord. It was the only part of the garden Agnes did not resurrect.

CHAPTER FOURTEEN

The end of August caught Agnes by surprise. Where had the time gone? Joan had begun calling with more frequency, telling her she was missing some good hikes with their friends and was about to miss the Labor Day bluegrass extravaganza if she stayed away much longer.

"I'm sorry, but I need to stay," Agnes told her.

"That much trouble getting your father moved?"

"I came to help him move, and now I want to help him stay. This place grows on you."

"Aren't your brothers on your case?" Joan asked. "Seems like they were calling here every day to get you out there."

"They don't care if it takes ten years as long as they aren't the ones dealing with it. I'll be back sometime soon—I need some warmer clothes."

After talking with Joan she thought she ought to check in with Patrick, who had not yet returned her last call.

"You were going to get back to me after your vacation to wherever it was," she said.

"Yosemite. It was beautiful, but crowded."

"And I never heard from you."

"Sorry, Ag—busy. Kids are in school now, I got behind at work so I'm putting in extra hours."

"Patrick, why don't you come see your father? If any of us suffered because of his temper it was me, and I'm managing to put up with him."

"Don't be so sure. He was a prick to all of us. Want to talk to Ginger?"

"I called to talk to you," Agnes said. "Don't keep putting your kid on the line."

"Jeez—so sorry. What's going on?"

"What can you tell me about Mother? Did she ever try to help—you know, protect us from him?"

"Are you kidding? She was his servant. Nothing in that pretty little head of hers besides duty. I think she might have been on tranquilizers."

"Really?"

"She drifted around the house half there. Don't you remember that?"

"I saw it differently."

"Clayt was hitting the bottle pretty hard by the time John and I grew up, so we were glad to get out of there. Sorry to leave you behind, but—"

"Not your fault."

"Old man ever hit you?" he asked.

"Once."

"I hope you hit him back," Patrick said with a laugh.

Agnes didn't see what was funny about it, and told him so.

"I can laugh or I can get pissed off," Patrick said. "If he whacked you as much as he did us boys, you'd know why none of us are anxious to come buddy up to him."

"He misses the family. He doesn't have anyone."

"Please. If he's got nobody, it's because he drove us all away."

"He's changing. Not drinking anymore."

"For somebody who didn't want to go—"

"I was the only one willing." Agnes felt her anger rising.

"Able," he corrected.

"Just because I didn't have the same excuses you did."

"We all have good reason to steer away. Don't let yourself get sucked into his little whirlwind of self-pity and condemnation, or you'll end up just like our mother. Ginger wants to say hello."

"Good talking with you, Patrick," Agnes said. "Let me know when you're coming. Bring Ginger and the other kid…"

"William. Certainly you remember his name."

"How could I not? Bring them. See you soon."

Forest fires kept the air dense with smoke and soured the mood of people Agnes talked to—cashiers at Helen's, customers at Rion's. Every conversation seemed to begin with *When it is going to rain?* But she couldn't help smiling. Hunter was part of her life now, and she knew it wasn't the smoke that had shortened his backcountry trips to two or three days. She had become an ad hoc employee at Rion's, filling in for her three mornings of the week—three in a row so she could spend the night in town, and over weekends so she could spend those nights at Hunter's.

For a change, life was full and fun. The weekly music evenings continued to draw crowds, though smaller ones as August ended, the college kids who worked seasonal jobs now starting to leave. She missed their energy and enthusiasm for things she loved, the way they came into the Raven's Roost before work to let her know they were heading up to one of her favorite places, and their reports of the wildflowers upon return. She felt like a den mother, and was sad to watch them leave, but with their departure rentals had opened up, and off-season rates were in effect.

The only thing that intruded on Agnes's contentment was her concern about Rion. She had taken a couple of days off to drive to Spokane, and when she returned her cheerfulness did not come back with her.

"Everything all right?" Agnes asked one morning at the Raven's Roost.

Rion squeezed her face into a smile. "Fine."

Things weren't fine, Agnes knew. "I'm here anytime if you want to talk," she said.

"I know."

"If I can do anything to help, please ask. I'm worried about you."

"Coming into the shop three days a week is a huge help," Rion said. "I need some quiet time to process a lot of things, and you are giving it to me."

"All right, then. You mean a lot to me, you know."

Rion nodded and turned her head. Then she brightened. "I damn near forgot," she said. She pulled a sticky note off the wall beside the telephone. "This guy has a cabin for rent, said to have you call."

Agnes called and the man told her to come right away.

"Back in a few," she said to Rion, and paused to hug her. "Thank you."

The cabin was part of an old resort gone to long-term rentals on a bench above the Methow River. It had what Clayt needed: a living room with a foldout bed, a kitchen area, one small bedroom and a bath. A patch of grass and a trail to the river. Rustic with its creaking wooden floors and sawn-log exterior, it pleased Agnes enough that she paid the deposit before calling Clayt. If he wouldn't move in, she would.

When she arrived at War Creek after work, Clayt was in the same place she had left him early that morning. Along with Rion, he had gone quiet, spending most of his time alone, sitting on the porch steps and staring at the newly repaired barn roof, the singed but surviving pines he had planted forty years before, and the empty corral. Jasper and Agate and Socks had been trailered downriver to Twisp, and without them to nicker in his direction when he approached, Clayt looked bereft. Agnes could hardly look at the corral. War Creek Station was being vacated.

Agnes stocked up on honey and sweet rolls from the Raven's Roost and tried to keep Clayt busy filling boxes of belongings for the move. "You're going to love this place," she told him, but he didn't answer.

She spent one morning on the telephone finding homes for the barn cats tame enough to catch.

"Rion says she'll take one," she called to Clayt.

His muffled voice came from a back closet. "Give her two. She might not notice. What the hell'm I supposed to do with all these uniform shirts?"

Agnes found a box for feline transport to town. Paint, a mostly white calico with coin-sized patches of black and orange, could be coaxed into the box with a saucer of half-and-half.

"Rion'll spoil the hell out of you," Agnes promised.

Hunter was bent over a newspaper at the far table when she arrived. He pushed himself to his feet and hugged her until it felt as if she might disappear into his bulk.

"How've you been?" He kissed the top of her head and released her.

"It's been a whole two days since I've seen you."

"Feels like a month."

Rion came around the counter and took the box, lifted Paint out, and held her up. "What a sweetie," she cooed. "You two are sickening, by the way."

"She's used to living in a barn," Agnes warned. "Better watch her with all those goodies sitting out."

Rion took the cat through the door to her apartment and Agnes could hear her voice, high-pitched as if she were talking to a baby.

"Why does a cat bring out the mother in just about anyone?"

"They're manipulative little predators, as far as I'm concerned," said Hunter. He gestured to the table where he had been reading. Agnes helped herself to a cup of coffee and sat across from him as he folded the newspaper and gathered notebooks to make room.

"Kind of late in the morning for you to still be in town," Agnes said. "What are you working on?"

"Paperwork's caught up with me. The report on that so-called bear attack is finally coming out and they want my input. I hate writing." He smiled and sat back. "Having you to look at helps."

Agnes turned her head, embarrassed by the attention he paid her in a public place. Then she met his gaze and said, "Thank you."

"News," he said. "I finally saw a copy of the investigation from when the Service was here, and found the name of the man who said he shot the bear. I called him up this morning."

"I'll bet he was glad to hear from you."

"He was all right. But he might have been blowing smoke."

"He didn't shoot it?"

"Says he shot *at* a bear."

Agnes sat up and leaned forward on her elbows. "That's great. Maybe he didn't hit her at all."

Hunter shrugged. "I'm not sure what to believe. That kid was lying to me when I talked to him earlier, so this might be another line of crap. He might be covering for somebody."

"Like who?"

"Part of why I'm staying in town today is to find out. Clayt say anything about it?"

Agnes held her breath. A knot formed in her throat and a chill ran along her scalp. Hunter would not ask about Clayt unless some line of evidence led in his direction.

"Clayt certainly didn't shoot that bear. He couldn't have managed it without me knowing, for one thing. His hand was still healing and he couldn't have picked up a rifle, let alone shoot one."

"I didn't imply that Clayt did it. You're defensive all the sudden."

Agnes thought about that. Why had she leapt to Clayt's defense? "I've spent my life thinking the worst about my father, and now I'm starting to see another side to him. I don't want to believe he had anything to do with it."

"Not saying he did, but he does seem to know everything that goes on around here."

"I know one thing: if one of his old buddies is in trouble, he'll do whatever he can to help him out. Collins comes to mind."

"Guy I talked to wasn't Collins."

Rion came back, announcing that Paint was settling in. "I showed her the litter box and she knew what to do from there."

"Let me know if she needs company," Agnes said. "We've got a shitload of barn cats to get rid of."

Rion brought pieces of apple muffins that had fallen apart when she took them out of the pan.

"We're going to have a ton of apples, too," Agnes said. "I'll start bringing some if we can find any place to store them."

Hunter corralled his stack of notebooks with one arm to keep them from tumbling into the muffin pieces. "Being organized was never that easy for me." He watched Rion moving behind the counter and nodded toward her. "She doing okay? It looks like she's been losing weight."

"I don't know what's up. I told her the other day she was getting skinny and she said she was glad people noticed. She hasn't been dieting, I know that much."

"I expect that when she's ready to tell you, she'll speak up."

Agnes sipped at her coffee and couldn't help breaking into a smile. "You're sweet for a bear."

Hunter cocked his head, puzzled.

"You've never noticed your bearlike traits?" She wasn't going to say big and heavy and hairy.

"Bears are loyal," he said.

"Speaking of bears."

"I've been flying this week—cover more ground that way. I want to take a look around the far side of Twisp Pass. It'll be a day hike, and I can do it on my time off."

"Why would you take time off to do your job?"

"So you can come. Remember when you told me early on that you wanted to get Clayt settled and then go play in your old haunts? I figure this was one of them."

"In all the time I spent in the mountains as a kid, I never went there. It's one of those spots I've always wanted to see."

"Even better, then. One thing I should ask: if we find the bear injured—or worse—could you take it?"

"I've had to help put down horses I was best friends with. I imagine I can deal with the death of an animal I've never met. But I sure hope that doesn't happen."

"Not saying it will. But it's something I ask myself every time I go out."

Agnes and Rion watched Hunter's truck back away and turn down the highway. A wisp of cloud angled across the sky. Rion laid her chin in her hand and sighed. "Is it ever going to rain?"

"I've heard that question a hundred times this week," Agnes said. "But there is a cloud up there for a change."

Rion grabbed her hand and squeezed it. "You were only going to stay a week. Couldn't wait to get out of here, remember?"

"I never want to leave. I'm sick of trying to teach math and science to thirteen-year-olds playing grab-ass in the schoolyard. I don't want to look for another job—I have one now, with you. I don't want to babysit Clayt from five hundred miles away." She realized she must be whining like a child and cut herself off.

"And you don't want to leave Hunter."

"Why should I? He makes me happy."

Rion raised an eyebrow. "Nobody can make you happy except you, lady."

"It's not just Hunter, Ri. The longer I'm here, the more I realize I've been trying to find another place just like this. I bought my house in Helena because it reminded me of War Creek Ranger Station, with its covered porch and double-hung windows, even if half of them were painted shut. Most of my friends there are hiking buddies, people I met working for the Forest Service. It feels like I've spent my life in an effort to reconstruct what I had here—minus Clayt."

"And now that Clayt's being less of an old ogre…" Rion smiled. "He's sweet underneath it all."

"I wouldn't go that far, but he is a hell of a lot better to be around since he quit drinking. He's always been one of those mean drunks who turns into, like you said, an ogre—and, well, it isn't pretty."

Rion got up to wait on a customer and Agnes watched the wisp of mare's tail out the window. Heading east, and she should be following it. She had just told Rion with conviction that she thought she belonged here, but if Hunter left for a job in say, Montana, wouldn't she be going too?

"I have a favor to ask," Rion said when she returned to the table. "Long as it doesn't interfere with your bear hunting."

"Sure."

"I have some personal business out of state and I'll need someone to keep shop on a more regular basis. Might be easier for you once Clayt's settled in a few blocks away—you can stay here."

"I think it would be a blast," Agnes said. "When?"

"As soon as everything's arranged. During the offseason a few hunters might show up early, but it'll be dead in the afternoon. I'd open at six and shut her down by one. If you want to close for a day to run off into the hills with your man, go for it."

The bells jangled at the door and Rion jumped up. She patted Agnes's shoulder.

"Thanks, sweetie. You're the best pal a girl could ever have."

Agnes's chest convulsed with a repressed sob as if she were about to collapse in on herself. She had drifted through most of her life feeling like a loner: the only girl in a family of older boys; an opinionated student in Catholic institutions where opinions were not encouraged; a single woman with few close friends, all of whom were introverts like her. But the friends she had were fiercely loyal. Like bears, as Hunter had said. She stared out the window with unfocused eyes and noted that the mare's tails were spreading into a general overcast. Maybe rain was on its way at last.

Hunter and Agnes had packed for a possible overnight, with bivouac gear so they could use daypacks. Hunter brought his bear-tracking equipment, lightweight but awkward, so he was inclined to take as little else as possible. Agnes borrowed a pack from him, too long for her frame, but it easily fit their clothing and she managed both sleeping bags, strapped on top and below. He would carry the smaller, heavier items.

They drove to the end of the Twisp River road, another dozen miles above War Creek Ranger Station. The upper valley closed in on the road as the glacially carved walls stood closer and more vertical.

"I remember going as far as North Creek," Agnes said. "We might have camped at Scatter Lake. It was a very long time ago."

"I flew that country the other day," Hunter said. "Looked like a nice spot—though not particularly bear-friendly."

The road made a turn to the northwest and impressive peaks rose above. For all her time in the mountains, Agnes never stopped being awed by the view from places like this. To her it suggested limitless possibilities, high routes and ridge walks in all directions.

The trailhead was a bulldozed patch of gravel in the forest. Two horse trailers and two cars were parked there, beside a vault toilet and a sign. Five miles to Twisp Pass.

"I know that doesn't sound far," Hunter said. "But we'll gain a few thousand feet. That's why I wanted to get an early start, in case it gets warm."

The overcast remained from the previous few days, and the weather report said rain was falling on the coast. The mountains usually wrung the clouds dry by the time they reached the Twisp Valley, but a cooling rainfall would be welcome.

"Let's hit it, then," Agnes said.

Her stride was long and eager, as it always was when she traveled a trail she hadn't hiked before, especially one that promised spectacular mountains and alpine parklands. The end of summer was the time to be up high: the snow had melted from most of the trails, the fords were easy to skip across, and the nights were cool enough that the insects were rarely troublesome.

The first mile consisted of a lovely walk through deepwoods, where the trail stayed north of the main drainage. The side slope began to open up, with scattered conifers and brush, rock outcrops, and views to the water far below. The route dipped back into the forest where it crossed the north branch of the Twisp River headwaters, a tumbling brook that started high above, at Copper Pass. A footbridge spanned the creek, and the surrounding forest looked as if it had been misplaced from the west side of the mountains, thick with large-diameter cedar, fir, and spruce. The water was clear and cold, the rocks a light gold-yellow under turquoise pools where the sunlight caught and reflected back. Through the deep forest and tall alders, Agnes caught tantalizing glimpses of the mountains into which the trail would take her.

The trail ascended a steep spur ridge, with full-frame views of bare south faces, shattered bedrock and snow-clad cliffs. Crags and towers and arêtes crowned the rugged mountainsides, while their skirts were dressed with talus and long, narrow stands of larch and subalpine fir. Knobs and knuckles of polished stone stuck out from the thinning forest, evidence of past glaciation. Above the spur ridge the trail leveled off and followed a bench of gneiss. The path had been blasted into solid rock, perhaps by Roger and his crew or the men of the Civilian Conservation Corps. Now above timberline, the trail was lined with late-blooming wildflowers, dogbane and bracken fern starting to turn yellow.

Clayt had never brought her here because he didn't want to look over the pass at what used to be his district. *Plenty a' good mountains in our own back yard*, he'd say.

Crescent Mountain, South Creek Butte, Hock Mountain, and Twisp Mountain formed a ragged ridge, the rocks dark and dusty blue in the late August light. Alpine sedge and rushes turned bronze and gold, and a few huckleberry plants were starting to go crimson. Glacier-polished slabs of gneiss, its minerals arranged in deformed bands like squirts of multicolored toothpaste, jutted up from the brush beside the trail. The rock faces were a map of the geologic past for those who knew how to decipher them. Agnes knew enough to see, in the tight meandering streams of quartz pushing aside the darker minerals, the evidence of a long, violent history deep underground. The slabs she walked over might once have been part of an ancient seabed. Now they stood nearly seven thousand feet in the sky, exposed to sun and rain and snow, encrusted with dark lichens and surrounded by the maroon leaves of autumn huckleberry.

Hunter left the trail before they reached the park boundary to get a better view. By the time they stopped at a high point, it was close to noon. The ridge north of the pass was strewn with boulders nesting in wildflowers gone to seed. One of them was flat, resembling a tilted dance floor.

"This looks like the perfect lunch rock," Agnes said. "And I'm starved."

"Ditto," Hunter said. "It wasn't easy keeping up with you."

"I was dawdling." Agnes produced a couple of ripe peaches and a McIntosh apple. "Too bad you don't eat fruit," she said. "Or I'd share this."

"I would try one of those peaches."

She peeled and sliced a peach, dribbling juice over the surface of the gneiss. Hunter took a slice and held it in his teeth.

"You can have the other half," he said.

She guided her lips around the peach slice until her teeth met his. They each bit off half the peach and ate, then performed the trick again—this time without the peach.

"How can I ever get enough of you," he said. "May I have this dance?"

He took her hands and they stood on the rock platform. His voice was a startlingly clear baritone as he began to sing *you fill up my senses* and led her in a slow circle.

The people whose horse trailers they had seen at the trailhead were riding over the pass from the west. They stopped to take in the view and to whistle at Hunter and Agnes, who waved back.

"We ought to decide if we're hiking out or staying," he said.

"If I thought there was a chance we wouldn't stay, I'd have left these sleeping bags behind."

He smiled. "Just checking," he said. "I'm used to doing this kind of thing alone."

They set up camp near a shallow pond just below the pass. Hunter had a permit to bivouac anywhere he needed to, so they found a sheltered spot among stunted trees and boulders. With no one else in sight, they took advantage of the chance to rinse the sweat and dust off with a splash in the pond. They chased each other through the shallows, laughing, until Hunter took Agnes's hand and pulled her into a patch of whortleberry. He cupped her face in his hand and leaned in to kiss her, and then stopped, searching her eyes.

"Is everything all right?"

"I had a strange moment," she said. "When you grabbed me and pulled me down, it reminded me—a whole different time and place and feeling."

"I don't mean to be clumsy or scary."

She leaned into him. "You're not. There's no one I would rather be with than you."

"You're safe. This is now."

"I know," she said. "I love you."

"Likewise," he said. He sat and held her for a long time.

Later, Agnes and Hunter picked enough huckleberries to sprinkle on oatmeal the next morning. Apparently wild berries agreed with Hunter just fine—perhaps because bears ate them. With an hour of daylight remaining, Hunter took the antenna to the ridge for a final check while Agnes wandered the pond's still shore alone. A crescent moon high in the sky became brighter as the daylight faded, and a hazy, bluish glow infused the mountains to the west, distant snowfields suspended in the cooling air.

A shout from the slope above. Hunter was hurrying to meet her.

"I picked up a signal," he said.

He led her to a rock rib above the pond, from which they could look down onto the upper valley of the East Fork. Dagger

Lake, dark and still, lay like an obsidian arrowhead set onto a bed of timber. He pointed at the lake.

"She's right down there. She must be feeding in those wet meadows." His voice was filled with wonder, as if this was the first time he'd ever tracked a bear.

Agnes imagined the bear nibbling sedges on the lakeshore and feasting on huckleberries high on a ridge as autumn passed and the nights grew frosty. A picture developed in her mind, the scene vivid, the location precise: a curve of glacier-polished granite, pale as a sand dune and dotted with alpine larch. A mountain stood at the apex of the long ridge like a petrified wave, the bedrock itself a cornice even without snow. Below the imposing headwall lay an amphitheater of stone, its floor a rubblescape of house-sized boulders. Protected from wind and sun, it would hold deep snow all winter, a perfect den site for a bear. Agnes imagined the War Creek sow sleeping away the memory of her troubled first summer in the North Cascades.

She and Hunter went to sleep that night under the stars and the setting crescent moon, knowing that the War Creek sow was foraging in the darkness less than a mile away.

CHAPTER FIFTEEN

Labor Day weekend brought a spate of late-season backpackers, giving Clayt an excuse to pull on his uniform cruiser jacket and meet them at the picnic table. A younger crowd, they knew Clayt only by reputation and none knew they should bring cookies, although one young couple offered to share their dried bananas. Regardless, their company was a welcome distraction for Clayt during his final days at War Creek. By midweek they were gone, and the hunters who followed did not need his advice on where to find a trophy buck. He was on the verge of becoming do-less, and his melancholy invaded Agnes. The barn was repaired, the tack room organized and reluctantly locked. The cats were off to new homes, except the wild one that had torn into Agnes's shoulder. She set a live trap with plans to have him neutered before letting him go.

"Declaw th' little bastard while you're at it," Clayt suggested.

"We're going to have to cull some of this stuff if it's going to fit into your new cabin," Agnes said. The rooms had looked plenty big before she started moving boxes. Though War Creek Ranger Station was nearly empty at this point, Clayt had yet to spend a night at the new place.

"What's the rush? We still got a week. Got nothin' left but files an' crap to go through."

As the house emptied, it took on the shadowed appearance of an abandoned small-town museum. The main room, for decades the hub of activity at a busy ranger station, held an unfamiliar echo when either of them spoke, each word circulating around the room as if from the distant past. The interior became a vacant space where life once took place, the windows pitted by years of sand and hail, the floor planks dark with decades of patina, worn smooth as wooden scoops at the front door and kitchen sink. Agnes imagined a fresh-faced intern with the historical society dressing up as a ranger's wife, a young man out in the tack shed posing as Clayt. Tourists with no idea what had happened at War Creek would be charmed by the picture of the olden days, when foresters worked in the forest and their wives at kitchen gardens. Tears quivered at the edges of her eyes. Her history would be erased, traded for a sanitized version of a past that never was.

Along the Twisp, the cottonwoods and spreading dogbane had begun to turn yellow. Agnes went to the porch for a box of apples from the tree beside the garden, breathing in their rich vanilla-spice scent. Early apples—perfect for making the chunky, cinnamon-laden sauce her mother used to can. Half the harvest had already been delivered to Helen's Market, the rest to Rion and Hunter. She had kept one box to make a batch of sauce.

A car turned off the river road and over the bridge, Seattle plates. Another pilgrim, coming to see the master. Agnes waited for the woman to leave her car, offered her an apple, and told her she would go fetch Clayt.

She found him in the office off the living room, sorting through papers. He started when he saw her in the doorway and quickly stuffed them back into a folder.

"You have a visitor," she said, and took the apples to the sink.

Clayt donned his cruiser jacket with its many pockets for maps and compasses and timber measurement devices. In his faded cotton cruiser and straw hat, he stepped out onto the porch like a man twenty years his junior. Agnes stood at the screen door and watched him striding to the steps where the young woman waited, wearing hiking shorts and a t-shirt that advertised the state's largest outdoor store. A blue bandana held her long blond hair. Agnes could tell she was a veteran hiker from the tone of her leg muscles and the scuffed boots she wore. It took a moment to recognize her—she had come into the Raven's Roost the day Clayt met with Mary Lynn.

"Where you headed, young lady?" Clayt asked as he shook her hand.

Agnes could see how pleased he was with his performance, and his appreciative audience. She was surprised Clayt didn't trot out his brogue and call her a lassie.

"Home," the woman said. "I wanted you to know what I found up there."

He lowered himself onto a bench at the picnic table and gestured for her to do the same. "First you got to tell me where y' mean by 'up there.'"

The woman unfolded a map across the table. Unable to contain her curiosity, Agnes fixed lemonade for both of them and took it outside.

Clayt ignored his, but the woman accepted her drink gratefully. "I'm Serena," she said. "You work at the coffee shop."

"Agnes Clayton. Where did you hike?"

"I did a Sawtooth traverse," she said with pride. "Hoodoo Pass to Reynolds Creek in five days. I climbed Star Peak and the Camel's Hump."

"That's impressive," Agnes said. She wanted to hear more, but the whistle of a teakettle sent her back into the house.

She made herself mint tea and glanced out the front window. Clayt was bent over the table and appeared to be questioning Serena with great intensity, the muscles of his back taut under the cruiser jacket. Agnes slipped into the office space where he had been working, the office that had served as her bedroom when she was a girl. The close, familiar darkness of the space, the blind pulled down over the window, made her shiver. The desk had been removed to accommodate her twin bed—more of a cot, really, but the stuffed animals had hidden the metal headboard. An unused oak door blank turned the cot into layout space for the folders Clayt was sorting. The one he had hastily set aside lay under Agnes's fingertips.

She monitored the discussion at the picnic table through the blind's slats and glanced through the folder. She found a disciplinary memo from around the time he had shot Brownie. It was written in standard bloodless bureaucratese, chiding Clayt for having taken things into his own hands when he knew proper procedures. Attached to the memo was a handwritten note signed by the same man who had signed the letter of reprimand, the deputy forest supervisor. *I covered your ass on this one, Clayt,* it read. *Don't let it happen again.*

Agnes couldn't tell by reading them what Clayt had done. Shooting his own dog for chasing cattle would have earned him an award, not a reprimand. Along with the memo she found a typed transcript of what must have been Clayt's statement on the incident. He had never been one for bureaucratic obfuscation, so at a glance Agnes knew what had happened. A bear had gotten into Brownie's grave. Clayt went after it and shot it. Such an action would not have been cause for discipline, except the bear had been a grizzly.

Agnes moved as if in a dream, floating in slowmotion. Carefully she placed the memos in order and put them back into the folder where she found them. She heard raised voices outside and got up to investigate.

"Everything okay here?" she asked.

"This ranger guy—is he your father?" Serena demanded. "He just told me to go fuck myself."

"Clayt wouldn't say something like—"

"He sure as hell did." The woman turned to Clayt. "I'm reporting your ass, mister."

"They can't exactly fire me, now. I'm a volunteer."

"What're doing wearing that uniform, then? I heard you were the one to see about anything going on around here. If you're not the boss, who is?"

Agnes couldn't help herself. "Fred Flintstone," she said. "You're much better off talking to Clayt."

"Not if he treats me like this."

"He must have had a reason."

"I was reporting a mess I found in North War Creek."

"Sounds like them search-'n-rescue boys could a done a better job cleaning up," Clayt said.

"Then I wanted to know how come everybody around here is so against this bear. All the hunters I ran into up there: *We can't wait to shoot a grizzly bear.* We're talking about a single bear in thousands of square miles—a threatened species, the only one in the whole North Cascades that we know of, wearing a collar, my tax dollars went to pay for that, and now some bozo has run off and shot her. I was wondering why the ranger didn't seem to give a damn, but I guess if he's just a volunteer he doesn't have to."

"Afraid you landed on a sore spot with my father," Agnes said. "If he won't apologize to you, I'll do it for him." She walked Serena to her car. "I was in the upper end of Bridge Creek a week ago," she said. "We found grizzly tracks. I think she's okay, and I hope she stays in the park. Away from all these bozos, as you call them."

"I'm glad to hear it. Sorry I flew off the handle."

"I'll take a pack horse up War Creek to clean up," Agnes said. "Thanks for that information. And believe it or not, a number of us care about the bear."

Serena got into her car and rolled down the window. "Somebody like you ought to be working out of this ranger station. At least you know how to talk to the public."

"Thanks, but I'm capable to telling people to fuck off too." She smiled to be sure Serena knew she meant no harm.

She passed the picnic table where Clayt sat with the map folded under one arm.

"Done with your lemonade?" She picked up the glasses and started for the house, then paused. "You used to lecture me about watching my tongue. I can't believe you said that to her."

Clayt came into the house while she was washing the lemonade glasses. When she turned from the sink he was standing at the table with the folder she had been rifling through.

"So, you been nosin' around affairs that don't concern you, missy."

Agnes didn't answer. In her haste to vacate the office she must have neglected to lay the folder exactly as it had been. The sort of thing Clayt never failed to notice.

He started into the office to put away the memo.

"You might have told me what happened," Agnes said. "It explains a lot of your strange behavior."

"What strange behavior?"

"Every time I—or anybody else—mentions that bear-shooting incident you start shuffling your feet and changing the subject. Even Mary Lynn noticed it that day at the coffee shop. Or else you start yelling, like you did to that lady. You must still be feeling guilty over something that happened years ago."

"I got nothin' to feel guilty about," he said. "About what happened years ago or what happened a minute ago. Now if you'll mind yer own damn business, I'll get back t' work."

"Fine," Agnes said. "I'm taking the rest of these boxes. God knows where we'll put them."

She filled her car and then paused, ready to leave.

"Clayt," she hollered from the bottom of the steps. "I'll see you later."

He came out the front door. "Phone's for you." He looked annoyed. If it had been Rion or Hunter, Clayt would have said so.

She took the porch steps two at a time.

"Hello?"

"Agnes, it's Mary Lynn."

"Uh-oh."

Agnes's thoughts flicked back to Serena and her promise to report Clayt. Perhaps she hadn't managed to smooth any feathers after all.

"Yeah, we need to talk. I'm in Winthrop for a meeting today— can you meet me for lunch?"

—

There was nearly no traffic on the state highway heading north. As Agnes drove, she sought familiar landmarks among new businesses and real estate offices. On the surface, Twisp hadn't changed much in the years since she left as a teenager. The town continued to shun the Western-kitsch image that its neighbor to the north, Winthrop, had adopted, with false-fronted saloons and wobbly boardwalks, opting instead for a take-it-or-leave-it town that invited tourists to buy a tank of gas and move on. The newspaper reported that an ad hoc beautification committee sought to redevelop the old sawmill—an abandoned eyesore along the main highway—but the only fix the town could afford was to fence it off so travelers wouldn't see it.

In spite of the best efforts of the town and county governance to avoid it, the vacation home market was on the rise. Subdivisions were being platted and advertised as getaway lots with national forest access. New roads wound their way into the foothills, inviting would-be homeowners to take a look. Agnes hoped the recent fires would discourage the trend.

But she liked the new people she met. In the two months since she had come back to War Creek, she'd spent a good deal of time at Helen's Market, the post office where she picked up general delivery mail from Joan, and the Raven's Roost. She had been surprised to see so few familiar faces. If anyone in her high school class remained in the area, she had yet to encounter him or her, which suited her fine. The last person she wanted to see was that half-tamed kid of Collins's—Pete Junior. She imagined him now, a drunk like his old man. He'd probably moved up to Winthrop to join the real-estate parasites tagging along behind the development of ski areas and four-season resorts. He would look good in one of those fancy cowboy hats whose bands were stuffed with gaudy feathers.

Once beyond the subdivisions, the highway passed scattered fields, farms, and stands of ponderosa pine, the Methow River flowing clear and bright beside the roadway. The view she remembered well calmed Agnes as she drove to meet the forest supervisor. The river was low and shot with sunlight between banks cloaked with golden aspens and cottonwoods, and with so little traffic, Agnes could slow down and absorb the river's peace. Too soon, she crossed the bridge leading into Winthrop.

She arrived a few minutes early and sat on the edge of the restaurant's wide plank porch. A Forest Service vehicle pulled into the lot, and she saw Mary Lynn was followed by her usual entourage. As more green fleet vehicles turned in behind her, it was clear there would be no meeting with the supervisor. She watched the group file into the restaurant and tried to make herself invisible when she saw Flintstone. She caught Mary Lynn's eye.

"I'm sorry about this," she told Agnes. "Everyone wants my ear at lunchtime."

"Shall I just drive back home then, or what?"

"Give me a minute. I told them I had an appointment."

Flintstone was holding the door for the last few stragglers, including his boss. With great willpower Agnes resisted giving him the finger. One inappropriate outburst from a Clayton was more than enough for the day. She shot him a mock smile instead.

She dangled her legs over the edge of the porch and swung her feet. Town was quiet with the summer tourists gone. The amber light of autumn fell through a row of cottonwoods, beyond them the prattle of the Chewack and Methow rivers flowing together. Agnes drifted in a state of pleasant suspension to help the time pass.

At last Mary Lynn came through the door and took a seat beside Agnes. She had a sandwich and a plate of fries and offered to split her lunch. Agnes was charmed by the supervisor's lack of pretension, game for sitting on a wooden deck in her uniform skirt and heels with the daughter of the Forest Service's primary pain in the rear.

"So," Agnes said. "You must have heard from Serena. That was quick."

"This summer's been hellish. Forest fires on every district, missing hikers—and not only that poor fellow who was chewed up down your way—and in the middle of a busy season we're doing a study on consolidating districts. That's the main thing this bunch is stewing over." She pointed with her elbow toward the restaurant.

"Seems like you already did that once," Agnes said.

"Now it looks like Twisp is going away—the office will most likely be here. For all I know the whole forest is about to get absorbed by the Wenatchee."

Agnes savored the thought that Flintstone might follow Clayt in being kicked out of the ranger's chair, but she hoped Mary Lynn would not be removed from hers.

Mary Lynn squirted ketchup onto her fries from a plastic envelope. "Anyway, the reason I wanted to meet with you. Apparently Clayt sounded off in a rather rude manner to a visitor."

"I tried to smooth things over. He never acts like that—well, not with the public."

"We can't have anyone in uniform telling tourists to go fuck themselves, and he knows he's not supposed to be wearing a uniform in the first place. That would be impersonating a forest officer."

"In his mind, Clayt was born a forest officer."

Mary Lynn offered her a sympathetic smile. "I know it must be hard on him. I've done all I can to cut him some slack, but we're getting too many complaints."

"More than Serena?" It was true Agnes had been spending more time in town than at War Creek. What else had she missed?

"All I know is what the ranger reported." Mary Lynn urged half of her sandwich on Agnes, who, famished, accepted.

"You're aware that my father doesn't exactly get along with Flintstone," Agnes said.

Mary Lynn put down her sandwich and laughed into her napkin. Agnes flushed, realizing she would no more have heard this nickname than her own.

Attracted by the sound of his boss's laughter, or the length of her absence from the table, Flintstone himself came out the door.

"You slipped out on us to talk to her?" He said it as if Agnes wasn't there.

"She had an appointment—you guys didn't."

Agnes stood with all the dignity she could muster and directed her outstretched hand toward Flintstone. "Pleased to meet you, mister ranger. I didn't get the chance when I made an appointment with you and you stood me up." She offered him a crimped smile and an outstretched hand until he reluctantly shook it.

"Care to join us?" Mary Lynn asked. "This is about what you told me this morning."

"Thought it might be."

"So what did Serena say?"

"Who?"

"The woman my father supposedly told to go fuck herself. They seemed to be having a congenial conversation when I was there."

"She accused him of shooting the War Creek sow."

Clayt hadn't told her that part. "I guess that would have made him mad," Agnes said.

"He's done it before, you know. Or maybe you don't."

"Told somebody off? Of course I know that, he's done it to me often enough."

"That's not what I'm talking about." Flintstone crouched on his heels, sadness in his eyes.

Mary Lynn wiped her hands on a crumpled napkin. "You've lost me, guys."

"Back in the old days." Flintstone spoke wearily, as if he had told the story many times before. "We had a bear problem and Clayt took care of it in his usual way, off by himself and not asking first. Shoot, shovel, and shut up. Turned out it was a griz and he could've got his ass in a sling without a buddy upstairs taking care of him." Flintstone spit tobacco juice into a paper cup. "So anyway, we got to get Clayt's ass out of there so he doesn't create any more headaches for me. This gal Serena isn't the only one I got complaints from."

Agnes could do nothing but stare into her hands, lying in her lap like a pair of broken wings.

"I'm sorry," said Mary Lynn. "But it looks like your dad has done this to himself."

Agnes nodded and stood. "We're almost packed up. He'll be out by the end of the week."

"Wait a second," Mary Lynn said. She nodded toward the restaurant door to indicate Flintstone's presence was no longer needed. "I'll join you shortly." She turned back to Agnes. "Sit down for another minute if you have time. I gave Clayt my word he could stay until we turn the water off."

"I won't be there to keep him out of trouble. Besides, I have nearly everything moved—it won't make any difference."

"Can you give me some insight on how to handle him? I don't want to make this any worse. He could be a good ally; I know how he reveres the Forest Service. One thing you can tell him is there won't be any demolition at the site until a thorough investigation of the historical significance is completed. That could take a good long while."

"I thought that would have been done ages ago," Agnes said.

"We had a report, but no one knew about that album of your father's. Now copies of some of those photographs are starting to turn up."

"Where is it, anyway? I promised Clayt—"

"I'll see that he gets it back as soon as he's moved in. I don't want it getting lost in the shuffle."

Agnes started to stand again, then paused. "He's been cleaning out old files," she said. "I found one this morning, and Flintstone was right—he shot a bear when I was a kid, and the deputy forest supervisor covered it up. That's the way the good-old-boy system worked."

Mary Lynn rolled her eyes to indicate she was all too familiar with the good-old-boy culture in the Forest Service. "How it still works," she said.

"He didn't have anything to do with what's going on now, though."

"It's hard to tell exactly what is going on."

"If I find out, I'll let you know," Agnes said.

On the drive back to Twisp, Agnes's thoughts raced. She called Clayt from the Raven's Roost.

"Mary Lynn told me about your little conversation on the phone," she said. "I need to get some boxes unpacked, so I'm staying in town tonight, and not with Hunter—he's in the woods."

"I don't give a damn who y' stay with."

He sounded hurt. "Unless you need me there for something," she added.

"Nope," he said. "I'm givin' that old truck to Collins. Takin' it for a final drive this afternoon."

"You don't have to leave this minute. She told you that."

"Place is empty as a cave. Don't see much point in hangin' around talkin' at my own damned echo."

"See you tomorrow, then." She hung up slowly, in case Clayt thought of something more to say before she put the receiver down. His tone had her worried.

CHAPTER SIXTEEN

At the cabin Agnes began to unload boxes. Clayt would like it once he got used to living in town, she thought. It even had a river view—of the Methow, not the Twisp—from the front window. The cottonwoods were bright yellow now, and they reminded her that she had to make a trip to Helena soon, to gather clothes and boots for the colder weather that would soon descend on the Methow Valley. As long as Hunter was here, she would stay.

She found the boxes that held contents from the filing cabinet—heavy things, full of old papers Agnes tried to get Clayt to leave behind. Each folder was labeled with a Forest Service file designation number: *2200 Range Management; 2500 Wildlife Management; 1900 Administration and Planning.* Smeared carbon copies of decades-old memos and directives. Why on earth was he keeping this junk?

With the folders she found a shallow metal box. She opened the clasp and saw that it was divided into dollar bill–sized compartments, as if for making change at a yard sale. Instead of bills the compartments held letters. When she saw the woman's handwriting she knew she had found correspondence from her mother.

She waited for her heart to slow. What she had sought was in her hands at last, but she hesitated. Just holding them, tangible connections to her mother, was enough for a moment, but the moment soon passed and she began to read.

She didn't pause to contemplate, but simply read each letter in sequence, looking at the dates and recalling how old she would have been. Most of the letters came during her first year in college. When she finished, she felt vaguely disappointed and wondered what she had expected. Great revelations, she supposed, of why her mother left and where she had gone and what had happened to her. Instead, the letters contained small talk and trivial news, not written in the tone of an estranged wife but of one who had to leave on a temporary errand and was checking in as a formality. Someone who barely knew the man she was writing to. At the end of each letter was a brief—and Agnes thought breezy—*Take care of her, now.*

Take care of whom? By the time these letters were written Agnes could take care of herself. One of them included a comment that Mary was relieved to know her daughter had gotten into Gonzaga, where they "might teach her some morals."

Agnes sighed. Convinced that Mary had left for reasons other than what Clayt had told her, she forgot to consider one possibility: her mother had condemned her as much as Clayt had. Her image of Mother Mary, with her gentle ways, now evaporated, replaced by a tight-lipped, judgmental, and unforgiving woman. Agnes did not think her memory was faulty, or that a person could change so suddenly and completely. She realized she had no idea who her mother was.

She folded the letters and pressed them together and stared out the window to the cottonwoods. For all she knew, "Take care of her, now" referred to someone else entirely. Another woman, a dog, a fucking barn cat. She had preserved in her mind a mother who was the opposite of Clayt, delicate and fine-boned, dark-haired, quiet. An accurate portrait—she had photographs. But what had her mother really been like beneath the surface? As Patrick confirmed, she had considered herself Clayt's partner, supporter, and fellow enforcer. Clayt's rule held when it came to raising children. As far as Agnes knew, Mary had never opposed her husband when he dished out corporal punishment. She had not intervened when he slapped Agnes.

She felt the place on her cheek smarting as it had when she was sixteen, her throat clenching to hold back sobs while her tears dropped onto the family table. Clayt, exasperated by her helpless bawling and angry with her for what she had done, had stood up and smacked her across the face. "Shame on you," he hollered. "Shame and shame again. You're no child a mine." Mary wouldn't look at either of them.

Agnes had run into the bathroom, where she locked herself in. She buried her face in a towel and cried until she was exhausted. When she looked in the mirror, her entire face was red, but his handprint still showed up. She wanted Mary to knock gently on the door and ask to come in, to sit with her on the edge of the bathtub or take her into a bedroom and rock her, tell it was all right and God would forgive her if she repented. That she—Mary—forgave her. She wanted her mother to love her, that woman who sat with her on quiet evenings and showed her piano chords so she could play them on her toy organ.

None of this had happened. No one spoke when she left the bathroom and went into her room and closed the door.

No one had spoken the next day, except in low tones to each other. It wasn't long before Agnes was driven to Spokane, the three hours passing mostly in silence, and delivered to Mother Cabrini House to wait out her pregnancy far from the scrutiny of classmates and their parents. Her mother did not hug her before she and Clayt got back into the car. Agnes watched them drive away out the window beside the front door of a cold, dark, unfamiliar house. They were going back to War Creek without her, and glad of it. She cried for her mother—the one she had wanted, if not the one she had—until one of the nuns came and showed her to her room.

She called Hunter's number to leave a message. To her surprise, he answered.

"I thought you were in the hills," she said.

"I came out a day early so I could be with you."

"I'm on my way to you now."

Hunter opened the door and pulled Agnes inside. He let her cry into his shirt until her sobs quieted, then ushered her to the folding table, stacked with clipboards and notebooks and equipment. He whisked a stack of papers away and sat her in a chair and stood beside her, massaging her neck with one hand.

"Something bad happened while I was out," he said. "Clayt?"

She shook her head.

"What, then? I'll get you a beer."

"Just water, thanks."

He perched on a chair next to her and held her hand as he watched her drink the water.

"I'm okay—really."

"Could have fooled me."

She set the empty glass on the table. "Better."

"You don't need to talk about it now."

"I'm not sure where to start," she said. How could she put into words a lifetime of memories that had been turned upside down?

"There's a time to talk and a time to just be."

"In that case, I be miserable."

"I know one thing that might help." He took her hands and helped her to her feet. "Just let me hold you a while."

He was right. What Agnes needed was intimate, prolonged closeness to another human body. To be held and held tighter, compensating for years of never being held at all.

Hunter listened as she told him about the letters she had found, the reason she had come to his door in tears.

"I grew up afraid of Clayt—his anger was so unpredictable. The way he swatted my brothers. The way he got when he had a little too much whiskey in him. My mother was the opposite. She kept us out of his hair while he worked, made us all sit down for meals together, loaded us into the car for Mass. She was like an oak mast, and he was a loose sail flapping in the wind. Strong, but erratic. I see now that being Clayt didn't mean he didn't love us. Maybe more than she ever did."

"He loved you all the time. How could he not?"

"He didn't love me when I came up pregnant," Agnes said. "He disowned me."

Hunter smoothed her hair and kissed the top of her head. "I doubt Clayt had the best of childhoods," he said. "You never know what makes a person the way they are. Maybe your mom had it worse."

"I never knew my parents as people. I had no idea what their hopes and dreams and battles were—they kept all that under the rug so they could provide us with a stable home. And we did have that. I grew up thinking everything was pretty good—I loved my childhood, in fact. When things started falling apart I blamed it all on Clayt and his drinking. I know there's more to the story, but he hasn't been willing to say."

"Probably too painful," Hunter said. "You don't have to know everything to know you survived. You're going to be all right."

"You must be tired. I'm sorry to dump all this on you."

"Not as tired as you are. Come on, let's go to bed."

The next morning she called War Creek Station around seven o'clock, when Clayt would be up making coffee. No answer.

"Maybe they turned the phone off already," Hunter suggested. "I'm out of eggs—oatmeal okay?"

"I had a feeling when I talked to him yesterday...something wasn't right. I hope he didn't go and drive that old truck into the river."

"Clayt's not going to do something like that. Let's go have a look. I'll take you."

She hugged him hard. "I have so much to thank you for. You know what I need before I do."

"I know you need plenty of support right now."

He served two bowls of instant oatmeal, one piled with dried apricots and raisins, the other plain.

"I have to get to Montana soon," Agnes said. "These summer shirts aren't going to do forever. I'm going to try to keep it short—a week, tops."

"Maybe it will work out so we're both away at the same time. Then one of us won't be sitting around wishing the other was here."

"Where are you going?"

"North American Bear Symposium. That's in Albuquerque—then I have to give a talk at a meeting in Missoula."

"Perfect. I'll grab my winter stuff and meet you there."

"Sounds like a plan. Now, let's get our asses up to War Creek."

Clayt's truck was gone and Agnes saw no evidence that he had been home. Tuck was standing in the yard between the house and corral, the white tip of his tail wagging tentatively, as if to ask what was going on. When he saw Agnes and Hunter he ran toward them.

"I can't believe he'd take off and forget about his dog," Agnes said. "This isn't like him at all."

She gave Tuck his breakfast while Hunter checked around the buildings for clues that Clayt might have stopped in and left again. The wild tomcat stared from the barn loft.

"One place to try," Agnes said. She opened the passenger door for Tuck. "Collins."

Before they reached the turn into the Collins's place, Agnes spotted Clayt's truck parked in the weeds. Hunter pulled into the long drive and parked beside it. A curtain moved at a back window. Collins came out and closed the front door behind him.

Agnes rolled down the window. "How long's he been here?"

She heard Clayt's voice coming from inside the door. It sounded as if he were crying into a pillow. She caught a whiff of whiskey.

"You've gone and gotten him shitfaced," she said. She leapt from the truck. Collins started to speak but Agnes cut him off. "Save it," she shouted.

"He was shitfaced when he got here," Collins shouted back.

Agnes turned in a circle, as if to find a magical ladder coming from the sky to lift her out of this nightmare. "I knew there was something wrong. Damn it—I should have come up yesterday. You have to let me see him."

"I don't know how else t' put it, but he don't want to see you."

Hunter got out of the truck and wandered down the drive with Tuck. He surveyed the little farm and its neat rows of old apple trees, heavy with fruit.

"We were doing so well," Agnes said. Tears sprang to her eyes and she looked away, not wanting Collins to see.

"Ain't because a' you, girl. He just don't want you seein' him like this."

She gathered herself and pushed past Collins and through the front door. Clayt was sitting on a broken-down sofa with the heels of his hands in his eyes, moaning. Collins followed her in.

She sat on the sofa beside Clayt.

"Get him some water," she told Collins. "Clayt, listen. Can you hear me?"

Collins brought a chipped china cup and Agnes held it. Clayt took it with a trembling hand and sipped. It slipped from his hand and Agnes caught it before it hit the floor.

"Thanks," she said, passing the cup to Collins. "Maybe you could get Tuck in here."

Collins went out and returned with Tuck a minute later. The dog wormed his way between Clayt and Agnes until he was on the sofa, licking Clayt's face. Clayt clutched his supple ruff and hugged him, now openly crying.

"It's all over," he mumbled. "All over."

"Nonsense," Agnes said. "What you need is more water and some sleep."

Clayt didn't answer but continued to clutch Tuck.

Agnes stood. "Now what?"

"I'll take care of him. Promise. No booze."

She studied Collins's face. "How can you expect me to believe that?"

"Fer one thing, he drank it all. I don't want to see him hurtin' like this any more'n you do."

"I'm not sure I have a choice. He's in no shape to move."

"I kin get 'im into town once he sobers up. Hell, he kin stay here with me long as he wants."

"Got something decent to feed him? And Tuck? I can take the dog with me but I think it'll help Clayt if he stays."

"Freezer full a venison I been needin' to eat up."

"Call me at the Raven's Roost—number's in the book and I'm there before six. I'll be staying at the old River Bend Resort—cabin five. If you need anything from town, call. Call to let me know how he's doing. If he starts getting too bad he's going to have to go to the clinic. His heart's on the blink, in case he didn't tell you."

"I know it when I see it. Don' think we haven't talked about it."

"Well, he wouldn't talk about it with me."

They went outside and Agnes gave Hunter a weary look.

"Under control for the moment," she said. "I think."

CHAPTER SEVENTEEN

When Agnes opened her eyes the next morning, Hunter was stroking her hair and watching her.

"Thought I'd have to wake you," he said.

She lifted her head off the pillow so she could see the alarm clock, then lay back. "I have at least three minutes before I have to get up," she said.

"Wish my flight were later," he said, and leaned in to kiss her.

"If you do that again, you're going to miss your flight altogether."

"Wouldn't that be too bad." He kissed her again on her lips, then her nose and ears, until they were both laughing.

"Okay, on the count of three, we get up," she said. "One…"

Hunter flung the sheet back and bounded out of bed. "Beat ya."

"Only because you cheated."

Agnes sat up and frowned. "I don't know if I'm doing the right thing."

"What, being with me?"

She stood and embraced him, pressing their bare bodies into one another.

"Letting Clayt stay with Collins. The two of them have never been a good combination."

"Given the options, what else could you do?"

"I know. But I don't like it."

"I thought things were going better than you expected."

"They are, so far."

So far, Clayt had recovered from what Collins described as his "bender." Agnes made sure the house was well stocked with coffee, juice, and her homemade applesauce. Clayt was sober, but unsteady on his feet. His stocky frame was slack, the skin hanging off him. Agnes had agreed to let him stay with Collins while she was in Helena, and ordered Collins to force-feed him if necessary, and to get him out fishing.

Hunter loaded his travel bags into Agnes's car and they took off for the airport.

"I'll see you soon," she said as she saw him off.

"Be good. Best to the old man." He blew her a kiss and she drove away, feeling empty without him. Glad that it was nearly six, she drove to the Raven's Roost and let herself in.

Rion looked surprised. "Aren't you the early bird."

"I just took Hunter to the airport."

"I don't know what I'm going to do for the next couple of weeks without the two of you to make fun of."

"When are you heading back to Detroit?"

"I might get out of here as early as next Monday."

"But I won't be back in time to run the shop."

Rion flicked her hand dismissively. "Not to worry. It won't hurt to close the place for a few days—not like I have a ton of customers this time of year."

A truck pulled into the parking lot.

"Want to bet?"

Agnes went to the door to unlock it and found Roger striding toward her.

"First and freshest cup is for you," she said.

"Better make it to go—son has a buck down on Wagner's place and we're off to pack it out. I wish he hadn't done it so late in the day, but he had a good shot."

Rion poured coffee into two large cups and fitted lids onto them. "One for your kid too," she said. "Bet he didn't sleep a wink."

Roger thanked her and asked Agnes how Clayt was doing.

"You don't want to know," she said. "He's better than he was a couple of days ago."

"I'll fix 'im up with some jerky." He started for the door, then turned. "Been good havin' you around. Good for your dad."

"Thanks, Roger." She waited for him to leave, but he stayed where he was. "Is there something the matter?" she asked.

"That time my kid shot 'is mouth off in here?"

"I remember. Some friend of a friend or his father…"

"Well that friend was hisself and th' father was me."

Agnes stared at him.

"He was tryin' to show off in front of the brass."

"Roger, I can't believe—"

"I didn't shoot at no griz—even I ain't that dumb. Had some hives knocked over though, even with a hot fence around 'em. Black bear come into the place one night lookin' to grab his snack of honey and I let a couple of shots loose over 'is head. Wasn't tryin' to hit him, just scare 'im off. Whole thing got rolled into the flap about that griz."

"Did you talk to Hunter about this?"

"He called. I didn't say much, scared my kid was in hot water."

"If you told him it happened on your property—"

"I told them other fellas that come here to ask everybody in town what was going on. I figured he knowed that much."

Agnes shook her head. "What a mess. Why're you telling me this now?"

"Guess this thing about Clayt come up."

"You knew about that, back then?"

"We all knowed it. Bear ate your little dog—Clayt was broke up about that."

"Your coffee's getting cold," Rion put in.

He started, as if he had forgotten entirely that he was supposed to be packing out deer meat. "I'm off, then," he said.

"He's a funny fellow," Rion said when Roger left.

"It's hard to imagine Clayt being that upset about a bear eating a dog's carcass when he's the one that shot him."

"Clayt shot your dog?"

"Had to, he said. Brownie was getting into trouble with cattle."

"He shot a dog he knew you loved. No wonder he was upset. Certainly he didn't want to do it."

"No, I'm sure he didn't."

"He loved you, Agnes. As much as any father would. Maybe more."

"More than he ever let me know."

After stopping at the post office to pick up her general delivery mail, Agnes sat on the cabin sofa sorting it. Another envelope from Joan, but this one held no bills. Only a note to say she couldn't wait to see her, and thought she ought to forward along the letter that had come. Agnes looked at the return address and felt a ripple of anticipation. She didn't recognize the address itself, but she knew the letter was from the old nun. Jaz must have written her.

She couldn't get past the first line without stopping to grind the tears from her eyes with the heels of her hands. *Agnes Clayton—of course I remember you, my dear. I remember all the girls.* The letter was typed, perhaps dictated. The tone was warm and conversational, as if a much younger Sister Magdalene Cecilia were sitting beside her. Perhaps, in a world that must still hold a miracle or two, she was. Agnes felt her presence as surely as she had felt Hunter's enveloping her for most of the night before. The sister mentioned the number of young people she had put in touch with birth parents, who later sent thanks and even came to visit. *At last I am doing God's work*, she wrote.

Finally she got to Agnes's question.

My dear, about your child. I pray for your forgiveness for withholding the truth, but the decision was made to handle it that way in your case. You were one of the sensitive ones. Our purpose was to find loving homes for the children and send the young women back to repair their lives. Unless the girl's parents agreed to adopt the grandchild as their own, we did not let anyone take a baby home. After many difficult situations arose, we began evaluating the girls. With a few of you, we thought it best to tell you that your baby didn't survive.

The sister went on to say that she had no information about where the grown child might be, and records of the adoptions were not available to her. She offered, with Agnes's permission, to include her on a registry of birth mothers, which adopted children could query once they came of age.

Agnes sat back and absorbed this information. She had a child out there in the world somewhere, an adult by now, assuming he or she had not met with untimely disaster. Perhaps this young man or lady still lived nearby—Spokane, Seattle. Her pulse quickened with possibilities. She would write to Sister Magdalene Cecilia immediately with permission to place her name on the register.

The kindly worded letter notwithstanding, she understood how places like Mother Cabrini House operated. By necessity, she supposed. She would carry the baby to term, have it taken from her, and then be expected to return to high school as if nothing had happened. Adoptive parents paid considerable sums, so there was no backing out of the deal. The girls were made to sign away their babies while still under sedation. "We're nothing but handmaidens," Jaz had told her at the time. "It's a business, and we're the worker bees."

Mother Cabrini House was long gone, but it stood in Agnes's mind as dark and imposing as the day she'd arrived, a plain-looking four-square house on a bare lot. Lace curtains behind tall double-hung windows, a heavy oak door, shadowed from the street by a deep, covered porch. She had faced it from the sidewalk, and two small windows under the upstairs dormer stared back. A social worker accompanied her as far as the porch steps, where they were met by a sad-faced nun in a black habit. Agnes wanted to wrest herself from the grip of the woman beside her and run, but she was too confused and terrified to do anything but march up the steps and allow herself to be taken inside. Iron railings surrounded her as she ascended the porch steps. Then the front door closed behind her.

CHAPTER EIGHTEEN

The outdoor light was on and Joan was waiting for her when Agnes arrived in Helena.

She ran to the car and hugged Agnes before she was completely standing.

"It's great to see you," Joan said.

"Likewise. I never expected to be gone so long."

"Need help carrying your stuff? You must be exhausted."

"Long drive," Agnes agreed. "But pretty. The fall colors are amazing." She opened the back of her car. "Take these," she said, passing Joan a box.

Joan peeked inside to see twelve pint jars filled with chunky applesauce. "Can't wait. Come on, I have a surprise."

Joan led her to the house, dark but for the porch light. When Joan opened the front door, the house smelled like baking bread. The living room light popped on and a chorus of female voices shouted *Welcome home!* and broke into laughter. Friends spilled from hiding places behind doors and furniture.

Agnes accepted hugs from all of them.

"Sit," Joan ordered. "Unless you have to…" She nodded toward the bathroom.

"Thanks."

The house's single bathroom smelled like lavender, from a bottle of essence sprayed on a basket of pinecones. The ceiling light gave off a familiar pinkish glow, and the sink and tub were loaded with bottles of various toiletries, the way they had been the last time she was there. For a disorienting moment, it was as if she had never left.

When she emerged, she was steered to her favorite chair and a glass of champagne was placed in her hand. As soon as her champagne glass emptied, another would appear.

"Enough," she said. "Or I'll fall right asleep."

"Good timing," Joan said. "Dinner's ready."

Seven women sat in a circle in the crowded living room, some on chairs, others on the floor. Agnes answered questions about her summer and took some teasing when she mentioned Hunter. Mostly, she listened to the news, much of which she had already heard from Joan. More exhausted than she realized until finishing her second glass of champagne, she was glad to sit back and be entertained.

After the party Agnes and Joan washed and dried the plates and let the lasagna pan soak.

"It was so good of you to do this," Agnes said. "It makes me sad I'm not going to stay for very long. I'm supposed to meet Hunter in Missoula next week."

"At least you're going to be here over the weekend, so we can get out for some hiking. I'm going to take Friday off. But right now, I have to go to bed—work day tomorrow." With another long hug, Joan excused herself. "Your bedroom's just the way you left it," she said. "Except I dusted and vacuumed."

"You're sweet. Good night."

Agnes wandered around the house, looking at the craft-fair art she and Joan had hung on every wall, the windowsills covered with river-washed glass shards and bits of driftwood, smooth round stones from their walks along the upper Missouri. The house seemed to embrace her as her friends had, as the familiar hills surrounding Helena had when she came into town with dusk falling fast.

But she found she could not return the land's welcoming embrace. Driving over MacDonald Pass a few hours before, she had begun to feel strangely out of place. The scene beyond the highway was one she knew well, but in the way of a dream or a distant memory, a landscape of the mind and not of the heart. Now, as she thought back on it, she realized her sense of dislocation had struck just after she crossed the Continental Divide. No longer in the Columbia River watershed, she felt as if a door had closed behind her. Mountains rose in the rearview mirror, blocking her view to the west. Moist Pacific air had followed her as she passed Spokane, Missoula, and the forest-cloaked foothills of the west slope of the Rockies. The air felt different east of the divide—drier, scented by the salt and alkali of drawn-down reservoirs, of bunchgrass and juniper and lodgepole pine. Helena had once reminded her of home, and she had stayed for that, but a surrogate would no longer do. She flicked the window blind to look out over the lights of town, the silhouette of a long, dome-shaped mountain in the distance. "Not your fault," she whispered.

Agnes took a shower and went into her room. Tired but not sleepy, she started sorting wool socks and thermal underwear, laying them in a neat stack on the floor. She searched a drawer with old papers until she found what she was looking for: the pocket notebook she had kept while at Cabrini House, filled with quotes from Christ and her scribblings about what each meant to her. She hadn't remembered the inscription she'd written on the cardboard cover—*All That Matters*. What had she been searching for when she assembled this collection? Maybe nothing more than words of comfort: *Believe in me and you will see Heaven. Your sins are forgiven.* At a time when forgiveness was unattainable for her, she had tried to believe in the power of those words, so fervently that she convinced herself. But when she returned to War Creek, she discovered there was someone whose forgiveness she needed more than that of Christ—one whose blessing would never be conferred.

Her guitar was in its case under the bed, the one thing that Joan hadn't gotten around to dusting. She opened it and sat on the edge of the bed with the instrument, testing its tuning after months without having been played. Quietly, so not to bother Joan, she laid her fingers on the strings. Her mother used to enter a trance-like state while playing the piano, and sometimes she didn't notice when Agnes slipped through the front door after school. Perhaps she had pretended not to hear, reluctant to forsake her time alone when she had no one else's needs to respond to.

True to her quiet nature, Mary wasn't volatile like Clayt; she kept her anger submerged below the surface. While her quietude was mostly mild, she was also capable of stony silence. It had been harder for Agnes to take than Clayt's temper. Agnes wanted the gentle mother, the shared quiet that wrapped them in contentment when no one else was in the house. Maybe that contentment had lived only in Agnes's imagination. She didn't want to pursue that thought. but she understood how Mary could be transported to another place sitting at the piano, because she felt the same thing with the guitar.

A small auditorium-style classical, it had a mellow tone. She could lose herself in music of her own making, and would feel refreshed after twenty minutes, as if she had been in a state of deep mediation or under hypnosis. Her fingers led the way through a memorized sequence of chords as Agnes considered why both she and her mother sought escape through music. Agnes played to soothe herself, to settle the sadness of her early life the way pollutants could be made to settle to the bottom of a pond. It did not make them go away, but life was easier when they weren't at the surface. Perhaps Mary had also tried to bury her disappointments this way.

Agnes strummed gently, stopped to turn a peg, and strummed again. She fell unconsciously into the same tunes she always played—snippets of old folk songs, a few bars of Bach. She was playing her usual opening notes and suddenly stopped, recognizing the melody and its significance. Slowly she began to play again, with more intention. She plucked the entire melody once, then started again, this time singing along in a barely audible voice. *The Lord is my shepherd, I shall not want.*

—

Agnes walked into the hotel lobby and found a seat from which she could watch both entrances. After a minute pretending to read the crumpled front section of the *Missoulian*, she asked the front desk to call Hunter's room. He wasn't in and had left no messages for her, so she went into the gift shop and bought a copy of the current bestseller by Larry McMurtry, the story of a middle-aged man confronted by a daughter he has never seen. A story she imagined could be similar to her own.

It was after eight when a group of boisterous men swept through the double glass doors. Hunter spotted Agnes and peeled away from them. She laid her book aside.

"How long have you been waiting?"

She stood and he opened his arms for a bear hug.

"Shall we find some grub?" he asked.

"Weren't you just coming back from dinner?"

He glanced toward the elevators where his group waited. "We were having a beer. But I'm starved. You?"

"Can I put my stuff in your room first?"

He carried her duffle and opted for the stairs rather than the elevator. She slipped into the bathroom, and after scrubbing her face with a hot washcloth she felt ready to present herself at a restaurant. When she emerged Hunter was sitting on the edge of the bed perusing her novel.

"Any good?" he asked.

"So far. How's the conference?"

"They're all the same. Best part is connecting with people, seeing what else is going on. Job market is tight for anyone looking for a permanent job."

She looked at him questioningly.

"Someday I'll have to consider it. For now, I couldn't ask for more." He held his hand out and she took it. He pulled gently and she sat beside him for a long kiss.

"I missed you," he said. "How are you holding up? And Clayt?"

"Collins surprised me. Both of them are on the wagon, and

Clayt sounds good on the phone. Still weak, though. I tried to talk my brother Pat into going there for a few days until I get back. Excuses, excuses—I'm sick of them."

Hunter squeezed her hand. "You're the only one of the bunch with a heart," he said. "Clearly your brothers are determined to leave it all to you."

"Pat and I have talked a couple times about how things were when we were growing up—of course, with eight years between us, his perspective was different. He's mad at Clayt but seemed angrier with Mother."

"You look tired. Want to say the heck with dinner?"

"I thought you were starved." She kissed him. "I missed you too."

Agnes expected the restaurants to be empty by nine, but the one she chose was packed. The only seats available were at a table with a group from the bear conference who were working their way through shared snack dishes and pitchers of beer. Hunter introduced her to the man she ended up sitting next to, and took a seat across the table. For the next hour she sipped at her beer, rummaged through carrot sticks and Buffalo wings and listened to the talk about wildlife management and the shortcomings of certain practitioners who were not at the table. Agnes wished she had stayed at the hotel. She had wanted to find a quiet table for two—a candle would have been a nice touch. An unrealistic scenario in a town full of bear guys. In any public place, one of them would have found Hunter and barged in on their conversation.

They left the restaurant late and walked back to the hotel.

"Dinner wasn't exactly what I had in mind," Agnes said.

"You could have ordered something else."

Agnes laughed. How dear he could be, and how clueless.

"I was talking about the company. It felt like I was sitting in on your conference."

"I couldn't help that."

"I know."

He stopped and turned to her. "I hope you also know I love you."

"Yes," she answered. "I do."

Hunter flew to Twisp the following day. Agnes's car was packed with gear—winter clothes, hats, gloves, a pair of skis, her guitar—but she managed to make space for him and his baggage.

"You might get home before I do," he said. "I've got a long layover in Spokane."

She gave him the McMurtry book to read while he waited and headed for the freeway westbound.

She drove ninety miles to Lookout Pass before stopping to stretch her legs. She walked along the lower edge of the grassy ski area and was about to get back into her car when a state patrol vehicle pulled up behind her. The patrolman was looking at her license plate as he got out of his car.

"Agnes Clayton?" he asked.

Emergency scenarios flashed through her mind: Hunter's plane had crashed. Joan was hurt. Her house burned down.

"Yes, what's wrong?" She fished in her wallet for her driver's license.

He looked at it and handed it back. "Is your father Bradford Clayton?"

She nodded. "Oh, Clayt, what've you done?"

"He's at Sacred Heart Hospital in Spokane." He gave her a sheet of paper with telephone numbers and an address.

"Do you know what happened?"

"Apparent heart attack. I'm going to call dispatch and let them know we found you. They'll tell the hospital that you're on your way."

Agnes made it to Spokane in two hours. The main entrance to Sacred Heart, floodlit and glowing from every window of its fourteen floors, stood like an angel with its wings spread. She drove most of the way around the imposing structure before finding a place to park. She retraced her route on foot to reach the main entrance.

Collins was slumped on a sofa when she found the nurse's station.

"How is he?"

Collins looked at her as if he didn't recognize her. His eyes were red at the margins and he didn't look as if he'd slept. "Outta surgery," he told her. "Can't see him yet."

"Tell me what happened—were you there?"

"We were down at the river, fishin', like you told us. He wasn't feelin' well, he said, and sat down. Face all pale—I had a hunch what was happenin' and got 'im back to the house. EMTs fetched him right out of there."

"You saved his life."

Collins dipped his head. "S'pose so."

Agnes stood at the nurse's station and leaned on the counter. A Sister of Providence regarded her from a mural-sized photograph on the wall. Her head was wrapped in a tight-fitting black hood with a wimple of starched white linen encircling her face. It reminded Agnes of the high collars that dogs wore to prevent them from chewing on sutures. The sister who came to the far side of the counter looked more comfortable than her forebear in the grainy photograph. Her headgear was reduced to a simple band and short veil, a bit of her dark brown hair showing.

"Can I help you?" the nun asked, and Agnes realized it was the second time she had done so.

"I'm here to see Bradford Clayton."

"No visitors yet, I'm afraid. He's still in the recovery room."

"He's my father." Agnes heard her voice crack.

The sister nodded. "I guessed that. We heard you were coming."

Gingerly Agnes settled onto a blue upholstered chair across a low table from Collins. "I tried to get him to the doctor about his heart," she said.

"Nothin' as stubborn as an old man," Collins said. "Gettin' the boot outta War Creek broke his heart. Just broke it all to hell."

"There were a lot of things that broke his heart over the years."

"Y' don't get to be our age without a few." Collins turned his attention to the newspaper he had been reading.

Agnes sat back on the chair and closed her eyes. Not that many hours ago, she was kissing Hunter and putting him on an airplane, expecting to see him before the day was over. She ought to call and let him know what had happened.

"Miss Clayton? Follow me, please."

Agnes walked down the polished linoleum hallway, enveloped with the quiet, methodical sounds of urgent medicine. She felt her pulse in her throat as she was led to a dimly lit room.

Clayt was sitting up. Instead of the many tubes and wires she expected to see, he was tethered only to an IV fluid bag. He looked surprised; then his head and shoulders fell back onto the pillow.

"Hello, missy."

She pulled a chair close and took his hand.

"I'm glad to see you," she said.

"I don't know what th' hell happened. I was fishin' with old Collins one minute an' the next I wake up here."

"He told me. He's out there waiting to see you."

"Why'n the hell don' he come in, then?"

Agnes turned to the ICU nurse. "Wouldn't that be okay? He's as much family to Clayt as I am."

"I'll bring him down."

Agnes told Clayt what Collins had told her. "You've had a heart attack. But it looks like you pulled through."

"What'd they do t' me?"

"I don't know exactly—I assume I'll have the chance to talk to the surgeon."

"They patched up your balky ticker," Collins said.

Agnes made room for him and Clayt started to talk but ended up coughing.

"Don't bother," Agnes said. "You need to rest."

"He does need to rest," the nurse said. "But he needed to see you."

Agnes stood. "We'll be right down the hall," she said. She bent to give her father a kiss on his forehead.

"Thanks, missy," he said. His eyes were clear and watery. Collins turned away, blinking.

"A breath of fresh air around this place," the nurse said as they walked back. "When they brought him in, he was cursing a blue streak at all the sisters trying to help him. 'What th' hell ya doing to me? Get that damn thing offa me!'" She laughed. "He doesn't care what he says or who hears it."

"Never has."

"We lost some staff recently—a terrible helicopter crash. His carrying on and sense of humor made everybody smile."

Agnes knew this about her father—regardless of what was going on with him, he was able to give what others needed, particularly if they were strangers. The ranger stepping up to do his job, serving the public.

She and Collins took their seats again.

"Guess we're here for a bit," he said.

"Who's minding your place?"

"Got one a' the boys over for a couple days."

She didn't want to know which one. "That's good of him," she said.

"An' good o' you to be there for your old man. Where the hell are all your good-for-nothing brothers? He's been spending every Christmas and Easter with me for lack of any family that gave enough of a good Goddamn to come visit."

The nun at the desk shushed him.

"Sorry, Sister." He picked up his newspaper.

"I need to make a phone call," Agnes said.

"As long as you reverse the charges." The nun passed her a cordless phone.

"No problem."

She dialed Hunter's number and he answered on the first ring. "I'm in Spokane," she said. "Clayt's had a heart attack."

CHAPTER NINETEEN

Agnes waited in a seat next to the nurse's station while Collins and Clayt said their so-longs. She was staring out a floor-to-ceiling window at a slate gray sky when someone walking toward her caught her eye.

"There you are," Hunter said. Agnes ran to meet him. "What's the news?"

"He's doing okay for somebody who just had bypass surgery. He's out of the ICU."

"And what about you?" He kissed her forehead.

"I'm fine. It's been kind of peaceful. Give me another hug."

"In front of the nuns?" he whispered, and she laughed.

"Let's sit."

She went back to the row of chairs beside the window. Hunter sat close and took her hand.

"When do they say he can go home?"

"A few more days."

Collins appeared at the nurse's station. "Guess I'll be headin' out," he said to Agnes. He nodded to Hunter. "Damned if half a' town ain't here."

Agnes thanked him for what he had done. "He's lucky to have a friend like you."

"Changed yer tune about me, eh?"

"The two of you can help each other stay off the bottle."

"Don't plan to quit cold turkey. But ain' touching a drop around Clayt. You let me know when y' git home—Tuck'll be mighty anxious t' see somebody besides me."

An early dusk fell with the overcast and it looked as if snow was a possibility.

"They'll be wanting us out of here soon," Agnes said to Hunter. "Want to say hello?"

When they entered Clayt's room, he was asleep. Hunter put a finger to his lips. "Let's let him rest—you can see him in the morning."

Clayt was finishing breakfast when Agnes arrived at the hospital.

"Hunter's on his way to Twisp with all my worldly goods," she said.

"Y' shoulda gone too. I'll get Collins to come back down when it's time."

She took his hands. Her desire for Hunter was matched by his for her; it was her relationship with Clayt that needed attention. She and Hunter had plenty of time, and Clayt did not.

"I think it's more important for me to be here."

"Well, if you're gonna hang around, missy, it's almost time for Mass," he said. "Didn't expect t' damn near die before you'd finally come."

She glanced at her image in the mirror above a free-standing sink. "Am I dressed all right?"

He chuckled. "Most of 'em'll be in hospital gowns."

Agnes found that she was moved by the simplicity of the ceremony, truncated and without a lengthy sermon, stripped to the essentials, like the quotes from Jesus Christ she had once gleaned from the matrix of warlike verbiage in the Bible. It was a small congregation of worshippers, a dozen or so, some in wheelchairs, some struggling to stay awake. There was no pretense, only goodwill and acceptance in a group of survivors humbled by age or illness. Like the service, they too were stripped to their essence. Agnes thought these were the people Christ would have chosen to be his friends. Hospital Mass was a weekly reminder of human vulnerability and interdependence, giving each person a reason to have hope that he might recover, or at least die in a state of grace.

Thin hosts dissolved on the patients' tongues and they bowed their heads. The priest's hand was like the branch of a great tree, each tongue a small and temporary leaf, sustained by the wafer. When the priest came around to Agnes and held up a host, she hesitated. It was a mortal sin to participate in the sacrament when she hadn't gone to confession in decades. Should she turn her head away while the priest was murmuring *The body of Christ*? Make a scene and destroy the communion among these people?

"Amen," she said, and opened her mouth.

She would hear all about it from Clayt, but that didn't worry her now. No bolt of lightning from the heavens struck her down for her sin, and she thought she might be forgiven, given the circumstances. For a religion that touted forgiveness and redemption, the Catholic Church had had little to offer along those lines when Agnes was a child. Its resounding themes were all about shame and blame and guilt and condemnation. Only perfection brought favor, and no one was perfect. Church and home and Mother Cabrini House had offered her the same grim message: a disapproving oversight of wild, unruly children, a careful doling out of affection, a stern and humorless presence. There was no place for such attitudes in the hospital, where the gift of life was not taken for granted. Forgiveness was assumed, and no one in the congregation would dispute that assumption.

By Wednesday Clayt was declared fit to go home. Agnes stood beside the open car door as he was wheeled to the passenger side. Having survived a heart attack that could easily have killed him, his spirit was subdued. Ranger Bradford Clayton, lord of the War Creek Ranger District, lived no more. In his place was a sober, gentle, aging soul. As she drove out of town and onto Route 2, Agnes smiled at the thought that this was the second time she and Clayt had shared a ride back from Spokane. Now, she was in charge, and she wouldn't treat him the way he had treated her. She looked over at him and smiled.

"Heading home."

"Always hated this stretch a road," he said. "Hours before you start t' see some mountains."

He slept as they passed through miles of blond wheat stubble and plowed fields, the farming towns of Davenport, Creston, Wilbur. Some of the settlements were small enough to make Twisp seem like a city, and Agnes wondered what people did there, with no access to public land and only dirt roads and mile-wide wheatfields as open space. Yet the country had its own austere beauty. A mile ahead of them, scattered squalls dropped rain that didn't hit the ground. Undulations in the prairie gathered shadows and sunlight, and in places that weren't cultivated, the seedheads of native grass and wildflowers bent before the wind. Agnes rolled down her window to take in the clean scent of Columbia Plateau air as they approached the crossing of Grand Coulee at Banks Lake.

The road dropped into the gorge between walls of layered basalt. The wide, choppy lake spread out of sight to the north, while south of the impoundment the creek seemed to go underground. Scoured topography remained from the Pleistocene Epoch, when a massive pluvial lake named Missoula broke through its dam of retreating ice and flooded this country, a geological catastrophe of such proportions it was hard for Agnes to picture. Beyond the coulee, more wheatfields, tiny towns, grain elevators, abandoned houses and one-room schools.

Clayt stirred. "That's more like it," he said, pointing at the windshield.

"All I see is powerlines."

"Christ sake, over there."

The Cascades had begun to come into view, a dusty blue silhouette on the horizon.

"Soon as I see that, I know I'm home," Clayt said.

"Once we're on the other side of the river, I'll know it."

"You and me, we ain' so different that way. Always loved them mountains."

At Chelan Falls, they crossed the Columbia and headed north. The Methow emptied into the Columbia after another twenty miles, and as she turned into its valley, Agnes fought tears. "I don't know how I ever stayed away this long."

"Didn't exactly make y' welcome, then, did I? I wished all that hadn't a happened."

"Me too. But it did, and now we're dealing with it. I just wish I were driving back to War Creek."

"Not half as much as I do."

"It's not going anywhere—we'll get you up there for some more fishing."

An early snowfall had frosted the mountainsides above town and low clouds hugged the Twisp River valley. The cottonwoods were dark along the river, most of their golden leaves blown off.

Agnes helped Clayt to the cabin and settled him onto the sofa where he could look out the window to the river.

"First night here at last," he said as he looked around. "Might do."

Agnes had most of his belongings put where they belonged, old photos hung on the walls—whatever she could do to make the interior feel like home to him.

"Ain' so bad," he said. "But I'm glad t' be damn near anywhere at the moment."

"Let me get Collins on the horn for you—he'll be bringing Tuck by."

Clayt lay down on the sofa and Agnes covered him with a woven throw she'd brought from Montana. "You talk t' him," he said. "I've had enough for one day."

CHAPTER TWENTY

The end of October was a bright flare of color in the mountains, the trails lined with scarlet huckleberry bushes, scree fields outlined in mountain ash. Agnes took Clayt up the North Cascades highway, before it closed for the winter, to see the larches turning yellow and amber. More snow had fallen, and the larches glowed like candles in the gloom of a misty day. Clayt was getting stronger, heartened by the people who stopped in to visit. Agnes spent her nights at Hunter's and brought Clayt dinner and breakfast, made at the Raven's Roost. With Rion in Detroit, Agnes opened the shop for a few hours in the morning and took Tuck for long walks in the afternoons. Unable to answer any of the questions about Rion that came from customers, she called and left messages for her. Rion would invariably call back in the late afternoon when Agnes wasn't there. *It's been hard to get to the phone*, she said. *I'll call again when I can.*

The brilliance of autumn faded and the storms began to tumble over the crest of the Cascades, bringing deeper snow to the high country. Hunter followed the War Creek sow, now moving south near the crest of Sawtooth Ridge where she had been back in June. He found her tracks in the snow, high on the east side of the divide. He came back from a ride in Reynolds Creek with news that he had found blood staining the white drifts.

"I hope she didn't run into some deer hunters."

"I've talked to a lot of them," Hunter said, "letting them know she's around and trying to get some cooperation."

"Things calmed down around here since she went back to the park. Now it looks like that might change."

"She might have scoped out denning spots a long time ago. I'll bet she's going to end up in the South Fork. What I don't like is how slow she's been going the last few days."

"Can I do anything from the Raven's Roost? People have been picking up those brochures."

"That's a big help. Take some across the street to the greasy spoon, if they'll stock them. I'm going to be spending a lot of time in the backcountry until she dens."

Agnes was used to him being gone a good deal, but if he actually told her she wouldn't be seeing much of him, she knew what that meant. Things always took longer than planned.

Clayt had settled into the cabin with more satisfaction than Agnes would have predicted, but the space he had to move around in, and the small patch of lawn, took some getting used to. No horses nearby, nowhere for Tuck to run off leash, except to chase a stick in the river.

Agnes watched her father from the cabin's picture window as he bent to run his hands over Tuck's ruff. She was dialing her brother Matt.

"You still planning to come?" she asked when he picked up the phone. "You can stay at the little apartment at the coffee shop—it's cozy and you'll have some privacy."

"How is he?"

"Physically, doing fine. Better every day. But I think you'll be surprised by his change in attitude."

"Nothing like a little heart attack to get your attention."

"It started when he sobered up. If I can get along with him, anyone can."

Clayt came in while she was talking to Matt and she handed him the phone. His side of the conversation consisted mostly of grunts and the occasional *yep*. Agnes thought he would belie what she had told her brother, but he surprised her before hanging up, saying, "It'll be damn good t' see ya, son."

He turned to Agnes.

"I've got cabin fever. Got time t' take an old man for a drive?"

She knew what this meant: he wanted to go see War Creek.

Before they reached the bridge over the Twisp River, Agnes knew something was not right. There was a vacancy in the tall pines whose crowns had been continuous, too much sky showing above the barn and the corrals. Beyond the bridge the road was gated, with a sign reading U.S. GOVERNMENT PROPERTY—NO PUBLIC ENTRY. Agnes slid a glance in Clayt's direction to gauge his mood.

"Why do they have to rub our noses in it?" she asked.

She imagined one of Flintstone's minions keeping guard, hiding out in the barn and ready to write her a ticket if she dared to cross. Tuck had no such worries. As Agnes crept forward he began to whine in the back seat. She reached around and opened the door and off he went, tearing down the road and sniffing furiously. Agnes stared for a minute at the planter barrels she had filled with geraniums and petunias, turned on end and emptied of flowers and topsoil. One petunia still fluttered a violet bloom in the chilly wind. The windows were shuttered and a sheet of plywood blocked entry to the barn's loft. Agnes worried about the cat that remained, and then figured he was probably more content than he'd ever been with the place to himself.

She took all this in while Clayt stared straight ahead. She followed his gaze and saw the reason for the open sky: the place had been clear-cut. The ponderosas that Clayt had planted were gone, their branches stacked into teepee burn piles.

"That fucking asshole," she said.

Clayt leaned on one elbow, face in hand.

Agnes turned the car around and called Tuck.

"Wait," Clayt said. "I damn near forgot the reason I came."

She helped him out of the car and he leaned against her as they squeezed between the gate and a boulder. He directed her to the back of the toolshed and a box of split kindling.

"Behind there," he said, pointing with his toe.

She found the kindling lighter than she expected, and realized it was a decoy, the box only a few inches deep. She set the kindling box aside and found a bundle wrapped in oilskin and tied with baling twine. Clayt had tied the twine to form a handle on the top, and Agnes lifted it easily. She replaced the kindling and they retreated without a word.

When they were back in her car she asked, "Why didn't you get whatever that is sooner?"

"Forgot all about it till we talked t' yer brother."

"Are you going to tell me what it is?"

"You'll see."

Agnes was closing the Raven's Roost for the day when Clayt called.

"Guess who just showed up?"

"My brother, huh? Be right over."

Matt and Clayt were engaged in an awkward conversation when she arrived, Matt perched on the edge of the sofa and Clayt at the table. Matt looked deeply relieved at Agnes's arrival. She gave him the closest approximation of a bear hug that her slender frame would allow. He was tall, as slender as she was, and his bristle-cut hair had begun to show some silver. He wore a tiny diamond in one ear.

"You have no idea how good it is to see you," she said.

Matt held her shoulders and inspected her. "Baby sister. Look at you." He gestured around the room. "Sorry I couldn't have been more help with this."

"You're here now, that's what matters. Did you two eat lunch yet?" She held up a bag of unsold bran muffins.

"She's been bakin' up a storm over there at the Robber's Roost," Clayt said. "Tryin' to put some skin on these bones."

Agnes saw that he had strewn the table with stacks of notebooks and a writing tablet that he covered with one arm. He looked tired, as if he'd already had enough company.

"You want us out of your hair for a while? I can get Matt settled in over at Rion's."

"We had a good talk. Now why don't you two visit a while. We'll have lunch in a bit."

Matt drove her the few blocks in his fancy new Accord, still smelling of plastic fumes.

"Wonder what he's working on," Agnes said. "Did he tell you?"

"He was busy mulling over what I told him."

"You told him?"

He turned to face her. "I was afraid he might go before I had the chance. It just seemed like the time."

"What'd he say?"

"Not much. He just sat there nodding, as if it explained a lot. One thing he didn't do was jump out of his chair and call me a damned heathen and tell me I'm going straight to hell."

"I told you, he's gotten better about that kind of thing. Just make sure you take him to Mass if you're still here on Sunday."

They arrived at the Raven's Roost and Agnes let them in.

"Watch the coffee beans," she said.

Matt looked around, taking in the wild-faced stoneware masks on the wall, tapestries of wool and driftwood and the rest of the oddball items Rion called her *redneck hippie décor*.

"Cool," he said. "Never expected to see a place like this around here."

Paint came out from the back room and wound her lithe little form around their legs. Agnes reached down to pet her, but Matt didn't seem to notice her at all. He examined each piece of art as if it were endlessly fascinating.

"How long's it been?" she asked.

"Since I saw the old man?" He shrugged. "Five, six years."

"I've spent more time with him in the last six months than I did in the first fifteen years of my life. He's pretty broken up about having to leave War Creek, but getting used to it, I think."

"We should go have a look while I'm here. I have these memories, but who knows how accurate they are."

"It doesn't look the same. The Forest Service—well, Flintstone—cut down all those pines he planted."

Matt laughed, a full-throated eruption from deep in his chest, and his gold fillings glinted when he threw his head back. "Flintstone! I forgot all about him."

"Oh yeah, he's the ranger now. That really gets Clayt's goat."

"I don't remember any pines."

"You won't miss them, then." She thought for a moment before asking, "What do you remember about growing up?"

He sat on one of the stools beside the counter.

"Want coffee? Look at me, going into Rion mode as soon as somebody sits down."

"No thanks. What's 'Rion mode'?"

"Rion owns the place. I'm covering while she's out of town."

"What I remember is having trouble fitting in," Matt said. "Being good enough. The sun set on Will, you know, and when I came along I was always compared to him. Later, I could fade into the crowd. Mom was always calling me Luke, the way she called Patrick John. Whether we were twins or not, we were pretty interchangeable to her—except for Will."

"What was Mother like?"

"Distracted. She was always busy with something."

"Pat told me he thought she was on tranquilizers."

"Not that I know of." He folded his arms on the counter and laid his head on his hands. "Long drive."

"Why don't you take a nap. We can talk more later."

Matt sat up. "It's fine. Maybe coffee's not a bad idea."

She brought him a cup and a serving of Roger's honey.

"You want to know why she left."

"Of course I do. But you were long gone before that happened, so I was asking more about how she was with you. Or the rest of them. I couldn't get much out of Pat. It's as if everyone assumes I know everything that you guys went through."

"I expect we all feel that way—that each of us is in the dark."

"I was certainly the black sheep of the bunch."

He laughed bitterly. "That's the family trait if there is one: none of us thinks we're worth a damn. We had to learn late what love is all about, how to make it last, how to say yes to it when it's staring you in the face. We all pretend, make sure everyone else thinks we're having the most wonderful life possible. It's all such crap."

Agnes stared at him and felt her body sagging, as though her skeleton had gone soft. "I know Mark's as hard on his kids as Clayt was, but—"

"Let me fill you in, little sister. All that shit they send with their Christmas cards? Forget it. You do the same thing—telling us all how great life in Montana is, your house is sweet, your friends are dandy—"

"Touché."

He sipped at his coffee. "Not too bad, for this town."

"You're just spoiled."

"Dad expected all of us to snap shit. He whipped us boys when we pissed him off, which was often—little things most kids would've gotten away with. Mom was remote, cold as a cucumber. So here we were with one parent always mad at us, the other one unreachable.

"I knew what I was early on," Matt said. "It took a long time to come to terms with it, to feel like a decent human being capable of giving and receiving love and not feeling guilty about it."

Agnes thought about her other brothers and the circumstances of their lives. Luke had stayed in Germany after serving in the Air Force, twice married and divorced. John was in Guatemala, helping the poor under the auspices of a left-leaning charity that Clayt would never have approved of. Agnes knew John considered the Vatican to be one of the most harmful and corrupt institutions on the planet. Patrick was a devoted dad and apparently content with his practice as a chiropractor. Her wallet was stuffed with photographs of Will and Ginger, his beautiful half-Irish, half-Japanese children. But, as she had discovered over the past few months, he was in no way prepared for reconciliation with his father.

"Clayt blamed everyone except himself when things went wrong at home," Matt said. "I suppose he couldn't face his own failures."

"I always thought of him as a great success," said Agnes. "King of his fiefdom at War Creek."

"I'm talking about his failure as a father."

"He was good at blaming people, that's for sure. But it couldn't have been easy with seven kids and a job where you worked nights and weekends."

"Shouldn't have had so damn many kids, then," Matt said. "Not that I'd wish you away."

"He probably thought being strict would make up for being gone all the time."

"There was nothing he loved more than work."

Agnes conceded that rangering was Clayt's life. Family had been his ticket to legitimacy, an outward sign that he was a regular person, when he would rather commune with pack mules and herding dogs than with other human beings, especially those he was closest to. The wall of protection around his deepest self was so thick and calcified that even he could not penetrate it. With the loss of War Creek Station, Clayt was left with nothing to do but watch television.

"It sounds like he had a hard childhood himself, to be the way he was," Agnes said.

"That didn't give him an excuse to be such an asshole."

"I know. But I'm tired of being pissed off about it. I'd rather hear about what you're doing," Agnes said. "Now that you're all grown up and gone."

"Middle-aged, you mean? Right now, all is well—I have a good job, a happy home, and I'm learning how to scuba dive. But life can change in a heartbeat. What about you? You don't seem to be in any hurry to get out of here."

"I'm looking for a way to stay. For some reason I seem to be the only one of the bunch to have been bitten by the mountain bug. I can't live in a place without mountains, and I've discovered over the summer that they have to be these mountains."

Matt nodded. "I had a certain feeling of nostalgia when I was driving over the pass. In spite of how things were at home—and I don't mean to tell you I thought it was all bad—I felt comforted somehow. *Welcome home*, the hills seemed to say. It was a good feeling. But there's no way I could live in this little podunkville."

"Maybe you'll have the same good feelings when I take you up to War Creek. Forget about the family stuff and remember the river and the woods."

"I'm counting on it," Matt said. "Better get over to Pop's place."

He brought his bags into the apartment and Agnes gave him the key.

"Who's this little squirt?" he asked. He picked up the cat.

"This one's called Paint. I gave her to Rion when I moved Clayt out of War Creek. There's still one left up there, the orneriest of the bunch."

"Sounds like my kind of cat," Matt said. "Or maybe Clayt's."

They brought roasted chicken and a pumpkin pie from Helen's and called it an early Thanksgiving. After lunch, Clayt got up and went into his bedroom. He came back to the table with two handmade booklets, stapled at the crease, a picture of War Creek Station on the front. He laid them next to the pumpkin pie.

"What's this?" Agnes said. "Is this what you've been working on?"

"Well," he started. His voice broke and he composed himself, hacking loudly to clear his throat. "Best an ol' buzzard could do."

Agnes scanned the document in her hands, its pages written in his Palmer-method cursive, a series of short paragraphs with an inch of white space between them, dates on the left margin. A chronicle of the family from the time the young ranger and his bride moved into War Creek Station to the present. A pocket envelope was glued into the back cover and labeled in Clayt's hand: *Agnes Cecilia. Birth Certificate, Baptism, First Communion, Confirmation.* The documents lent their earthy smell to the book and Agnes knew what had been buried under the kindling.

"Shall we read these now?" She looked at him uncertainly.

Matt was already reading, nodding his head at what he either recognized or agreed with. "Everybody get one of these?" he asked.

Clayt nodded. "Goin' in th' mail tomorrow."

Clayt had his own booklet on the table in front of him and his finger trembled slightly where he rested his hands on it. Agnes read.

"Oh, God," she said. She looked at Clayt.

He glanced at the page. Looking at it upside down was no impediment to understanding what his daughter had just read. "Ain't th' sorta thing you want t' brag about, now is it," he said.

Will had not died a hero's death in combat. Agnes didn't know what to say.

Matt was reading the same section of the history. "I talked to him not long before he died. There was something wrong and he wouldn't say what."

"I can't believe he killed himself," Agnes said.

Clayt leaned forward on his elbows. "Whole thing was my Goddamned fault. Pushin' him to be a priest—I knew he didn't want to, but back then, I guess I didn't give a damn. Sure as hell didn't want t' join the Army neither. But gettin' that letter from the seminary that said he was in—that was it for Will. He joined up just t' get outta that."

Agnes could understand why her mother would be devastated, and angry at Clayt. When she became pregnant a few weeks later, it must have been the final blow. She reread the paragraphs that followed Will's death—her pregnancy, Mary's departure.

"She left because of him, not me."

Clayt dipped his head in confirmation. "A bit a both. And neither one."

"What do you mean?"

"I blamed myself, she blamed me, we got t' fightin' and said some things t' one another that never should of been said." He paused. "She told me when she married me that only one thing would make her break her vows. If I ever hit 'er."

Agnes sat in silence, stunned. As much as Clayt had knocked the boys around, it was impossible to picture him laying a hand on Mary.

With a wavering voice, he continued. "She packed bags th' next day. I said what about Agnes an'…"

"You don't have to finish," Agnes said. "She has made it clear since the day she walked out on you that she didn't give a shit about me."

"Y' know that ain't true," Clayt said. "We both made sure y' got through school."

"Where is she now?"

"I answered that a hundred times, now, haven't I?"

"You truly don't know. She hasn't been in touch at all?"

"Got some letters for a while. Then nothin'."

"We ought to be able to find her," Matt said. "If you're sure you really want to."

Clayt turned his face away, eyes shining.

Agnes was slow to answer. "Yeah," she said. "I think I want to."

CHAPTER TWENTY-ONE

Hunter didn't come home from the mountains on the evening he had planned, and Agnes stayed up reading until after midnight, hoping to hear his truck pulling onto the gravel pad out front. She fell asleep on the sofa and woke before it was light. Wet, heavy snow fell, and from the look of her car under several inches, it had been falling for most of the night.

The driest summer in years had been followed by a spectacular early autumn, but by November the snowfall was on its way to setting a record in the high country. This was the first night of deep snow in the valley.

Agnes tried to calm herself. It wasn't the first time Hunter had been late getting out of the mountains. The weather made her worry more than she would otherwise: perhaps his truck had gotten stuck. He had told her which drainages he would travel, by snowshoe now instead of horseback, so she drove up to each trailhead in turn. Seasonal gates were in place, but Hunter had the combinations. Agnes did not, so she parked at each gate and hiked.

After checking the War Creek trailhead, she decided to try an old logging road that headed to the south. The road was gated, so she parked and started walking. A mile above the gate she rounded a tight switchback in the road and saw the hood of a white pickup truck that had been backed into the forest.

"He's in the South Fork," she told Clayt when she returned to town. "I'm going up there tomorrow if he doesn't get out tonight."

"Why in the hell don't y' call the sheriff instead a' goin' up there yourself?"

"I already did. They don't consider someone missing until they're more than a day late. It'll be spring before they get organized."

Clayt sighed. "No talking y' outta this."

He insisted she take Tuck along, which she was glad to do.

Agnes reached Hunter's truck the next morning at first light, pulled her climbing skins tight onto her skis, and shouldered her bivouac pack. She hadn't counted on needing winter camping gear, but she had brought most of what she needed from Helena. Among Hunter's things she had found a candle lantern, waterproof matches, miner's candles, survey flagging, and a stuff sack that she filled with cookies and granola bars.

The remnants of his tracks led up a steep, forested mountainside at the base of Snowshoe Ridge. She followed, stopping to tie bright flagging to the branches so she could navigate on the way out. The tracks Hunter left led over obstacles she had to skirt with her long, awkward skis. Tuck wallowed in the deep, fresh snow.

She took a break and looked at her topographic map. In an hour and a half she had traveled less than a mile. The ridge ahead would soon leave the forest, and its south face would offer steep but open slopes where her progress would improve.

As Agnes gained elevation, she looked down into the valley of Eagle Creek, much transformed after the fires of '89. There would be plenty of falling snags to keep the trail crew busy next year. The mountaintops were shrouded in cloud, and she could see neither the upper reaches of the creek nor the top of Snowshoe Ridge. After another hour she reached a break in the slope where the ridge became gentler. The south side had been nearly scoured of snow by strong winds. The beginnings of the winter's cornice formed along the leeward side above dark, continuous forest. The windblown snow was dense enough to hold her weight, and both she and Tuck found the going far easier than the first part of the climb. Agnes was able to actually ski instead of bushwhacking, and she made good time. She stopped to feed and water Tuck, and ate a candy bar on a bare high point along the ridge, wishing the clouds would lift so she could have a view.

For a short distance the ridge dropped and she enjoyed a brief downhill run, able to carve turns on the firm, consistent snow. She remembered telling Rion, when they looked in this direction from Eagle Pass, how much fun this ridge would be to ski. In other circumstances, it would have been. Now she was simply trying to hurry. Ahead of her stood a series of rocky knobs, culminating in a tall, faceted peak with cliffs on all sides. She could see no more than the base of the peak.

She looked at her topo map again. She had skied five miles and gained four thousand feet, and going farther was not an option. Hunter must have found a way off the ridge, and she had missed seeing his tracks, or the wind had filled them in. She looked over the edge to a small frozen lake high in a cirque above the South Fork. The slope above the lake was dizzyingly steep, a long talus slope cut by cliff bands. Agnes took off her pack and blasted on her whistle, so shrill she had to cover her own ears. Tuck laid his ears back and squinted with a canine wince. No reply came—only the silence of the mountains, the dense windless quiet that comes before a storm.

Agnes started to backtrack down the ridge and had gone less than a tenth of a mile before Tuck began sniffing the ground. The ridgeline dipped into a saddle here, an obvious place to abandon the top before it became too difficult to navigate.

It was after noon and time to make a decision—if she was going to get home before nightfall, she had to turn around within an hour. She gave herself until 1:30 and started down the forested slope on the north side of the ridge, looking for a safe route into the cirque. She side-slipped for a hundred yards, keeping to a barely perceptible convex rib whose trees did not appear to be flagged by avalanches. She carved a few turns in an open meadow and looked up at them, pleased with her first downhill skiing of the year. Tuck had run behind her, straight down the center of her ski tracks, and the combination looked like a column of dollar signs. At last she reached the base of the slope and crossed the frozen outlet of the lake. A stringer of timber large enough to offer shelter covered a bench on the far side. She nearly skied past the camp before she caught a glimpse of his tent, tucked behind a six-foot windbreak he had made from branches and a tarp.

Snow lay against the fly. Agnes unzipped the tent and looked inside to find his sleeping bag and some clothing tucked away into one corner. His gas stove was set up behind a secondary wind screen, and a neat pile of firewood stayed dry behind the tent. A nylon stuff sack hung from a high tree branch, out of reach of bears. She called out a few times, her hands around her mouth to amplify her voice. Silence followed, until she heard her voice returning as it bounced off the crags above. Already past two, she knew she would not be able to climb back to the ridge and ski back to her car before dark. A deep sense of solitude enveloped her. She had never felt more alone.

To distract herself from the foreboding that clutched at her throat, Agnes prepared to spend the night. She swept the floor of the tent, tightened the tie-downs and tucked the tarp around the corners of the firewood pile. She shook out Hunter's sleeping bag and laid it back in the tent beside her own. She took off her skis and punched her way partway up the mountainside, tying extra flagging to tree branches in case she faced whiteout conditions in the morning. By the time she finished, the wind was on the rise and a light snow had begun to sift from the blank gray sky. The clouds lowered, cutting off the limited view she had of the lower cirque basin. She circled camp, calling for Hunter.

With an early dusk falling fast, Agnes made a small campfire, for its light as much as its warmth, taking her time so she had something to do for as long as possible. One thing she disliked about winter camping was the hours of darkness beginning in late afternoon, with nothing to do but sit beside a campfire or lie in the tent, trying not to glance at her watch and see how much of night remained.

The dial told her it was pas time for Hunter to return to camp, if he was going to. What could have happened? Perhaps the bear had gone over the Sawtooth Crest and Hunter had followed her. He had brought bivouac gear. But his food was here, his heat and shelter. None of her scenarios made sense.

Tuck barked and she turned around. Out of the dusk and snowfall the figure of a man resolved.

"Hunter," she cried.

"What on earth?" He scratched Tuck's ears and looked around the campsite. "I wasn't expecting room service."

He laid the antenna aside and took off his daypack. Agnes ran to him and burrowed into his embrace.

"The snow, you were late…I worried."

"I told you not to." He held her for a minute and neither spoke. "Mmm," he said. "I reach camp late, it's cold and wet. But wait, there's a little campfire burning. Beside it sits the woman of my dreams."

Agnes laughed and stood back. "I'll bet you're hungry."

"Only for you." He held her temples and kissed her. They stood beside the fire passing kisses back and forth for long enough that neither of them gave a thought to dinner.

"I almost forgot to tell you the reason I'm running late," Hunter said. "I found her den."

"I was sure you wouldn't have come off the mountain until you did."

"The way the weather's turned, this trip was my last chance." He kissed her again and took her into his arms, swung her around and they danced. "I found the den," he sang. "Found the den, found the den." He stopped. "And here's the best part: she's in it."

With Tuck curled between their feet, for the second time Agnes and Hunter spent a night within a mile of the War Creek sow. Dawn seeped into the tent where the fly sagged under the snow that had fallen overnight. Hunter punched at it until it slid free. Outside the door was a world of white, even under the shelter of the trees. Clouds hung over the tops of the mountains, but the amphitheater where the bear slept was pristine with fresh snow and the growing light of day. The air was barely below freezing, but it felt damp, the kind of chill that penetrated.

Hunter started packing gear while Agnes dressed. She pulled on her wool hat and stuffed her feet into her stiff, cold ski boots. They each drank a quart of water and had granola bars for breakfast. Agnes gave Tuck the food she'd brought for him and started organizing her gear for the homeward trek.

She hung the tent fly from a branch to let it dry while Hunter wadded the wet tent into its stuff sack. Slowly the clouds lifted, revealing flocked cliffs and snow-covered talus slopes shining in the morning sun. A col dipped just under the floor of the clouds, outlining a patch of blue round as an eye.

Hunter stuffed the handle of his antenna into his bulky pack. For the first time Agnes noticed he had a shotgun.

"Hell of a nice day for a ridge walk," he said.

"Even better for a ski." Agnes pulled on her pack. "You picked a great campsite," she said. "We'll have to come back next summer."

"Is that a promise?"

She looked at him. "If you want it to be. Why?"

He left his pack leaning against a tree and walked over to her. "I wondered if you ever thought about getting married."

"I don't know—I never met the right person. Until now."

"It's the same for me."

"We haven't known each other that long," Agnes said.

"I'm not talking about next month or even next year—but I want us to be together."

Agnes felt the heat in her face spreading into her chest as she understood that he had just proposed to her. "Me too," she said.

"Time to move on, then," he said with a smile. "We'll talk some more later."

"I'll break trail."

She started for the flagging she had left, but the open meadow she had skied now looked easier than climbing through the forest. She headed for it at a gentle angle, waiting for Tuck as he tried to stay on top of the tails of her skis. In contrast to the cold Montana powder she had grown accustomed to, this snow was deep and heavy, and Agnes was glad it would slow her as she skied down the steep sections at the bottom of the ridge. Hunter followed on snowshoes, leaving in his wake a wide beaten path.

The clouds broke into shreds of mist and the air was fresh with the scent of lichens hanging from the trees. It felt more like spring than the start of winter. Agnes turned to look back at the camp and cirque basin. A broad ray struck the north face of a pyramidal mountain that stood over the frozen lake. The picture that had come to her when she stood watching darkness fall above Dagger Lake returned: that curve of glacier-polished granite, the long ridge, the amphitheater of stone. It was the place she had imagined, where the War Creek sow lay sleeping. The ray of sunlight slid down the snowfield above and paused for a moment where Agnes stood. The warmth she felt was not imagined.

Below the crest of the ridge the forest opened into a sunny glade. Snow had blown from the ridge into deep pillows that buried Tuck, so Agnes slipped her ski poles under one arm, lifted him, and held him tight as she climbed.

"Wait while I cross," she told Hunter. "Just in case."

He paused, watching her. All at once she felt the snow shifting beneath her and heard a muffled sigh as it collapsed. A line spread across the top of the slope like a crack in a windshield. Tuck leapt from her arms and scrambled away.

Agnes lost her balance as the avalanche gained speed. It ripped off one ski, then the other, and yanked her pack off her shoulders. She flailed with arms and legs to stay near the surface. *I've done it now,* she thought. Before she could close her eyes in despair she slammed into a tree.

For a moment her vision sharpened and blue sparklers dancing before her. Tuck, being lightweight and unburdened by packs and ski gear, had stayed on top of the moving snow. He sat beside her and watched her intently. The dog was the last thing she saw before sparklers filled her head.

When Agnes regained consciousness, her first attempt at movement made her wince. It hurt to breathe. Tuck licked and nuzzled her as she started to show signs of life, and his presence reminded her of where she was, what had happened. She went over each detail of the moments before the snow caught and nearly buried her, leaving her on her side, her back against the solid trunk of a larch and her legs sprawled at odd angles, uphill. She wiggled her toes and felt them moving in her ski boots. Her fingers wiggled too. Tuck's anxious licking roused her and she noticed more sensations. The sharp pain when she took a breath. A gradual awareness of feeling very chilled. She reached to the top of her head and found her woolen hat missing and her hair soaked from the wet snow.

It hurt to move, but she did, to relieve the discomfort of lying with her feet elevated, and because she knew she must. She squirmed around until her feet were downslope and she could sit up against the tree. Her body heat had melted a firm cup into the solidified snow. She took shallow, tentative breaths, feeling her way to the limit of breath before her cracked ribs cried out in pain. After a few more breaths she felt able to think.

A wave of panic overtook her. "Hunter," she yelled.

Clutching the tree trunk for balance, she pushed herself up and stood trembling. Dizziness threatened to send her back to the ground but she fought it, fought the fogginess in her head, the ache at the back of her skull and the sharp pain that came with each breath. Her vision cleared and she looked up to the crown of the avalanche, only a foot deep and consisting of the loose snow that had fallen overnight. She traced the crown of the slide to its far side, where she saw the tracks of her skis and Hunter's snowshoes before they both disappeared. She could see no sign of him. She called him again, more urgently.

The tree she hit had kept her from traveling farther downslope as the avalanche gained material and momentum before launching itself over a cliff. The place where Hunter had been caught offered no such protection. Her awareness sharpened to the most urgent parts of the situation, pushing her pain aside. She had to find him.

Her skis and pack were nowhere in sight. A ski pole basket protruded from the snow, and she crept toward it. The pole was buried in snow that had set up like concrete after the avalanche came to rest, and she could not budge it. She retreated into the forest and found a stout fallen branch, then dug around the pole until she freed it. If nothing else, she would have a serviceable walking stick. She used the bent ski pole and branch to steady herself as she walked across the avalanche, calling for Hunter. The obvious revealed itself, but she kept searching for him anyway, on the edge of the forest where he might have retreated, beyond the snow that had slid away. If he wasn't there, the only place he could have gone was deep under the snow and over the cliff.

She was shaken, hurting and disoriented, but had the presence of mind to know she had to find help as soon as possible. She made her way to the top of the ridge. With a few hours of daylight remaining, she began to march as quickly as her legs would take her, alternating between firm, windblown snow and bare, windswept ground where she could find it. Tuck led the way and she followed numbly. The ridge rose behind her, and when she looked around in hopes of spotting Hunter up there somewhere, it surprised her to see how much elevation she had lost. She crossed the snow line where the night's precipitation had come as rain. Abandoning the deadfall she had traversed the day before, she headed straight down the open slope to Eagle Creek, where there was a real trail.

The trail was snow-packed but had been beaten in by hunters on horseback. She fell into the semi-conscious state of hiking she thought of as autopilot and followed the path to the road. By the time she and Tuck reached her car at the gate, dusk had fallen and she was exhausted. Then she realized the car keys were in her pack, buried in the avalanche.

There was nothing to do but continue her long trudge, another mile to the river road and pavement, where she might be lucky enough to catch a ride. With her last reserve of strength she put one foot in front of the other, not allowing herself to look up and see how far she had to go. She failed to hear the vehicle approaching from behind until it was even with her.

A young man rolled down his window and looked her over.

"Looks like you could use a ride," he said.

She thanked him as she climbed in and held Tuck in her lap.

"Where you headed? I'm on my way to town."

She nodded and the man reached over to scratch Tuck's ears.

He commented on her attire, ski boots and parka, no other gear.

"Avalanche," she said. "My partner's buried."

He whistled softly and stepped on the accelerator. He glanced over at her. "Looks like you're hurt. Take you to the clinic?"

Agnes didn't respond. Her physical exhaustion and injuries paled in comparison to the deep grief that seeped through every cell of her body. She hugged Tuck and cried.

CHAPTER TWENTY-TWO

Dawn feathered the hem of the window curtain. Agnes raised herself onto one elbow and tried to make her eyes focus. Her body ached, as if she'd been shaken up like a pea in a coffee can. A pot lid being clapped onto a sizzling pan and the smell of bacon frying brought her around, and she saw that she was on the sofa in Clayt's cabin. Tuck was curled up on the floor below her, his tail gently slapping the floor.

She lay back on the sofa and tested her ribcage with a deep breath. The pain was sharp but tolerable as she pulled the cabin's cool air into her lungs. But thirst and a full bladder demanded her attention and prodded her toward the bathroom, where she peed and drank three glasses of cold well water.

"How ya feelin', missy?" Clayt asked. His eyes were wide with concern as he steered her toward the table and set a cup of coffee in front of her. "Y' slept fer a day an' a half."

No wonder she had to pee. "I need to take a shower." Her voice sounded as if it came from another room.

In the shower she noticed blood running down the drain. She checked for wounds and saw a bruise blooming around a wide scrape on her forearm. She put a washcloth to her face and it came off stained with blood. She touched the spot with her fingertips and found that it had been bandaged. At the back of her head was a lump the size of a crabapple. Gingerly she patted herself dry and put on Clayt's old bathrobe.

Clayt noticed the blood on her forehead. "Looks like y' got that bleedin' again." He ordered her to sit down and inspected the damage as if he were checking out a pack horse after a fall. "Let's get a bandage on that arm," he said.

"Did you do this?" she asked, fingering the tape on her forehead.

"Young feller took y' to the clinic. He told me what happened."

She stared out the window, where snow was falling. "I found his camp," she said. "We were coming out together." Tears came and she couldn't say more.

"Search 'n Rescue's up there," Clayt said.

Agnes knew the snowstorm that must be engulfing the high country would prevent them from getting anywhere near the avalanche site. But she let her mind drift into the kind of magical thinking that accompanies sudden and devastating loss. Scenarios involving his rescue were like balm on a burn, dulling the pain. When she faced the inevitable, it made her raw inside, her throat in a constant clench to hold back the sobs.

In a week's time, Agnes had healed enough to drive, and she began going back to War Creek for solace. She would park in front of the bridge gate and walk the old trail to the cottonwood log. With a foot of fresh snow on the ground, the path was kept open by her frequent trips. The armchair was waiting for her, as it had been since the day she hacked it into the fallen tree. It was crumbling with age and now filled with snow, so Agnes brought a square cut from an old Insulite pad and used it as a cushion while she sat on the thickest part of the log.

In her fleece, waterproof ski pants and jacket, a thick wool hat and gloves, and a scarf wrapped around her neck, she could sit on the log in relative comfort, listening to the sound of flowing water muffled under layers of snow while the winter wind rattled the bare branches of the cottonwoods. In a few months, the river would thaw and by June it would rush with snowmelt. The cottonwoods would start to grow again, first with the sticky red bud scales that would fall into the river and gather in eddies like tiny boats as the trees began to bloom. The spiders and warblers would return, filling the branches with life and motion and song. All of that could wait as far as Agnes was concerned. The season of darkness and cold, with a merciless wind coming down the canyon, was all that she wanted. She could not have borne the bright exuberance of spring.

Search and Rescue had failed to find any traces of Hunter. The search had been called off after another set of storms, and now it would be spring before the recovery could commence. It was no longer possible for her to hope the worst had not happened, though some nights she reverted to her dreams of finding him in order to get to sleep. How would she ever stop wishing she had died in the avalanche instead of him? Or at least with him?

Hunter's parents, Bart and Cora, arrived from opposite coasts, and Agnes met them at the Raven's Roost.

"He was our only child," Cora told her in a voice that was barely audible. Her face was drawn and her eyes swollen, but for the moment it seemed she had run out of tears.

"I'll take you over to his place," Agnes said. "Coffee?"

Bart shook his head.

"Maybe later," Cora said. "This will be hard enough without being wired."

The Fish and Wildlife Service had already collected anything that was government property, including the truck Hunter had left at the South Fork trailhead. Agnes struggled for words, trying to offer his bereaved parents assistance and condolences, but she was encased in her own capsule of grief. It held her so tightly that anything she said came out as a hollow echo. When someone spoke, the words were as muffled as the Twisp River prattling under its blanket of snow.

"We appreciate your being concerned enough to ski into the mountains to make sure he was all right," Bart said.

"He was so excited about finding that bear in her den. And I'm so glad he did."

"I guess we should be glad he died happy," Cora said. Her voice broke and she didn't say more.

"I keep wishing it had been me instead of him," Agnes said. "He had so much to offer—was doing good conservation work, while I was serving coffee."

"If you had gone instead of Hunter, he never would have forgiven himself," Bart said.

Cora nodded in agreement. "He thought the world of you."

"Likewise. We were talking about getting married."

Agnes sat on the sofa where Hunter had first kissed her and held Cora, both of them openly crying. Bart started the grim task of moving Hunter's personal belongings from the house. He came out of the bedroom with the banjo and offered it to Agnes.

"He told us you played guitar. Maybe you can use it."

"He was teaching me," she said.

When she held its case, running her hand over the same surface that his hands had last touched, she felt his absence the way she might have felt the absence of the earth beneath her feet if she had jumped from a high cliff. She thanked Bart, and thought about the grief her father must have felt when Will died.

"This has to be so hard for you," she said.

"There is no comfort for any of us now," Cora told her. "But someday, there will be."

"I don't know how we'll live through this afternoon."

Agnes threw herself into helping move Hunter's things, and her own, from the house and cleaning it once it was empty. Stripped of the life it had held, the house was just another vacant property, waiting for the next renter. She didn't want to see it again.

When Hunter's parents prepared to leave, she told Cora, "It's sad to think I could have been your daughter-in-law."

"I would have liked that," Cora said. "Why don't we just act as if you already are?"

The two women hugged like old friends, each aware of the other's profound sorrow over the loss of the man they had both loved.

—

Agnes returned to the cottonwood log to escape the false cheer of Christmas carols and holiday lights blinking at the greasy spoon across the street from the Raven's Roost. She found her personal form of cheer in knowing that Joan was on her way for a visit, and she would have someone to listen to her cry and hold her the way Cora had. She had not called Rion to let her know what happened, for whenever she tried and had to leave a message she would lose her voice. Her mouth would not form the words *killed* or *dead*. She understood now how a term like "passed away" could soften the blow. She promised herself she would leave a message before Christmas.

Agnes wanted to sit on the log beside the Twisp River until the wind brought another snowstorm, and another, until both the log and she were covered for good. But she had begun to shiver and knew she had to leave. *Live your life,* Hunter would have told her. *Go to the places that make your heart sing. Remember me, and how I loved you.*

Since returning to War Creek, Agnes had found meaning in her love of place, and now it gave her a reason to continue. Through art or community service or some kind of job she had yet to imagine, she had to find a way to express it.

She stood and swung her arms to bring circulation into her hands and fingers. Dark fell early, in the middle of the afternoon. She walked back to the station, boarded up and abandoned. No one had been there other than Clayt and herself.

As she drove down the snowy valley she thought about the bear that had inhabited her dreams, and how it had become more distinct with time. It had approached Agnes and she had reached out in return. With each repetition of the dream, the visage of the bear had come into clearer focus. Its first appearance was indistinct and hazy, moving toward her before retreating into the darkness. Later, she smelled it, and felt its breath on her face. The bear wanted something, she had told Hunter, but she couldn't guess what. Now it occurred to her that the bear had been asking the same question that had lain heavy in Agnes's heart since she woke up after giving birth: *Where is my little cub?* At last it sunk in that she had been the dream bear all along.

The dream had once brought solace, but she didn't feel qualified to be the source of her own comfort now. She wanted to believe the bear had been a messenger from the spirit world beyond her reach or understanding, a magical realm where immortal people and their animal kin spoke with and understood each other the way they did in Indian legends. She wanted to believe the bear had something she needed, if only she could decipher what it was. *Come with me; you will find peace.* The bear was looking for her little cub, so why wasn't Agnes? What could she do, other than to place her name on a registry and hope someone would seek her out? She missed Hunter more than she missed a child she had never known, but that child was her link to the future, just as Mary was a link to her past. She resolved to do her best to find them both. Perhaps the restlessly searching bear had been trying to tell her that all of her life's yearnings were wrapped together in a knot she had only begun to unravel.

CHAPTER TWENTY-THREE

When Bart and Cora were in town, Agnes had taken a carload of her clothing from Hunter's to Rion's and dumped it on the bed in her apartment. Now she began the process of moving in. Rion had been gone for over two months and the skiers had started to show up, giving Agnes reason to keep the shop open longer hours. She was glad for the distraction from her sorrow, and for the bits of gossip coming through the door.

"I heard a rumor that cheered me up," she told Clayt one evening after bringing him dinner. "Flintstone's being shipped to some backwater forest in eastern Oregon."

Clayt's eyes widened. "To do what?"

"Range con in the SO. I think it's only a detail, but it gets him out of here for a few months."

"I wonder what he did to piss off Sara Lee."

"Might not have anything to do with her. The districts are combining again and everything's going to Winthrop."

Clayt shook his head. "Glad I got outta the outfit when I did. They keep tossin' districts and forests together an' there's gonna be nobody in the woods."

"It's all about saving money, I suppose," Agnes said.

"Savin' money, hell. It's about spendin' what they got on gas and motels and Goddamned useless meetings."

"Clayt, part of my job in looking after you is to keep you from getting upset. Sorry to bring up a sore subject."

"Ain't upset. Tickles the hell outta me to hear Flintstone's out on his ass. Give 'im a bit a his own medicine." He chuckled with deep satisfaction.

Agnes sifted through a stack of mail, hoping for replies to the inquiries she had sent to schools and organizations that conducted environmental education programs from Washington to Montana and beyond. An Audubon Society field camp in western Wyoming sounded like a good option, except that it was in Wyoming and only operated a few weeks of the year. The one that held the greatest interest was a relatively new group that called itself the North Cascades Institute. Programs for children and adults on the natural and human history of the region she knew best—this was more than she'd hoped for. She had no way of knowing from the contents of the brochures if any of these nonprofits were seeking employees, but she had found an advertisement from the North Cascades Institute in *High Country News*.

No replies with the current crop of mail, but she was glad to receive a Christmas card addressed to her. Her brothers had all sent their cards to Clayt, with the assumption he would share them, thus saving them an extra stamp. The envelope carried a postmark date more than a week old: *Rochester, MN*. Agnes made the mental leap to the Mayo Clinic before she peeled the envelope off the card.

Rion wrote that she was attending her ex, who was going through a regimen of chemotherapy for breast cancer. It looked as if she would be gone longer than expected and hoped that would be all right. *If not*, she wrote, *just close the place up and do whatever you need to do*. Agnes was ready to close and go see Rion.

The letter ended with an enigma. *Not sure at this point when I will be back, or if*

Rion had omitted the period, as if interrupted before completing her sentence, leaving Agnes to ponder what might have followed the *if*. Maybe nothing.

She laid the card in a bowl with the others and picked up Matt's letter again. He had written a personal note to both her and Clayt, inviting them to visit.

"Sounds like Matt's serious about trying to find our mother," Agnes said. "How would you feel if he did?"

Clayt lay on his back on the sofa. He was quiet for long enough that Agnes looked at him to be sure he hadn't fallen asleep.

"I'm not sure how I feel about it," Agnes said. "What would I say to her?"

"She'd be happy t' know you ended up fine," Clayt said. "I think she'd want to know that."

"But not enough to inquire, apparently."

"I was readin' your little *All That Matters* book th' other day. Think you're on t' something with it."

She waited for him to continue.

"Seems y' found a way to forgive this old fart for all th' things he done. Might be time for us t' start workin' on your mother."

"I cried and cried for her once. Now…I'm almost as afraid of seeing her as I was you."

"Not much t' be scared about on my end, turns out."

"I'm afraid I'd chew her out so bad she wouldn't know what hit her."

"What'd I just say about forgiveness?"

"I know, you're right." Agnes pictured a reunion with her mother, the resentments of the past forgotten as she and Mary reached for one another and hugged. But she doubted it would be like that. "I could write, maybe. That would be a start."

"See what happens," Clayt said. "She may want nothin' to do with either of us."

"One way to find out."

Since Cora had been so kind to her, Agnes no longer yearned for an imaginary vision of Mary. Already her new mother-in-law had called twice to see how she was doing. Nonetheless she had already begun composing the letter in her mind. *I'm going to try to find my child*, she would begin. *But first I need to find you.*

—

SUSAN MARSH

On New Year's Day, Agnes was making coffee at the Raven's Roost when Rion appeared. A fine silver fuzz clung to her bald head, a sharp contrast from her usual salt-and-pepper hair, and it was clear to Agnes why she'd been away so long.

"Why didn't you say so?" Agnes asked as she rushed toward her. "I would have helped, I could have come—like you were supposedly doing for your friend."

"No supposedly about it," Rion said. She was thin and tired in the eyes, but she sounded confident and strong. "We decided we could help each other."

Understanding dawned and Agnes could think of nothing to say.

Rion continued. "I didn't want anyone to know." She hugged Agnes hard. "I came to find out about you—how are you holding up?"

"You got my message, then. I can't call it much more than survival," Agnes said. "I'm so sad all the time. No energy, no desire to move when I wake up. I thought I knew what grief was, but now I'm really finding out." She bent over and convulsed with sobs. "This is all I do, every day. Think of him and cry."

"It's what you have to do, girl. If you stuffed it all in and pretended everything was just wonderful, you'd go nuts."

"I feel like I'm nuts now. I spend my days in a fog, like a hibernating bear. Waiting for spring, waiting for them to find him." She looked at Rion. "We were being careful, crossing that slope one at a time. I keep going over and over in my mind what I should have done differently."

"Sometimes disaster strikes when you're doing everything right."

Agnes felt Rion's bony shoulder blades. "Like you and your friend," she said.

"It's the second time for both of us," Rion said. She stood back and raised both fists, lifting an imaginary barbell. "But I'm not giving up."

"What happens next?"

"Wait and see if any of this torture did some good." Rion

270

rubbed the fuzz on top of her head. "I'm going back next week for more."

Agnes poured them coffee and they retreated to their table, switching roles. "What about the shop?" she asked.

"Put it up for sale, I guess. Want to buy it?"

"No. I have another iron in the fire."

Rion smiled and cocked her head.

"I'm going to put in for a job I read about—there's an opening with the North Cascades Institute, environmental ed for science teachers. I'm waiting to get the application in the mail."

Rion beamed. "Sounds like you got your shit together, sister."

"Time will tell on that one. In the meanwhile, I'm fine with keeping the shop going for you. Not that it's raking in the cash."

"The bank statements look better than I expected. If this hospital crap goes on much longer I'll be selling the place regardless. How's Old Cranky doing?"

"Recovering. Slowly, and probably not completely."

"And you're still waiting on him hand and foot."

"It's different now. I want to help, and he appreciates it. He doesn't ask for much, and it's nice to have someone to eat a meal with once in a while." She fought tears. "Who else do I have?"

"Yourself, my friend. When all else fails."

"I know you're right, but without Hunter…"

"It's going to be hard for a couple of years," Rion said. "And then it will get better."

"Please be right. Each day is an eternity without him."

"You'll get through it."

Agnes wasn't so sure. She still found herself restless at night, clutching false hope to lull herself into sleep. She saw Hunter somewhere in the mountains, holed up in one of the sod-roofed cabins that dotted the deep woods, living on pine needles and wild grouse. Each night she fell asleep to another version of this scenario, ending with her skiing into the backcountry to find him waiting for her, wondering what had taken her so long.

A white pickup turned into the gravel lot and parked.

"Customers," Rion sang.

Agnes stared in silence out the window.

"What?" Rion leaned forward to look.

"That's Hunter's truck. For a minute..."

They watched as a lanky young man unfolded from the front seat.

"Must be the new kid they hired," Agnes said. "To replace him."

"You don't have to talk to this snot-nose," Rion said as she stood. "I'll give him his cup of Joe and get him the hell out of here."

Agnes smiled. "It's good to have you back—and being yourself again."

"Go feed the cat. I've got you covered."

The door's bell jangled and the young man ducked between bags of coffee beans. Agnes couldn't stop herself from staring at him.

Rion stepped forward, trying to get his attention, but he looked straight at Agnes.

"Good morning," she said, standing.

He held his hand out for her to shake and she offered hers reluctantly.

"Phil Sanderson," he said. "And I believe you must be Agnes Clayton."

"I've been expecting to meet you at some point," she said. She kept her tone even, her voice low, resisting the desire to turn and run out the back door. He seemed to sense her discomfort, for now he was saying how sorry he was about what had happened and how he would be hard-pressed to fill Hunter's shoes. Agnes heard half of what he said, and tried to smile politely as she listened.

"What can I get you, mister?" Rion asked.

He seemed to notice her for the first time. "Large coffee to go, black."

"Coming up."

He turned his attention back to Agnes. "Are you going to be in the mood to talk one of these days? I'm not trying to make things worse."

"Things can't get any worse. How about now?"

Rion rolled her eyes and brought his coffee to the window table.

"Ma'am, I wanted it to go," Phil said to Rion.

"You'll be here long enough for a refill. Then we'll give you one for the road."

CHAPTER TWENTY-FOUR

How quickly the light changed after the darkest months. The sun rose farther to the north and colors returned to the sky. Meltwater ran from snowbanks, allowing the smaller creeks, silent all winter, to find their voices. By the end of February the cottonwood buds were swelling and the air held the scent of newly bared soil. Willows, aspens, river birch, and alder dangled long catkins like fancy earrings from their branches. Chickadees courted and magpies grew noisy as they argued over nesting territories.

A small dark cloud intruded on the festival of spring. Matt had found an address for their mother. Agnes had sent her a ten-page letter. She had even talked Clayt into adding a note at the bottom. But that was a month ago, and she had not heard back.

March brought warmer days and Clayt spent more time outside, holding court as old friends came by to pay respects. Rion was living in Detroit with her ex—or ex-ex, Agnes understood. They would be there for each other, each determined to help the other enjoy whatever time they had. Rion had yet to decide whether she would sell the Raven's Roost, but Agnes was content to keep it open, to have somewhere warm and familiar to spend her time as the cold gray of winter gave way to spring.

The last week in March she played telephone tag with the director of the North Cascades Institute. He wanted to arrange an interview. When she finally spoke with him, he offered the job over the telephone. "No other candidate for this position can touch you," he told her.

Though flattered, she knew he was right. Knowledge of the mountains was second nature to her, and having grown up with Clayt, she had practical skills as well, able to read the country as well as a map. Her time with Hunter had given her expertise in an area of study that other candidates lacked, expertise that Phil had recognized after their first encounter. He had called the Institute to put in a good word for her.

The man who interviewed Agnes told her the Institute planned to open a field camp at Lake Chelan. She could commute, sort of, staying in Institute cabins and bunkhouses and coming home to the Twisp River on days off.

On a brilliant April morning Agnes postponed opening the Raven's Roost and took Clayt for a drive to War Creek. The station was still gated and there had been no apparent activity since fall, other than Agnes's frequent forays to the cottonwood log. She parked and they trespassed as usual, Tuck bounding ahead and claiming his old marking posts, her flower barrels still turned over. Some Johnny-jump-ups had gone to seed and their offspring were starting to bloom. The garden was a neat rectangle of tilled earth, the rhubarb plant defiantly raising its red-green fists. The buildings looked forlorn, the barn and corral free of the fresh smell of hay and horses. A pale streak in the shadows of the barn told her that old six-toes had wintered well. Tuck trotted out of the barn and the cat peered at Agnes from the loft.

"Good morning, you little bastard," she said.

The cat meowed.

"Must of missed us," Clayt said. "First time I ever heard 'im say squat."

They walked at Clayt's pace to the confluence with War Creek and what remained of Agnes's armchair. The log had split, pitching the front half of her seat forward in an unusable tilt. The chair had lasted longer than she imagined possible, and now, like many people and things that had come into her life since she returned to War Creek, it had completed its work. The log itself would last much longer, and as one bit began to crumble with decay she could pick another spot along its length to offer her rest for as long as she survived.

"Been damn near a year," Clayt said.

"I was planning to stay a week." Agnes smiled. "It turns out I needed a year."

"That bunch a hippies tell ya when t' show up yet?"

"Clayt—"

"I know—they ain' hippies, they're scientists."

"I'm lucky to get this job offer. I couldn't be more pleased."

"Glad fer ya, missy," Clayt said. "'Bout time somethin' good come your way."

Agnes agreed. Winter had been a slow progression of days and weeks, each dragging its way into the next, each beginning and ending with intense grief. The brightest moments of the season had come when Phil stopped by the Raven's Roost. Eager to learn, he sought her knowledge and advice about forest trails, valley politics, and Hunter's methodology. Hunter's understanding of his work ran so deep that it was intuitive rather than methodical, and Agnes tried to help Phil, fresh out of graduate school, understand. Phil told her on more than one occasion that he wished he had known Hunter, but having her to learn from was nearly as good. Now, at the North Cascades Institute, she would pass on Hunter's knowledge and love of wild things to others of Phil's generation.

When she got back to the Raven's Roost after dropping Clayt at his place, Roger was there, waiting.

"Sorry," she said. "I meant to be back way before now."

"Searchers found him," he said. "Thought you'd want to know."

Bart and Cora returned, and Agnes gave them Rion's apartment for their stay while she slept on Clayt's sofa. She and Cora put together dinner for the family of four—Clayt included—which they took at a table at the Raven's Roost, Cora sneaking scraps of chicken to the cat. Bart chose the seat Agnes told him had been Hunter's favorite work spot, near the rear of the shop and next to a window that faced west.

"We want to have a memorial for him here before we leave," Cora announced. "His ashes should be spread in the place he loved most."

Agnes thought of Twisp Pass, Eagle Pass, the many high points where she had stood with Hunter, all of which he called his favorite. "That would be the den site," she said. "But I'm not sure how we'd get you there."

"I damn sure know how t' get 'em there," Clayt said.

Bart and Cora were fit enough for people in their seventies, but unaccustomed to the elevation.

"It's a steep ridge," Agnes said. "Could horses manage it?"

"I can get us up from the bottom a th' South Fork—I know an old trail."

On the next sunny day Clayt sat tall in the saddle once again. Even the outfitter whose horses they had hired didn't know all of Clayt's secret trails. The South Fork had mostly escaped the wildfire the previous summer, but the trail had not been cleared of avalanche debris, and Agnes was afraid they might be in for another bushwhack.

Clayt stayed on the main trail for the first three miles, which was still snow-covered but surprisingly easy going, thanks to the search team's snowmobile tracks. The south-facing slope above them was bare of snow, but the opposite side of the valley was dense with forest and brush fields, and considerably steeper. Draws ran from the ridgeline to the creek, most of them choked with snow. Clayt left the trail where Black Ridge cleaved the valley of War Creek into its two branches. He led the way across a wide shallow ford and doubled back, heading parallel to the main trail as if he had changed his mind and decided to ride back out to the road. The outfitter shrugged and said he figured the old man knew what he was up to, and Agnes allowed that he'd better.

Soon enough, they both saw where they were heading. The trail climbed at a steady ten percent grade, following a crease in the mountainside that could not be seen from the far side of the creek. It made its way upward in a series of long switchbacks, with only two stops required to cut a log out of the way. The patches of snow were soft enough that the horses easily crossed them. Once on the crest of a spur, where old-growth forest remained after a forest fire had burned around it decades ago, the route went straight up. On the shaded forest floor no brush grew, and the trees had formed a shelter from most of the winter's snowfall. The spur leveled out near the top of Snowshoe Ridge. The place where Clayt's trail met the ridge crest was the only one without an imposing cornice.

"Pretty nice route," the outfitter said. "Might use this trail myself."

"It's a lot easier than the way I skied it," Agnes said.

The group dismounted to allow the horses to rest after the uphill push.

"Should be all right from here," Clayt said. "What is it—couple a miles?"

"We won't make it to the cirque itself," Agnes said. "But we'll be able to look into it."

She pointed out landmarks to Bart and Cora, the basin where they had camped when Hunter first hired Clayt to guide him, the peaks Hunter had climbed in search of a signal from the bear. She had made Phil a map of the place where Hunter had found the bear's den, but put him off when he asked her to take him there. This was one place meant only for close family—a family that included Clayt and Bart and Cora, and the War Creek sow.

Agnes was relieved to find much of the upper Eagle Creek drainage unburned. What had burned, directly below them, was a naked bowl of blackened snags, islands of old-growth ponderosas still alive here and there. Near the bottom of the creek, where snow had melted off, a fringe of silver-green had begun to sprout among the charred snags. The forest, born again after the fire, had already gotten down to the serious business of resurrection.

"Time to saddle up," Bart said. He was trying to be cheerful, but his face made it plain that he looked forward to having this day over with.

They reached the gap in the ridge above Hunter's last campsite. Deep snow lay on the north side of the ridge.

"I think we should take his ashes over there," Agnes said, pointing to a promontory of bare rock on the ridge. "That way he gets to spend eternity with everything he loved in sight." She indicated the place where the bear had denned, in the cirque barely visible through tree trunks, struck again by the accuracy with which she had pictured it before ever seeing the actual place.

"You go," Clayt said. "Doc says I need t' stay below six thousand feet."

"We're well above that now," Agnes said. "Back in a little while."

Bart carried what looked like a cardboard shoebox as the three walked in silence to the bulge of bedrock sticking out of the snow.

At the edge of the rock, Agnes stopped. "I don't know what we're supposed to say."

Bart opened the box and the plastic bag within. Cora put her hand in the bag and kissed a handful of ashes before raising it up to the wind. She tried to say something but her voice cracked and she shook her head. Bart offered Agnes a chance to do as Cora had done. All of them cried as he let the wind take the finest dust while white bone remnants fell into the cracks in the rock and bounced into the talus below.

"I'll leave the two of you for a minute," Agnes said, sensing their need to be alone. She followed the rock rib higher until it ended in a continuous snowfield. From there she could look into the cirque where the searchers had found Hunter. She wanted to yell across the mountains to him until her echo filled the valley. But what would she tell him? *Here we are, we love you.* Surely he knew that.

Avalanche debris spread across the cirque as the warming sun softened cornices and sent them down the steep faces, across a frozen tarn, and into the forest. She stood in silence for a moment, gazing into the snowy bowls, before turning back. Clayt and the outfitter sat on their heels at the gap. Bart and Cora slowly walked toward them, and Agnes hurried to catch up.

Clayt stood and reached for the outfitter's binoculars. He was pointing to the skyline and the rocky divide between War and Fish Creeks. Agnes turned and scanned the mountain in the direction Clayt pointed. Near the top of the ridge, in scattered larch and whitebark pine, she spotted a set of large, fresh tracks in the snow. She followed them until she saw a dark shape moving at a low angle toward the top.

"It's her," she whispered.

She absorbed the sight she had longed for, a glimpse of the elusive grizzly bear. No evidence of injury, no hint of a limp or awkwardness of gait. Then she spotted something else: at the bear's feet a small shadow moved along, running to keep up. The War Creek sow had found her cub.

ACKNOWLEDGMENTS

Of the many I have to thank for helping this book become reality, my editor Marthine Satris is primary. She saw the potential in the story and suggested ways I could bring that potential to fruition. My sincere thanks to her and her colleagues at MP Publishing, especially Briah Skelly and Michelle Dotter, who also gave me excellent feedback and suggestions.

Thanks to members of my longtime writing group for years of encouragement. Novelist Tina Welling read an early manuscript of *War Creek* and gave me valuable feedback. I appreciate the time given by authors Florence Shepard, Connie Wieneke, and Louise Wagenknecht, who read all or parts of the manuscript.

The Jackson Hole Writers Conference, an annual event, was helpful for me. Its faculty and guests provided useful comments on excerpts from *War Creek* and other works. The University of Washington offers an online certificate in literary fiction, and the University of Montana offered a course in storytelling techniques. Such programs made it possible for a full-time employee (me) living in an isolated community (Jackson Hole) to continue to learn and improve my craft.

Thanks to my husband, Don Plumley, who kept the coffee pot going on mornings when I rose early to write.

Deep appreciation and thanks go to Karen Fant, who passed away in 2006. She suggested Sawtooth Ridge for a backpacking trip in the early eighties, one of many backcountry explorations we shared in the mountains of northeastern Washington. The

Sawtooth became the setting for this book. Her tireless efforts on behalf of the state's wild lands led to the designation of the Lake Chelan-Sawtooth Wilderness.

None of the characters in *War Creek* are modeled on a living person. The setting is real, consisting of public land within a national forest and park, rendered as accurately as my memory can manage. War Creek Ranger Station, however, is a complete fabrication.

ABOUT THE AUTHOR

Susan Marsh is a naturalist and award-winning writer in Jackson, Wyoming. She has over thirty years' experience as a wild land steward for the U.S. Forest Service. Drawn to the wild from an early age while growing up in the Pacific Northweast, animals were her primary conduit to places of beauty and mystery.

"I have always associated animals with wilderness, even if the wild was only the five-acre patch of second-growth forest, where I grew played as a child. When I looked out the window and saw quail, or a fox, I knew all was right with the world. Not too many years later, the quail and foxes were gone."

She holds degrees in geology and landscape architecture.

Her writing has appeared in *Orion, North American Review, Fourth Genre*, and numerous other journals. Her work has been anthologized in books including *The Leap Years* (Beacon Press, 2001), *Going Alone* (Seal Press, 2004), *Open Windows* (Ghost Road Press, 2005), *Solo* (Seal Press, 2005), and *A Mile in Her Boots* (Solas House, 2006). Her nonfiction books include *Beyond the Tetons* (White Willow, 2009), *Stories of the Wild* (The Murie Center, 2001), *Targhee Trails* (White Willow, 2012), and *The Wild Wyoming Range* (Laguna Wilderness Press, 2012). Her upcoming creative nonfiction title, *A Hunger for High Country*, will be released by Oregon State University Press.

She received the 2003 Neltje Blanchan award from the Wyoming Arts Council for writing inspired by the natural world.

CPSIA information can be obtained at www.ICGtesting.com
Printed in the USA
LVOW13s2151220614

391190LV00003B/167/P